Dipped in Sunshine

Surfing the Waves, Book Two

Fearne Hill

Copyright © 2022 by Fearne Hill

All rights reserved.

No part of this book may be reproduced in any form or by any electronic or mechanical means, including information storage and retrieval systems, without written permission from the author, except for the use of brief quotations in a book review.

Chapter One

When Fifty meets the fluffball

Eggy's youngest brother's voice carried, whether due to his Scandinavian accent—more pronounced than Eggy's—or the higher-pitched, slightly too loud tones of a not-yet-full-grown man who was no longer a boy either. More likely, the topic of conversation was what garnered interest from pretty much every other diner in the bustling tapas restaurant.

"I want to be gay and proud. Like you, Ragnar!"

Yes, most definitely a subject guaranteed to turn heads.

"Thanks, Otto. You've outed me to half the population of Corralejo." Eggy sounded amused. In the few hours since Otto's plane landed, his unexpected arrival surprising all of us, I realised nothing Otto did or said could raise Big Brother's hackles. Already, the boy had Eggy totally wrapped around his little finger.

"Ragnar, you're holding hands and making gooey eyes with a man dressed like Morticia Adams. Love the eyeliner, by the way, Clem. How do you get the line so straight? Anyway, Ragnar, I think they've sussed you out by now."

"At the risk of being accused of pedantry," Clem interjected, also smiling good-humouredly at the miniature blond fluffball opposite, "your brother is bisexual, not homosexual. And he also has a thing for bacon."

"Ooh, no, I couldn't do girls." Otto wrinkled his nose in distaste.

Seemingly, bacon was okay. Since our introduction half an hour earlier, I'd been covertly observing young Otto. I'd seen the precious photo of him as a young boy several times. Eggy carried it everywhere in his wallet. Occasionally over the years, he'd spoken of him, always in tones filled with love. Since Eggy reunited with his brothers on his trip to Norway, he and Otto had exchanged hours-long phone calls, Eggy giggling like a schoolboy at some of Otto's antics back home. By all accounts, his baby brother was a lively lad. To finally meet him, all grown up, after so many years, was more interesting than I expected.

The risk of Clem being accused of pedantry? Precisely zero. Eggy and Otto were highly unlikely to know the meaning of the word, and I certainly didn't.

Not long after we emigrated, he began teaching Eggy basic literacy skills. With a stroke of genius designed to placate his boyfriend's enormous ego, Clem set me daily homework assignments too. My reading and writing abilities were perfectly adequate for my minimal daily needs, but if pretending a desire to increase my word power smoothed life on the home front, I wouldn't complain. Hence, word of the day. Today's, with a nod in my direction, was pedantry. I'd look it up later.

"Otto." I took a swig of my beer. "Could you not, like, could you not...um...be homo back in Vikingville?"

"Vestvågøya," Eggy corrected automatically. I'd jerked his chain about the name of his Norwegian homeland for coming up to nine years. I reckoned I was good for another nine.

"Hah!" Otto snorted. "Let me tell you something, Fifty, about Vestvågøya. Our village of Stamsund has a population of one thousand. Subtracting the women, kids, and old folk leaves less than two hundred men. I'm related to most of those—our pa is one of eight kids and our ma one of ten. Statistically, that leaves me with a choice of about three homosexuals, but fuck knows who they are. They're not shouting it from the fishing boats, are they, Ragnar? Nor are they on Grindr, I've already looked. And that's before we get onto the subject of my dad. He's not exactly the most modern of—"

Lips pursed, Eggy interrupted. "Otto, *lille venn*, for the love of Odin, please tell me you do not have a Grindr profile. I'll confiscate your phone if you do."

The fluffball laughed wickedly. "Nah, big brother, I'm only winding you up. I had to delete it. My dick pics took up too many pixels to fit on the screen."

Clem and I gaped at him, not sure whether to laugh. From Eggy's grim expression, laughter would have been the wrong call. Precisely how protective Eggy felt towards his favourite brother was fast becoming evident.

"Shit, the family do realize you're here, don't they? Otto, please tell me they knew you were coming."

Eggy's emotional range was as familiar to me as my own, and he was experiencing escalating anxiety. Generally, a precursor to a facial tic and fist clenching, themselves signalling an imminent, full-blown attack of the heebie-jeebies. Ah, there it was; his jaw tightened and his lips thinned into a determined line.

Flushing, Otto wriggled in his chair. "Um...I, well...I left a note on the kitchen table." He glanced at his phone nervously, which had been lighting up at regular intervals since we sat down. "Oh, look, it appears they've read it. Fancy that."

"Call one of the brothers. Now," Eggy ordered. "It doesn't matter which. They'll be going insane with worry."

While not physically resembling his oldest brother, Otto clearly inherited the Eggebraaten attitude gene. A rapid exchange in Norwegian followed Eggy's imperious command. To an English ear, it sounded as if they sang alternate lines of a complicated song to each other, whereas their facial contortions and body language strongly indicated they were enjoying a full-on argument.

Fascinated, Clem and I watched David and Goliath slug it out. Despite all the years I'd spent living with Eggy, the occasion marked the first time I'd ever heard him speak Norwegian at any length. Although we were both decent at Spanish and had passable French, the idea he also had all these indecipherable consonants and vowels with funny dots and squiggles flowing around his brain was crazy.

But neither Eggy nor his brother must have remembered their Bible stories, as Goliath finally won, folding his strong arms across his broad chest and glaring at his pint-sized sibling.

If Clem and I thought that exchange riveting, the following scene made compulsive viewing. Otto switched his phone onto loudspeaker, and Eggy helpfully translated. "That's my brother Dag he's talking to at the moment. He's only eighteen months younger than me. He won't take any shit. He found a packet of Otto's epilepsy tablets next to his bed, so he's been worried sick he's not brought any with him."

He listened briefly and shook his head. "Dag's gutted he hadn't picked up on Otto's little escapade. Fortunately, Otto's packed enough meds for at least two weeks. We'll have to register him with a doctor tomorrow."

Not a flying visit to Big Brother then. The fluffball evidently planned on staying a while.

"Those two trying to talk over each other are Arvid and Egil. The twins. They're so wrapped up in their own world, they probably didn't realise Otto had gone missing until Dag pointed it out. I don't know why he didn't bloody tell one of them, even if he was too scared to inform my dad."

"He is only nineteen," Clem pointed out reasonably. "Teenage boys aren't exactly renowned for making sensible decisions."

Eggy nodded again as the two voices back in Norway vied to be heard, both surprisingly upset. "They want him home, but he says he wants to stay here with me."

Otto's wide grey eyes—the only features immediately marking him out as Eggy's brother—flashed in anger at something one of the twins said. Thoughtlessly upping sticks and vanishing might not have been the wisest choice, but he was clearly capable of holding his own with his older brothers. This stroppy elf with his shock of blond hair was used to getting his own way.

"That's Erik talking now. He wants him to come home. They share a room." His voice softened. "He says he's sorry he wasn't around when Otto fell out with our pa."

As the phone call played out, Clem and I exchanged glances. Clem held Eggy's hand across the table, offering his silent support. Years had passed since Eggy's father had booted him out of the family home after discovering him with a man, but from the tension in his face, memories of that difficult time were flooding back.

"Poor Otto. I feel so guilty for not realising how unhappy he'd become. I should have picked up something was wrong last time we spoke on the phone."

I tried to hold back a snort. The fluffball had selfishly caused a whole heap of aggro, and somehow, these five big strong men all blamed themselves.

"Do you know what the fallout was about?" I asked.

Eggy nodded. "Yeah, although from what he told me when I met up with him last year, it's been building for some time. He wanted to go with a mate to Svolvær for the weekend. To go shopping and then to a club and stay over—you know the sort of thing. Teenage stuff's difficult to do in Stamsund. Since they all worry about his health so much, our pa said no."

A piss-poor excuse for causing this much drama. Otto gave one of his indulgent brothers an earful down the phone line, waving his skinny arms around wildly. I cocked a brow. "Looks pretty healthy to me, dude."

"God knows where he gets all that feistiness from," drawled Clem. "Seems perfectly capable of looking after himself."

Defending his brother, Eggy earnestly replied, "If you'd seen him as a baby, you'd understand. Heart surgery, epilepsy, endless chest infections. We didn't expect him to ever reach adulthood. He wants to stay here with me because he's fed up with the brothers being too overprotective."

In my opinion, all this older sibling attention had spawned a little monster, judging from the way he manipulated them in the palm of his hand, but keeping that blasphemous idea to myself seemed wise. And if he thought Eggy would be any less overprotective, then he was in for a shock. From the prideful way he'd eyed his youngest sibling since he'd stepped off the aeroplane, the testosterone-fuelled chest beating had barely begun.

Between us, we'd ordered about ten tapas dishes. Clem and I had finished our share, then stolen most of Eggy and Otto's as they passed the phone back and forth. Pinching the last of the *patatas bravas* earned me identical frowns from the larger and the smaller of the brothers. The smaller one could fuck right off. Catching the waiter's eye, I ordered some more for the larger.

When the phone call finally ended, I enquired of Eggy-the-younger, "So, how are you going to be spending your holiday here in Corralejo?" I needed to make an effort; I had the feeling I'd be seeing quite a lot of him over the next few days. "At this time of year, we're flat out with the surf school."

"And I'm on a strict deadline for the screenplay I'm working on," Clem added quickly, clearly determining here and now not to be cast in the role of babysitter and tour guide. To be fair, when he slipped into the writing groove, he squirrelled himself away from dawn until dusk.

"Oh, I'm not on holiday. I'm staying for good!"

Well, that was news. From the way his eyebrows disappeared into his hairline, it was to Clem too.

"And I've thought it through," Otto went on. "Ragnar says I can earn my keep helping in the shop, if it's okay with you, Fifty. I've been taking Spanish lessons for nearly a year, and I've already enrolled in more here—I arranged them online back in Norway."

Eggy gave his brother a look normally associated with a new father witnessing his toddler poo in a potty for the first time. What was the big deal? So the fluffball knew his way around the internet? He was a teenager, for Christ's sake, practically born with a phone glued to his hand. The extra help in the shop would be useful, though. When we were both out teaching, we relied on the hotel staff to fill in, and their dedication to the task could be hit and miss. And being Eggy's brother, I guessed he could talk surfboards and wetsuits with the punters as well as anyone.

"Great." I nodded, observing Eggy's pleasure at my agreement. "The Spanish will be useful."

"Oh, languages are easy! I'm Scandinavian. I'll be fluent in no time."

The Eggebraaten ego gene seemed to be fairly powerful, too.

"I'm hoping to go to college here eventually, to do my nurse training," Otto added cheerfully. "I've already researched courses and which qualifications I need. My Norwegian school-leaving exam results were good enough. I'll only need to pass a language test. I'm going to ask Clem to help me with the application forms when the time comes."

Now Clem threw him a proud look. Jesus, he'd got them both eating out of his hand. Mind you, his prior planning was pretty impressive for a nineteen-year-old boy on his first trip away from home. He'd got the angles covered. And if he really needed to escape his toxic father, then coming to stay with Big Brother wasn't the worst decision. At least he'd be safe.

"We need to establish some ground rules, Otto," Eggy began, as fresh plates of tapas arrived. Clem's head nodded up and down repeatedly.

Otto dived in, beating me to the steaming heap of *patatas bravas*. Hmm, I needed to establish some ground rules of my own.

"Fifty? You and Clem need to hear these rules too, so we're all on the same page. Firstly, Otto's not allowed to have an unsupervised bath. Showers only."

Okay, so, not what I'd expected. Curfews and keeping his room tidy, yes; running a hot bath, no. I shot Otto a quick look. In his shoes, I'd have told Eggy to fuck off, whereas he seemed unperturbed, happy to munch through my favourite plate of tapas while his big brother laid down the personal hygiene laws.

He caught me staring and grinned. "It's okay, Fifty. No one's going to ask you to supervise my bath time. I can play on my own with the rubber duckies in the shower."

Eggy carried on, sparing my blushes. "It's due to his epilepsy. He's not allowed to lock the bathroom door, no matter what he's doing in there, even if he's only cleaning his teeth. He's not allowed to use the cooker either, unless someone else is present, and especially not the barbecue. And no open fires. It's not that I don't trust you, Otto, and I know you are aware of all this already. But I'll never forgive myself if something dreadful happened."

Shrugging, the fluffball carried on eating. The ground rules clearly weren't new, but all the same, they were a bloody imposition on a nineteen-year-old lad. "Jesus! If there were four more of you back in Viking Land, Eggy, I'm not surprised Otto did a runner," I commented.

Eggy frowned. Apparently, one didn't joke about 'the rules'. Otto, however, giggled, then cheekily tweaked Eggy's ridiculously luxuriant hair, his conspiratorial smile lighting up his whole face. Which had me making a sound very close to a giggle myself. Perhaps there was more to the youngest Eggebraaten than I'd first thought.

No more rules-which-must-be-obeyed were forthcoming. Finishing the tapas and ordering another round of drinks, conversation flowed back and forth. After a while, I zoned out of Otto's excited chatter about his new life here on the island, and nobody seemed to mind. Eggy and Clem were used to me being quiet, Otto too full of zest to notice.

I vaguely wondered what that excitement must feel like. He wasn't to blame, but meeting him tonight had left me out of sorts and I couldn't pinpoint why. Unrequited love for Eggy, my best mate, used to be the cause; time was I'd end every evening wishing for something I'd never have. Thankfully—finally—I was over him, so it wasn't that either. Only as I walked home by myself, back to my empty, silent apartment, did I understand the root of my abrupt downturn in mood. Eggy was gradually building up a family around himself—his beloved Clem and now his cherished brother, Otto. Perhaps there would be a dog or a cat sometime. Maybe even a horde of baby Viking warriors one day. Who knew?

I, on the other hand, fast approached my thirtieth birthday still totally, one hundred percent alone. It sucked.

Chapter Two

When Otto develops an unhealthy interest in floor tiles

I woke with an erection. Hang out the bunting.

A lively internal debate with myself ensued; whether to do something about it or ignore it. If I ignored it, it would soon disappear of its own accord. If I attempted to enjoy it, the same outcome was likely, accompanied by a bone-weary heaviness I would endeavour to shake off before facing the world. Depressingly, my dick made the decision for me, softening before I'd even laid a hand on it.

With a sigh, I glanced at my phone for a time check. A couple of messages from Felipe awaited my response. I sighed again.

Over the last few years, there had been several Felipes in my life. Not all named Felipe, of course. The current one seemed perfectly pleasant, a handsome enough history teacher in his mid-thirties. Carlos, the hotel manager, had introduced us, imagining a young, single guy like me to be exactly the sort of fun his cousin Felipe needed. Clem and Eggy approved wholeheartedly, desperately hoping this Felipe would be *the Felipe*, that I'd finally meet my Mr Right and we could make up a cosy foursome or some such shit.

So, to please everybody, I continued the charade, charting the course of my depressing non-relationships with the Felipes of this world. They followed a predictable path. Text chats, flirty phone calls, drinks, then dinner. Some of the less pushy ones would patiently repeat this sequence a number of times before homing in for the kill.

And then I'd politely reject them.

Although interestingly, the current Felipe showed less predictability. A glutton for punishment. No matter how many times I ended our drinks dates or our dinner dates in an abrupt fashion, frequently around the point I sensed him psyching himself up to make physical advances, he insisted on coming back for more.

I'd apologised to some of his predecessors for leading them on, although I'd never offer an explanation. I'd stick pins in my eyes rather than reveal the truth. Even in the face of rejection, the nice guys would occasionally persevere. I had a miserable feeling this Felipe would draw out the awkwardness longer than anyone, being either incredibly lonely or extremely thick-skinned. On account of Eggy's brother, I'd called off our date last night, and his latest text suggested drinks in a few days' time. Agreeing was sometimes easier than making up excuses.

Another looming event, however, made me extra miserable and tense this morning—a doctor's appointment. Otto's arrival had proved a useful distraction, but now nerves plagued me. I was unable to contemplate breakfast. Not so much as a glass of water, despite the heat of the apartment, even at this hour of the morning. As I lingered in the shower, hoping the refreshing jets would soothe my soul, I mentally steeled myself for my ten o'clock appointment. How bloody difficult could it be?

Already, my fingers hovered over the phone buttons, contemplating cancelling. But I resisted. Having come this far several times already, only to back out with minutes to spare, this time I was determined to see it through. Doctors were professionals, I reminded myself, they dealt with much more embarrassing stuff all the time. And in a few months I'd be celebrating (mourning?) my thirtieth birthday. Life passed me by. I couldn't carry on in this unhappy limbo any longer.

The mirrored glass windows of the medical centre gleamed brightly in the mid-morning sunshine, the perfectly reflected, cloudless blue sky subliminally suggesting grubby problems like mine didn't belong in shiny new buildings like this. Boasting bilingual doctors, a spacious carpark, and its own pharmacy, the set-up catered mostly for foreign tourists. Childhood visits to old Dr Jones, our family GP in Woolacombe, in his creased suit in his crumbly back office, couldn't have been more different. Precisely the reason I'd chosen it—anonymous, professional, remote. Even so, my bowels had evacuated themselves three times that morning, I'd changed my sweat-drenched shirt twice, taken a second, hurried shower and smoked half a pack of fags. And, aside from mixing it with weed, I didn't even smoke tobacco anymore.

I locked the jeep, with five minutes to spare before my allotted appointment. I felt lightheaded—from lack of food, an unaccustomed nicotine buzz, the Fuerteventura summer heat, and crippling anxiety. Forcing myself through the shiny revolving doors, I reminded myself for the thousandth time the chances of bumping into anyone I knew here approached zero.

Eggy's favourite sibling, Otto, one slim, denim-clad leg casually crossed over the other, sat quietly perusing a magazine in the waiting room.

Fuck.

For a brief, joyous moment, I contemplated turning and fleeing through the revolving doors, straight back out into the

June sunshine. A plan immediately scuppered by an elderly lady attempting to negotiate the doors on a set of crutches, one leg encased in a plaster cast. Precious seconds ticked by as she practically brought the spin of the doors to a standstill.

I considered my dwindling options rapidly: barging through regardless, possibly rendering her even more incapacitated, or facing Otto. Despairingly, my good manners won.

"Hi, Fifty, what the hell are you doing here?"

"Oh, um...hi, Otto. Er...this is a surprise."

Shaking his head in disgust, Otto brandished the magazine at me. "I know! Tell me about it. I've got enough epilepsy meds to last for ages, but Ragnar insisted I register with the doctor immediately anyway! As if I haven't got anything better to do with my time."

To be fair, being new to town, I suspected he didn't.

"I'm not gonna lie—Ragnar's worse than the other brothers put together. He's even bought me one of those bloody pill boxes old people use, with a tablet compartment for every day of the week, so I don't ever forget one. Honestly!"

First-world problems. As he grumbled about how awful being so cherished was, I let him prattle and grabbed the seat next to him. Sitting elsewhere would have looked odd. And if he wanted to drone on about his tablets? Absolutely fine by me.

"Anyway, enough about me. My epilepsy saga bores me to tears. Why are you here?"

Shit. Beads of sweat broke out on my forehead. My heart danced a *pasodoble* against my rib cage, skipping one beat and then another.

"Erm... I..."

"Christian Grey?" a shiny young nurse, of a similar age to me, called pleasantly across the waiting room. Oh God, I hoped she wouldn't be sitting in on the consultation.

Dizzily, I stood, my heart racing, guts churning. Shit, I was going to puke. Wiping my sweaty palms on my jeans, I waved weakly in acknowledgment and took a step forwards. Then for some obscure reason my vision blurred. A ringing sound echoed in my ears. The world jerked, then tilted sideways. And I promptly fainted.

My first, and hopefully last, fainting experience. I didn't recommend it; it was an inexplicably panicky, uncontrollable sensation. I'd witnessed other people faint. My friend Zen once keeled over after she cut her foot open on a piece of jagged glass at the beach. In less than a second, her skin colour drained from tan to ash. I thought she'd died as she sank to the ground, and I'd never felt so helpless and scared before or since.

I must have looked the same way. When I came to, reclining on a narrow couch in the doctor's consulting room with a monitor pegged to my finger, Otto's horribly anxious face was inches away from mine. His extraordinary grey eyes peered at me closely, and he clutched my hand in both of his, which felt kind of weird, but kind of comforting too.

"Oh, thank goodness. Bloody hell, Fifty, you gave me the fright of my life! Here, drink this."

Orange squash never tasted so good. Fainting, it turned out, made me desperately thirsty. Or maybe that was all the sweating and lack of sustenance. The pretty young nurse fussed around with a blood pressure cuff on my arm. Groaning, I felt myself redden. Although girls didn't float my boat, I wasn't happy to appear an utter twat in front of one.

"Why the hell did you faint?" Otto quizzed me anxiously. "What's wrong with you? Are you properly ill? Ragnar is going to be in a complete state when he finds out about this. Aside from me and Clem, you're, like, his number-one favourite person. Odin's teeth, I need to call him."

Oh fuck, no. "Otto, please don't. Please. I'm not ill, I'm... I'm..."

I was what, exactly? Slowly turning mad? So fed up with obsessing over the state of my penis, my brain took a nosedive onto the floor?

Shit, could I *actually* be properly ill? Did I have something seriously wrong with me? Did I have a rare, fatal condition making me prone to fainting and causing my penis to refuse to function like a young man's should?

A movement at the door halted my further descent into panic, and a serene woman, about my mum's age, bustled in. Dressed in the universal symbols of doctorhood, pristine white coat and stethoscope slung around her neck, she introduced herself, in excellent English, as Dr Marchena. "Oh, you're recovered. Goodness me, you certainly livened up the waiting room this morning, Mr Grey!"

Having satisfied herself with the observations documented by the nurse on the chart, and after a cursory feel of my pulse, she settled in the chair opposite the couch and composed her face into a kindly expression of interest. Thankfully, the nurse left.

"I'll...um...hey, I'll leave you to it as well." Otto slipped his hands out of mine.

"Oh, I'm happy for your partner to stay." Dr Marchena smiled politely.

"Oh my god, no, I...um..." began Otto awkwardly.

"He can stay," I mumbled, throwing him a pleading look. "He's not my partner though. He's, he's...a friend. I don't...Otto, I'd like you to...will you hang around?"

"Goodness, of course! Ragnar would kill me if I left you alone now."

Whether my post-faint muzzy head prevented me from processing clearly, or whether the fainting episode had panicked me into believing I was seconds away from discovering I genuinely had a major, life-threatening health condition, I realised facing this by myself utterly petrified me. It was too late to invite Eggy or Clem along, but right at this moment, I didn't give a shit anymore who heard about my embarrassing problem. So what if Otto, a virtual stranger, knew? I'd shout it across the waiting room if it made me feel any better and made my problem disappear. I'd become so bloody sick and tired of carrying the deathly weight of it around with me. All those nights lying awake worrying about it, trying to resolve it, obsessing over it, googling it. All the appointments I'd made to come here and then backed out at the last minute. All the anxious nausea, the sweats, my bowels tying themselves up in knots over it. I was fucking done. If Otto pissed himself laughing and advertised it to the entire community of Corralejo, then so be it.

"So, Mr Grey, now you're not quite so green around the gills, what brings you here to see me this morning?"

Here goes. I shot Otto a nervous glance, which he returned with an encouraging smile. My next sentence would soon wipe that off his face. "I...um...I think I have a problem with my... um...my penis."

I could almost see the words 'oh my god' form in a cartoon bubble over Otto's head. He visibly shrank in his chair, his face a teenage mask of horrified politeness. Bizarrely, I had an urge to giggle.

"I see," said the doctor. "What sort of problem?"

"It...um...it's not working properly. I mean, I can wee out of it fine, but it doesn't do the other. You know, get...um...hard. Um...not for very long, anyway."

Otto studied a plain white floor tile at his feet as though he'd discovered the most fascinating artefact in the British Museum. The whiteness of the floor tile contrasted beautifully with the redness infusing his cheeks. Oddly, his utter embarrassment somehow lessened my own.

Dr Marchena didn't find the conversation awkward in the slightest. She scribbled a note on the pad next to her. "So, you are struggling to maintain an erection, am I correct?"

I gave her a quick nod.

"And this is a newish problem? You're, what, twenty-nine? So I'm assuming you have had successful erections in the past?"

I nodded again, thinking of all the nights I'd listened to Eggy in the van next door, pounding his latest conquest into the mattress, and the effect the sound of his pleasure had on me. Yes, very successful erections. Hundreds and hundreds of them.

Granted, since Clem had come on the scene, I'd made a conscious effort to stop eavesdropping. I wasn't a total creep. It had felt wrong, voyeuristic. Eggy's sexual antics had morphed into private, passionate lovemaking, and I'd worn headphones or turned up my music. "Yes, I've had...um...successful erections, but not for a while. Well...um...not when I've, er...wanted them."

"With a partner, you mean?" She glanced at Otto. His eyes were out on stalks. No way were they ever leaving that floor tile.

"I don't have a partner. No, I mean...er...on my own. Um... you know, masturbating."

"I see. How long has this been going on for?"

Fuck it. In for a penny, in for a pound. It could have been a post-fainting adrenaline surge but getting this shit off my chest felt almost exhilarating. "At least a year. It's getting worse. I sometimes wake up in the morning with an...um...an erection, but then it goes down again really quickly. And sometimes, I... um..." Pausing, I sucked a big breath in. "And sometimes I wake up, and it's happened in the night when I've been asleep. I've... er...had a...a wet dream."

Otto choked. I ploughed on.

"And I'm worried if I do find a partner, then I'm...er...I'm not going to be able to...um...get it up. And I'm trying to find a partner at the moment, but I'm scared to take it any further in case of what they might think if this were to happen. It would be excruciatingly embarrassing."

There. I'd got it out. The sky hadn't fallen in, the doctor hadn't sniggered, and I hadn't dissolved into a puddle of tears. And Otto hadn't fled, even though he most likely desperately wanted to.

After more jotting on her notepad, Dr Marchena ran through some basic questions regarding my past medical history, smoking and drinking habits, and occupation. I relaxed; even Otto dared raise his eyes from the floor tile. "If you can quickly slip your trousers and underwear off, I'll examine you, and then we'll discuss your options from here."

With Otto safely recovering from his traumatic experience on the other side of the flimsy curtain, Dr Marchena's cool fingers roamed over my block and tackle. It was kind of soothing. And while the certainty I wouldn't sprout an inappropriate boner comforted me, the knowledge the only hands, apart from my own, that had fondled my cock and balls since babyhood belonged to a middle-aged, matronly doctor was depressing.

Examination over, I sat up as Dr Marchena pronounced her verdict. A composed Otto appeared to be sitting up and taking note too. She handed me a form for routine blood tests, checking various hormone levels and my blood sugar, and reassured me they would likely come back as normal. She also delivered lifestyle advice regarding my weed smoking and drinking, which Otto nodded at carefully, shooting me a knowing look. Apparently, an excess of weed could exacerbate erectile problems. Great, now he'd be nagging me along with Eggy and Clem.

"This issue is more common than you would imagine in young men. Well done, Christian, for wanting to tackle it. We'll wait for the blood tests to rule out a few things, but I think you have a significant degree of anxiety related to performance, and that anxiety has been allowed to take over and got out of hand."

Understatement of the century. Otto nodded wisely next to me.

"This is made worse if you don't have a regular, understanding partner. Our frailties are easier to share with someone who knows us, rather than a stranger on whom we'd like to make a good impression." She gave me a warm smile, and I gratefully smiled back. This woman talked a lot of sense. I particularly appreciated how she frequently paused, checking I understood her. She continued, "We have several options we can try, to ameliorate your problem. Some of the strategies include drugs, although I'm reluctant to start medication in the first instance."

She waffled on a while longer. Lost me a little to be honest with the medical terms and the types of drugs, but we agreed to another appointment in a week's time after the results of the blood tests.

And then I was pushing through the revolving doors and into the carpark, with the glorious Fuerteventura sunshine beating down on me. Inhaling great lungsful of the fresh sea breeze felt like stepping into a brave new world.

"Shit, we never got your epilepsy stuff."

"Yeah, we did." Otto dangled a white paper bag. "When you were out cold, I took your appointment slot. You were booked in for the ten minutes before mine."

"Did you catch the bus to get here?"

Otto nodded. Despite Clem offering to take him, he preferred public transport. People watching, apparently, and an opportunity to improve his Spanish.

"I'll give you a lift, although you've probably had enough of my company for a morning."

He grinned at this, surprised I made a feeble joke. But I felt stupidly light and free. The expression 'a problem shared is a problem halved' felt clichéd, yet as I unlocked the car, it summed up my feelings exactly. The doc had been amazing—professional, calm, matter-of-fact. She hadn't cured me, but she hadn't fobbed me off either, or suggested I was a lost cause. She'd laid out options, medicines, blood tests, hope. I only regretted I hadn't visited her much sooner.

"Are you okay to drive?" Otto asked, not unreasonably, considering half an hour earlier I'd been laid out cold on the floor of the waiting room.

"Yeah, I'm fine." I sighed with relief as I took a seat behind the wheel.

Although I may have looked and felt much better, my young companion looked as if he'd welcome a stiff drink. He stared rigidly ahead, and I felt a rush of embarrassment for the first time since I'd woken from my faint. "Odin's teeth, Christian. I had no idea. Ragnar never said you had health problems."

For a fleeting moment I wondered who Cristian was, then realised it was me. I liked it; my name sounded nice in his lilting accent. "Nah, well, I guess not." I fiddled with the car keys in my lap, too wound up again to start the engine. "And your brother doesn't know."

"I mean...I suppose...how...did you...I mean..."

"It's okay. I get it. I should have asked you to leave, not made you sit through all that shit. My brain turned to wool. I didn't think straight."

"No, it's not that. I'm used to doctors and hospitals, I've spent my childhood in and out of them. It's...it's...why didn't you tell Ragnar or Clem? They would have been very supportive. Ragnar would have insisted on coming with you today." He shook his head in wonder. "I had no idea guys your age could suffer from...um..."

"Erectile dysfunction?" I supplied, making him cringe even further. "Nah, nor did I. It's a fucking joke, isn't it? Christian

Grey has erectile dysfunction. Fifty shades of fucked up. Maybe Clem could pen the screenplay."

"Odin's certainly playing tricks on you," Otto agreed sagely. Christ, not him too with the Odin crap. The Fifty Shades reference appeared to pass straight over his head, which was refreshing. No doubt the youth of today had newer touchpoints.

"I'm guessing young Vikings don't suffer these sorts of embarrassing problems, do they?"

"No," he replied gravely, shocked I'd even considered it.

Granted, the idea of a man as virile and as confident with his sexuality as Eggy ever drooping in the heat of the moment was laughable. I guessed good genes ran in families.

"If you...erm...would like me to...um...erase the last hour from my memory, then I'm happy to do so," he ventured carefully.

I thought for a moment before agreeing. God knew how he would erase it; images of my pathetic, flaccid penis would haunt his dreams for a few days to come. "Yeah. Probably for the best, Otto. Eggy doesn't need to know. I'd prefer he didn't."

"My lips are sealed."

I had my doubts, but it was too late now. In the brief time I'd known Otto, he never stopped bloody talking. His adventure at the doctor's had temporarily quietened him, though. I started the engine and put the car into reverse. Otto adjusted the air-con, then fiddled with the radio. His grey eyes darted everywhere apart from at my groin.

"Thank you for being there with me," I added. "It kind of made it easier in a way. Your face. Jesus. If you could have disappeared through the floor, I think you would have done."

"I'm not gonna lie, when you mentioned masturbation, I was worried she was going to ask for a demonstration of your technique." Laughing, he shook his head. "I'm not letting you do this by yourself, you know, Christian."

"What, try and fail to masturbate? It tends to be a lonely sport, mate."

Otto blushed beautifully, then face-planted dramatically into his hands. The fluffball had some finer qualities after all. "OMG, Christian! You are so embarrassing! I was thinking of the doctor's appointments, as you damn well know."

Chapter Three

When Fifty hits the dance floor

As if Otto hadn't endured enough of my company that day, Eggy invited me over for an evening barbecue. Declining would have seemed odd, so I dutifully turned up at eight, with a six-pack tucked under my arm. Thankfully, Otto was nowhere to be seen, and Eggy and Clem both behaved as if nothing unusual had happened. Seemed like Otto could be trustworthy after all. He'd given me his word and my secrets were safe, even from Eggy.

"Dude."

"Dude."

I slouched in a lounger next to Eggy, and we opened a beer each.

"Where's the fluffball tonight?"

Eggy frowned. "He's out in town with some Spanish girls he met at the shop yesterday."

"Blimey, he doesn't hang around."

"Tell me about it! I've told him to check in at ten." He glanced down at his watch anxiously. "Maybe I should have told him nine o'clock, instead. The girls seemed nice, young like him, but..."

"Dude, the guy's nineteen. He doesn't need Big Bro checking up on him."

Clem gave me a 'don't go there' warning look, which I foolishly ignored.

"Yeah, I know. But he's grown up in the back of beyond. In Vestvågøya everyone knows everyone. He's never had to learn any street smarts. And he's tiny. People have pet poodles bigger and stronger than Otto. What if someone tries to rob him? Or knife him?"

"Mate, calm down," I told him. "This is Corralejo, not the Wild West. It's safe enough. He'll have a great night out."

Eggy's grip tightened around his beer bottle and his chin took on a familiar jut. "I can tell you one thing; anybody who so much as lays a finger on my little brother will wish they'd never been born by the time I've finished with them."

I laughed—a wrong move judging from Eggy's fierce expression. I tried to pacify him. "Dude, he'll be with a whole gang of kids by now if those girls are local. He'll be making friends, meeting new people. Trust me, he'll be absolutely fine."

Eggy harrumphed. "And what about men? Sexual predators? He's such an easy target."

Behind Eggy, Clem rolled his eyes.

Eggy's big fists clenched around his beer bottle; the facial tic started up. "I'll say this only once. If any bloke even dreams of doing the jiggy with my Otto, without fucking wooing him with chocolates and flowers for approximately three years first, they will find themselves held down and their toenails pulled out with a rusty pair of pliers. Extremely slowly." Blimey, talk about dramatic. With that cool Scandi accent, he could be auditioning for the role of Bond villain. Aside from the 'doing the jiggy' part, obviously.

My own toes curled involuntarily in my flipflops in sympathy for whichever poor bugger foolishly threw in his lot with Otto one day. With four more overprotective older brothers like Eggy waiting in the wings, the fluffball might as well join a monastery now. "Chill, dude. He's gone into town with some mates for a couple of drinks. He's not pole-dancing at G.A.Y."

I wasted my breath. Eggy had the bit firmly between his teeth. Evidently, he took older-brother responsibilities extremely seriously. "And it isn't only him being attacked I have to worry about, is it? What if he has a fit? The bars with dance floors have strobe lights. He says they don't trigger his epilepsy, but how can he be so sure? The strobes in Vestvågøya are basically someone turning a light switch on and off really quickly."

Clem, hearing it for at least the second time around, busied himself serving the food. "Perhaps we should have gone out with him." He handed me a plate piled high with spicy chicken wings, a colourful rice salad and homemade coleslaw on the side. The smell alone had me drooling. Eggy was a lucky boy—his man had some serious kitchen skills.

"I suggested that. Social suicide, apparently. Which is fucking ridiculous. I'm not that bloody old and uncool."

I sniggered, imagining how that conversation went down.

"He'll be fine," I reassured him, digging in. "He'll text at ten. Try and relax."

Ten o'clock came and went with no communication from Otto. By now, we'd adjourned to the house. I scarfed down two bowlfuls of Clem's homemade apple pie and custard while Eggy's incessant pacing wore a groove across the limestone-tiled floor. Clem texted Otto, and Eggy left increasingly concerned voice messages. Even I had begun to feel on edge by the time Clem finally got through to him.

"He's fine," he said, relieved, reading out the text. "He says 'tell the hairy ginger Viking to go to bed and stop bloody worrying'."

I smirked; the kid was growing on me.

"And for your information, he's in Gators Bar, down on the front. Still with the girls. They are going to stay for the live DJ set."

The hairy ginger Viking reached for his jacket. "We should join him. I need to check out the people he's with. And the strobe lights. And his new friends. And whether he's drunk. He promised he wouldn't drink, as alcohol messes with his meds. Fuck, I don't even know if he took his tablets this morning."

"No, Eggy, you're staying here," Clem disagreed sternly, a hand on his arm. "Listen. He's told us where he is and with whom. We have to be able to trust him. If you turn up, he'll be really pissed off, which means that next time, he won't tell us anything, and we'll worry even more."

They were experiencing their first taste of parenting and, judging by their tense expressions, not enjoying the experience very much. I'd never had a particular affinity for babies, but I reckoned they were more straightforward than headstrong, lively nineteen-year-olds. Eggy still had his jacket in his hand, unconvinced.

"Why don't I go and check up on him?" appeased Clem. "I could pop into the bar for a quick drink. If I hide in the background, he may not even spot me."

I swear Eggy actually growled. Either that or emitted an especially windy belch. Whichever, his body language alone made the message crystal clear. No way on Odin's fine earth would any boyfriend of his go to a bar on his own. Observing the clenched fist and jaw tic, Clem and I both sensibly refrained from pointing out Clem had negotiated the world quite adequately alone before Eggy landed on his doorstep. So, even though he no doubt had a ready smart-arse reply on the tip of his tongue, Clem wisely remained silent.

"Oh, fuck it. I'll go." I reached for my car keys. I'd had enough of the alpha display from Eggy anyway. With my trip to the doctor still fresh in my memory, I'd only drunk one beer all evening, and I'd deliberately run out of weed. After the day I'd had, another drink wouldn't go amiss. I could always ditch the car and retrieve it tomorrow. Two pairs of grateful eyes watched me leave.

Gators Bar and Club was essentially a glorified pub catering to the northern European tourist market. Not a bad spot to while away a couple of hours after work, with a cool lager and a bowl of olives as the sun set over the Atlantic. During the winter, anyhow. Indeed, Felipe and I had spent a perfectly pleasant evening there only a couple of months earlier. Until, without warning, he'd placed a warm hand on my upper thigh, which had caused my dick to practically turn in on itself and my heart to beat so fast I checked whether the place had installed a wall-mounted defibrillator.

A hot June night, however, presented me with a sweaty wall of screeching noise, most of it emanating from groups of drunk, overexcited, sunburnt teenagers trying to make themselves heard over the relentless hammering of the bass. A small, tightly packed dance floor completed this earthly representation of hell.

Wading to the bar, my shirt wet and clinging to my back within five paces, I failed to spy Otto. Not surprising considering the number of kids crammed into the venue and Otto's unimpressive height. Using my own height to my advantage, I caught the barmaid's attention and soon had an ice-cold bottle of Tropical in my hand. After surveying the landscape around the bar area one more time and still failing to spot his blond head, I took a deep breath and ploughed my way to the edge of the dance floor.

A wave of relief washed through me as I finally located Eggy's errant youngest brother. Not because I'd found him. I knew he'd be hiding in here somewhere; all the supposedly cool kids hung out in Gators. And not even relief that the fluffball appeared relatively sober compared to the brightly coloured teens of both sexes swaying tipsily around him. Nor that the strobe lights were of a cheap, low-wattage variety, unlikely to trigger his epilepsy. No, my overriding emotion was to thank the Lord only I stood there nursing a beer, instead of Eggy. Mass murder on the dance floor had been narrowly avoided.

For as long as I'd known him, Eggy had carried around in his wallet that precious photo of his favourite younger brother. Before he made contact again with his family, I used to find him staring at it, kissing it lightly before carefully returning it to its special pouch. Kind of cute and kind of sad.

If Eggy still pictured his youngest brother as that angelic little boy in a grubby red T-shirt, delightedly showing off a crab toward the camera, then he had some serious catching up to do. Young Bjørn Otto Sigurdson Eggebraaten had grown up and moved on from crab fishing. The creatures now attracting his attention circled him on the dance floor, of the two-legged, male variety. Was Otto naively oblivious to the attention he garnered? Not bloody likely. As the twinkiest twink in the whole of twinkdom strutted his stuff, he knew exactly the effect his arse-wiggling had on the predators surrounding him. I'd have bet the surf shop on it. And he revelled in every second.

I enjoyed dancing, but rarely indulged in public. In the kitchen, yes, especially when cooking a late-night fry up after a few beers. Or even at a spontaneous beach barbecue amongst close friends after a particularly brilliant sundowner surfing session. Even Eggy had been known to shake his booty at one of those—more of a crazed, Viking-warrior jitterbug than actual dancing, not that any of us had the nerve to tell him. He could have learnt a few moves from his youngest brother because, Christ, could that boy dance.

An artfully placed rip in Otto's skin-tight white jeans, just below his left buttock, drew my gaze and held it. As he uninhibitedly shimmied his narrow hips to a growing and appreciative audience, an expression of utter ecstasy crossed his elfin features. I couldn't tear my eyes away either. My dick might have lay dormant, but my eyes and brain hadn't, and fuck me, I understood why the sharks closed in.

The ground under my feet reverberated to the thump of the bass. But the quivering of my own left buttock was actually my phone vibrating in my pocket. Eggy's handsome mug appeared on the screen. Keeping an eye on Otto, I pushed my way through the masses until I reached the less noisy and cooler terrace.

"Have you found him?" squawked Eggy. "Dude, please tell me you've found him."

"Yeah, bro, he's here." *Good Lord was he there.*

"Oh thank god. Is he okay?"

On tiptoes, I scanned the dance floor. Next to Otto, a big German-looking blond guy lumpenly shuffled from foot to foot. Like a brand-new dwarf planet orbiting the sun, the apple of Eggy's eye slunk around him, wiggling those bloody hips like they were on a piece of elastic. Two pretty girls, of a similar age to Otto and unremarkable in comparison, strutted their stuff alongside. From the German guy's expression, he'd thought all his Christmases had come at once.

"Yeah, he's...um...he's good. He's...er...he's, you know, sitting quietly with a few friends at one of the tables." Not enough. Eggy needed more. I looked up again. "Yeah, um, just sitting.

With two girls, one with long dark hair, another with short red hair."

"Sounds like Alicia and Celine." Eggy's relief was palpable. "Is he drinking? God, Fifty, tell me he's not drinking."

Why the hell did I cover for this boy? A tall, skinny darker man joined the butch German and greeted Otto with a cheeky tweak to his arse. His reward was a brief vertical lap dance, all the more impressive since Otto ground into his crotch while simultaneously swigging from a small metal hipflask.

"Nah, I think...um...he's having a can of Coke."

"Christ, I'm so glad you're there watching out for him. Clem says to ask you if there are any blokes hovering? Are you sure I don't need to come and sort them out? I can be there in five minutes. You only need to say the word."

The hip flask vanished, mostly because Otto required both hands around the dark-skinned guy's neck to facilitate his climb up his body. Any more of this and they'd be practically humping on the dance floor.

"Um...nah, not really. A couple of kids hanging around, that's all."

The German and the dark-skinned guy were both well into their thirties. I spotted another couple of men edging towards the dance floor, both of them ogling the fluffball. Talk about sharks circling fresh meat. Fuck, I would have to do something. Loyalty to Eggy compelled me to intervene. My mission tonight was to ensure the kid made it home safely, not watch the local sleazeballs seduce him. And most definitely not to gawp at him myself. I sized up the two new guys, praying they'd become distracted and wander off.

Absolutely slaughtered, one was almost too drunk to stand, let alone have his wicked way with Eggy's innocent pride and joy. He wasn't the problem. The German and the tall dark guy had thankfully backed off a bit too. Squinting through the flashing lights, I gave the other man on the side-lines a closer look, and my heart sank. Exactly as I feared. Old Ale-handsy himself.

Alejandro Abrantes. Bloody typical. That man could smell new blood from the moment the tourist planes touched down. Clem had dubbed him the Casanova of Corralejo. I'd dubbed him something far less literary. And to Eggy he would always be Ale-handsy, from his ill-judged attempt to paw Clem one night out about six months ago. With Eggy barely two feet away when Alejandro's wandering fingers had found their way onto Clem's arse, the man should count himself lucky he still had them. And now he unwittingly jeopardised his toenails.

I'd never admit it to Eggy, but I secretly admired the Spaniard's sexual confidence, most likely as I had none myself. Like most of the predators closing in on the dance floor tonight, his age was much closer to mine than Otto's, easily pushing thirty-five. No oil painting: he had a slab of a nose much too big for his face and severe acne scarring no amount of time in the sun could disguise. His family owned a couple of hotels in Corralejo, so he flashed the cash and dressed well. He talked a good talk too and had the bloody balls to have a crack at anyone he fancied, scoring plenty from what I'd seen. Tourists aside, I was possibly the only single gay man in Corralejo he hadn't tried it on with, most likely because he hadn't clocked we were on the same team. A lot of people didn't. After all, I wasn't exactly out there shaking my booty and waving a rainbow flag, like young Otto.

Ale-handsy practically licked his lips in anticipation, and I watched with growing unease as his palm fiddled at his crotch. Christ, the pissed kids here for the summer were easy pickings for the likes of him. As he handed his drink to his boozed-up mate and pushed through the throng of dancers towards his target, I began a pincer movement from the opposite side, never taking my eyes away from the top of Otto's blond head.

A perennial wallflower, I had spent years observing other men's approach to the dance floor. Hammered British guys favoured barging in *en masse*, taking over a space, and then busting some hideously uncoordinated moves without giving a shit about the ensuing carnage on either side. More sophisticated European men joined their friends with a sexy half dance, half walk, clicking their fingers and swaying their hips, already pretentiously lost to the rhythm.

Alejandro took that to another level, having perfected what I could only describe as an oily glide. As he oozed towards his target, hips undulating suggestively, the tight pouch of his groin preceded the rest of him, as if his dick were attached to an invisible thread pulling him in time to the beat towards the hottest new boy in the club.

We met in the middle. It wasn't pretty. My own approach to Otto had been closer to the unsophisticated, but effective, British barging-through technique.

On reaching his goal, Alejandro upscaled his naff dance moves, mostly centred around suggestive groin thrusts. Innocently greeting his new admirer with flirtatious delight, Otto twirled around him with eye-wateringly provocative hip action of his own. Blond fluffballs weren't generally my thing, but...I couldn't deny it. Sexy as hell. Eggy would have self-combusted on the spot. Anyone else's baby brother and I'd be on the sidelines scoffing at the blatant cheesiness of Alejandro's approach and Otto's cheesier response, but fuck, the dumb kid was Eggy's flesh and blood. No way this douchebag's hands would go anywhere near him.

From behind, I slid my own arms around Otto's slender waist, and the boy automatically sank back into me. For a brief second, the length of his warm body sashayed suggestively against mine. Looking up, the ready smile on his lips changed to jaw-dropping astonishment, followed by dismay, as I sternly mouthed the words "he's mine" to Ale-handsy, who was attempting some sort of body-popping manoeuvre in front of us. At times like this, looming easily over six feet tall and built on the chunky side felt like a distinct asset. Not only did my size ensure Alejandro rapidly melted back into the crowd, but it also prevented a very pissed-off fluffball from wriggling out of my grasp. I huffed with the effort to hold on to him.

The Eggebraaten stroppiness gene was strong in this one.

"What the fuck do you think you're doing?" he screamed after I'd marched him to the cooler, quieter outdoor bar area. His attempts to yank himself out of my stronghold were attracting attention. A lovers' tiff.

I loosened my grip a fraction, while keeping my arm still firm around his narrow shoulders. "Lovely view along the coastline from here at night, don't you think?"

Grey eyes flashed at me furiously, and a pair of well-shaped blond eyebrows joined in the middle in an angry vee. His full lips pursed into a pretty pout, making me smile. I'd seen another version of this annoyed, handsome face many times, a much more intimidating version. The smile only served to piss him off even more.

"Let me guess. Ragnar sent you to keep an eye on me, am I right? God, you are so embarrassing, Christian! I'm never going to live this down. You dragged me off the dance floor in front of my friends! In front of my *friends*, you arsehole!"

I nodded calmly as he stamped his foot, hands on hips. An angry, fire-breathing baby dragon.

"I don't need Ragnar's henchman watching over me! I'm nineteen! If I wanted babysitting like this, I'd have stayed in bloody Vestvågøya!"

"And saved us a whole load of aggro," I drawled, agreeing

with him. I spotted his girlfriends making their way towards us and attempted to placate him.

"Listen, dude. Yes, you're nineteen. An adult on your passport but still a fucking dumb teenager in your head. We've all been there, mate. When I was nineteen, I overturned my mum's car and got so stoned I slept in a dog kennel for two nights. No one would have described me as a grown-up back then. Spots were my biggest worry."

"You don't have any spots." His hand automatically went to a small red blemish on his otherwise smooth jawline.

"I'm no longer nineteen."

"Not all teenage boys do stupid things. When Clem was my age, he won an Oscar!"

I sighed wearily. "Sunshine, I didn't know Clem at nineteen, but I have a feeling he wasn't much like you."

Frowning, I studied at him properly, taking in the tiny, lime-green T-shirt, unfeasibly tight jeans, and that mass of spiky white hair. Nope, I couldn't imagine Clem ever dressing like that. I gestured vaguely back inside the club.

"Otto, listen. Take my advice. To local guys like him, cute blond foreign boys are easy meat. I know him—your brother knows him. He cruises the tourist bars all summer. He'll get you drunk, give you some of the sexy Spanish accent, all the chat. I couldn't stand by and watch that happen. Eggy would kill me."

"What do you have against Spanish guys?"

Obviously, I needed to spell it out further. "I don't. They're really hot. I've made some great friends amongst the locals. But stay away from that one. And ones like him. In any case, he's way too old for you."

"I can handle myself," Otto insisted obstinately.

The ensuing lip chewing and folded arms was also a familiar look. Time for the stranger-danger conversation. "Dude, you don't know him; you don't know if you can trust him. I do, and Alejandro is angling for more than a peck on the cheek, that's for sure. And you say you can handle yourself, but you weigh scarcely fifty kilos wringing wet."

Listening to myself, I cringed. Sage old man dispensing wisdom to a young buck. Christ, if he only knew how little I had to back up my wise words. One more groin fondle on the dance floor and Otto's sexual experience would have surpassed my own.

More cute pouting. "So what if I'm not very big? My brothers used to tell me the best things come in small packages."

I rolled my eyes, imagining five huge, muscly blokes jumping every time precious little Otto expressed a hint of displeasure. "Yeah, mate. And so does poison."

"Maybe I want to taste some of what's on offer," Otto retorted, ignoring me. "Maybe I want more than a peck on the cheek. Maybe I want to be ravaged by a hot Spaniard."

Join the fucking club.

"Maybe you do," I sighed. "And good luck with that. But it's not happening on my watch, buddy."

After much back and forth and a hell of a lot of pouting—him, not me—we reached a compromise. He could dance with his mates for another hour, under my watchful eye, and then I'd escort him home.

What can I say? It was a tough gig, sipping my beer and watching Otto do his thing. I manfully coped. At first, he threw me a few hard glares, but soon forgot, caught up with a gang of teens having a wild night.

He sulked for the beginning of the short walk home, trailing a pace or two behind. To be fair, I walked at quite a trot, and his legs were much shorter. We'd reached the far end of the beach before he spoke, slightly breathless.

"Can we stop somewhere for a minute? I've been dancing all night, and my feet are killing me. And if I go home now, Ragnar will still be awake, and he'll fire twenty questions: Who were you with? Where did you go? What did you drink? Have you changed your pants this morning? I'm beginning to think he's worse than all the other brothers put together."

I grinned in the darkness; he did a pretty accurate impression of Eggy throwing his weight around. Somehow, I had a feeling it was water off a duck's back with Otto.

"So, have you?" I asked him with a grin.

"Have I what?"

"Changed your pants this morning?"

"Odin's teeth, Christian! I'd started to think you were okay!"

"Chill, mate." I smiled at him. "I'm only joshing with you. Until Clem came along, your brother was a right dirty bugger. He used to turn his grundies inside out to make them last another day."

Otto laughed delightedly. "I'm going to save that nugget of information until he's really pissing me off."

We walked side by side a little farther. "I know. Let's go down here," he suggested brightly, pointing to the beach. "I found a secret spot on the rocks yesterday. No one can see you from the path."

I checked my watch. Just after midnight. Way past this old man's usual bedtime. But Otto had already headed off the pavement, so I followed, the refreshing cool sea breeze after the fug of the club making my mind up for me. Since he was working in the shop and living at Eggy's house, we'd be seeing a lot of each other. I didn't want to fall out with him any further. And, however tempting after I'd embarrassed him in the club, he hadn't scored cheap points by bringing up my consultation at the doctor's this morning.

His secret spot wasn't that secret, though well hidden from

anyone strolling along the pavement above. A set of very ordinary steep concrete steps led down to the beach, or what passed for one at this end of town. More of a rocky outcrop. I'd certainly never seen anyone sunbathing down here. At full tide, the narrow strip of sand disappeared, the jagged rocks hidden from the unwary. Only surfers with a death wish would dip their toe in the waters off this short stretch of coastline.

Next to the steps, a set of narrower, older steps veered off, most eroded away with only a couple remaining. In the UK, they'd have been fenced off years ago, before someone sued the council for injuring themselves. Settling on one of these, Otto swung his legs down towards the lethal rocks below.

"Not the prettiest viewpoint on the island, dude," I observed mildly. Nothing but the crashing waves of the murky Atlantic lay ahead. Boulders loomed to the sides, studded with illegible graffiti, and behind us stood a dull stone wall.

Otto shrugged, taking a generous swig from his metal hipflask before passing it to me. God knows where he'd secreted that—his jeans looked as if he'd sewn himself into them. Gingerly, I brought it to my lips and took a cautious sip, braced for whatever Scandinavian firewater he'd nicked from Eggy's alcohol stash. Fortunately, it was only the local sickly *ron miel* liqueur.

"I like it here. It reminds me of home. Except much warmer, of course." Features lighting up, he flashed me a grin in the dark. "The waves back in Vestvågøya are exactly like this at night. Harsh and rough."

He took another swig.

"I bet Eggy doesn't know about that." I indicated the flask. God, I sounded like a proper ageing fun sponge.

"Don't tell him, okay? I don't drink much, never enough to get sloshed. Believe me, I don't want to have a fit in the middle of a nightclub any more than Eggy does."

Possibly foolishly, I believed him. At that age, constantly being told you couldn't do entirely normal things for every other nineteen-year-old around you must have been hell.

Much happier now, having recovered from the humiliation of his older brother's mate pulling him off the dance floor, Otto became positively chatty. His singsong accent against the backdrop of the waves was strangely soothing. As we leaned together against the cool stone wall, passing the hipflask to and fro, I let him witter on about his dreams for nursing college, his brothers, his favourite brand of jeans, the spot on his chin, how much he'd missed Eggy, and how much he wanted to live near him forever (so bloody cute).

"Do you have dreams, Christian?" he asked, rousing me from a semi-doze.

"I'd be dreaming right now if you weren't keeping me from my bed."

He tutted at me. "Seriously, do you?"

"I'm living it," I said half-jokingly. "Coming here with your brother, that was the dream, and it turned out fine."

Erectile dysfunction and chronic loneliness weren't included in the original plan, but he could work that out for himself. Until my thirties beckoned, I'd always believed the old surfing adage. You only needed three things in life to be happy: your body, a surfboard, and a wave. After witnessing month after month of Eggy and Clem's utter contentment, I realised a fourth component was missing.

Frowning, Otto looked about to add something else and then thought better of it. He stayed silent awhile, kicking his feet against the rocks below.

"You said to the doctor that you were dating," he began, not looking at me. "Or hoping to, anyhow."

I inhaled deeply. I always found conversations like these so much easier after a spliff. "Yeah. That's the plan."

"Ragnar and Clem worry about you ever such a lot," he confided. "Ragnar says you're very nice once people get to know you. But you can be really grumpy too, apparently. Which puts men off."

"Good to know." I chuckled. "Anything else he says about me that I ought to hear?"

He kicked against the rocks again. "Only that you saved his life when he first came over to the UK, when he had nothing and no one. He says if you hadn't rescued him, he'd be dead or homeless or in prison by now."

The old, infatuated Fifty would have desperately clung to that snippet of verbal sunshine; the newer, improved one laughed. "I'm sure your brother would be thrilled if he knew you were spilling all his innermost thoughts."

"What was Ragnar like when you first met him? I remember him as wonderful—this huge older brother who tickled me and made me my favourite dinners and gave me piggybacks every-where. When I had a fit, he'd always let me sleep in his bed with him."

His childlike perspective made me smile. A very young Otto had idolised his cool, older brother. How his memory of teenage Eggy contrasted with my own! The seventeen-year-old Eggy I'd picked up at the motorway service station, all those years ago, had been a cold, hungry, frightened boy. A homeless kid, miles from Norway, who'd had the stuffing comprehensively knocked out of him. I didn't want to burst Otto's bubble.

"Well, for a start, he's never tickled me or given me piggy-backs. Or cooked my favourite dinners. Sounds like I need to have some strong words with him."

He'd never let me sleep in his bed either, but there lay another story.

"Yeah, but what was he like?" Otto persisted.

Eggy spent that first summer sleeping in a tent next to my

van, quiet and withdrawn, only brightening when we went surf-ing. He'd followed me everywhere, like a whipped puppy. My uncle Ray had needed another guy to help at work, so I'd spruced him up, sorted out a national insurance number for him, and taught him how to hold a paintbrush. Then promptly fallen in love.

In return, Eggy had made me his best mate, widened my horizons and comprehensively broken my heart.

"He was exactly as he is now. A cocky, opinionated, egotistical Viking. With way too much hair."

Otto laughed. "That's all for show, you know that. You should see the way he fusses over Clem. It's bloody nauseating. Anyway, you must be okay, because he's hung around with you for years. And Clem also adores you, and he hardly likes anyone. Ragnar says you're like another brother to him. Even though you fancy him, which is a bit weird."

"Did he say that?" I asked sharply.

Otto shook his head. "Nah, but I can tell. Everyone fancies him."

"Well, I don't," I replied firmly. "Don't say so again, please."

He smiled slyly, kicking his feet against the rock. "I'm only winding you up. I know you don't. He's not your type."

I let out a bark of laughter, piercing the cooling night air. "And what's my type, Mr Know-It-All?"

He raised an eyebrow knowingly. "Well, according to what you said to that Spanish bloke who was having a crack at me, 'I'm yours'. So I guess I'm it. And you called me a cute blond foreign boy." I shook my head in disbelief, and he shrugged. "Just saying."

Bloody hell, this kid was a real piece of work. Crab fishing? Delicate disposition? Not bloody likely.

"I'm getting a numb bum," he observed, shifting on the cold stone slab. After checking his phone, he climbed to his feet and brushed himself down. The hip flask disappeared, tucked below his waistband.

"I'm not surprised it's numb, with that massive hole in your trousers."

Yep, I sounded ancient. He pulled a face and wiggled his cute little arse at me, the rip just about on the right side of decency. Fuck, this boy was dangerous.

"Ragnar should be asleep by now, and if he's not, then I can legitimately say I spent most of the night with you, which would meet with his approval."

We retraced our steps in silence, until we were back on the pavement and heading for home.

"Why does everyone call you Fifty?" he asked, as we rounded the corner at the top of his road.

"Because my real name is Christian Grey," I answered, ready for the usual conversation which followed.

It didn't.

"So?" He frowned.

"So what?"

"I mean, is it a joke or something? If it is, I don't get it."

"Er, dude? Christian Grey? *Fifty Shades of Grey?* You know, the film, the books? The red room of pain?"

He shrugged. "Nah, never heard of it. Christian's a nice name, though."

Smiling, I shook my head. Kids these days.

Chapter Four

When Otto receives a lesson in how to wash up properly

Having Otto as an extra pair of hands in the shop greatly eased our summer pressures. Instead of relying on the hotel reception staff to manage lesson bookings, Otto arranged them directly through the shop. Being far better than Eggy and me at flogging stuff, our merchandise and clothing sales increased too. His knowledge of surfboards and repairing them rivalled mine, and his Spanish was coming along a treat too, practising confidently at every opportunity. All in all, I'd warmed to the kid, not that I'd let him know.

"Are you going out surfing later?" I asked him. My last lesson had finished sooner than expected. Both pleased and surprised at his work ethic, I'd given Otto permission to take the rest of the afternoon off. I'd seen his girlies hanging around, all kitted out in beach gear, and I'd overheard them making plans. "The waves are super clean this afternoon if you head down by the sand dunes. There's only a very gentle onshore breeze."

"I don't surf." He sighed miserably. "I suppose I might go down to the beach and watch Alicia and Celine, though."

My jaw dropped. "What? You seem to know everything there is to know about the subject!"

"Yeah," he agreed glumly. "Doesn't mean I'm allowed. I grew up surrounded by surfers. I also know a hell of a lot about fishing quotas, but I don't fish either. With my epilepsy, the brothers have never let me anywhere near the water. I can't even swim very well."

I was being even dimmer than usual. "Dude, there's nothing wrong with your arms and legs, is there? Epileptics can learn to swim, can't they?"

"Yeah, *dude,* but they can also drown if they have a fit and no one gets them out of the water in time. That's why I'm never allowed to take a bath. Not unless one of the brothers watches me, and you may not have noticed, but I'm getting a bit too old."

"But, like, haven't you got medicines and stuff? To control it?"

He shrugged. "Yeah, but I still have fits. Not very often, but it can happen. And I have focals all the time. I had one this morning while I sorted out that Irish family with their board hire, but you didn't notice."

"What the hell's a focal?"

"Some people call them partial seizures, but it's not actually. My mind goes blank for a few seconds. Or I act a bit weird and spaced out for a minute or two. The family most likely simply assumed I'd got distracted and lost my train of thought."

That had totally passed me by, but then again, I wasn't the sharpest tool in the box.

I'd never witnessed anyone have a proper fit. With my newly acquired expertise, I assumed it was similar to fainting. "Can't you go swimming or surfing with someone else keeping an eye on you?"

He pulled a face. "Ragnar thinks it's too risky. My pa always said the same. Especially in the sea. When I was younger, the brothers used to take me for a splash around in the swimming pool at our local leisure centre, but by the time I reached twelve or thirteen, it was a bit embarrassing, so I stopped." He gave me a sly look. "Not too dissimilar from having my older brother's best mate spying on me when I'm out at night."

My turn to shrug. "Yeah, well, I'm not apologising. And you're lucky I turned up. Next time, find a bloke your own age to hook up with."

The phone in the back office rang. Otto answered, switching to his ultra-polite and friendly telephone voice. Nodding, he held the receiver out to me.

"It's for you. A Spanish man called Felipe." Putting his hand over the receiver, he whispered, "I hope he's age-appropriate for you, Christian. Wouldn't want you being led astray by an older man."

Yanking the phone from him, I swatted his arse. "Oh, yes please, daddy!" he shrieked.

Little fucker.

"Daddy? Is there something you're hiding from me, Fifty?" Felipe purred.

Cringing, I rolled my eyes at Otto, who stuck his tongue out at me in return. I turned my back on him. "No, it's the annoying lad I work with, pulling my chain."

I'll give Felipe his due—he was persistent. To make up for blowing him off the night Otto arrived, I agreed to a dinner date. He then treated me to a pretty dull rundown of his working day, which I supposed was how prospective partners sounded each other out. Hopefully, I made all the right noises. Deliberately earwigging, Otto mooched around the shop, pretending to straighten a rack of wetsuits.

"Is that your new boyfriend?" he asked after I finally managed to hang up. God, how old were we, twelve?

"No. I don't have a boyfriend. You know this already. We're only meeting for drinks and some food."

"Most people call that dating. You said you wanted to date someone."

I considered this. "Yes. Possibly. Not that it's any of your business."

"He does a weird throat-clearing thing before he speaks."

"No he doesn't."

"Just saying."

His hand lingered on one of the wetsuits, and he made a guttural sound in his throat, exactly as Felipe had done. Smart-arse little fucker. I shouldered on my jacket, then began turning out the lights.

"Can I come back to your place for a bit?"

I snorted. "Five minutes ago, I was your older brother's horribly embarrassing best mate."

"Yeah, and you still are, but I don't wanna go home. I'm bored, and Alicia and Celine have gone surfing."

I shrugged. I didn't see why not. He'd worked hard, and in retrospect, he did appear a little glum. I felt sorry for him—I pitied *anyone* not being able to surf. Surfing was life, in my opin-ion. Nothing else came close.

Otto loved my tiny, rented apartment, cooing over every-thing, from my plain blue corner sofa with its bright yellow cushions to the pristine white kitchen units. His appreciation amused me, as my home wasn't that special—not compared to Eggy and Clem's. They'd bought a rambling old villa that (thanks to Clem's gazillions) Eggy had begun gradually over-hauling, room by room. Not intrinsically tidy by nature, Clem's books and papers spilled over every available surface. Shabby-chic rugs littered the floor, and the kitchen was a minefield of pots and pans and spices and cookery books. Bohemian clutter, Clem called it. Eggy adored the mess, as it epitomised the essence of Clem. Evidently, it didn't find favour with his younger brother though.

"Wow! You're so neat and organised. I'd like an apartment like this one day." He fingered the plain throw hanging over the back of the sofa, perfectly parallel to the floor. "It's so cool having a place of your own. I had to share a bedroom with Erik at home in Norway, and he had so much stuff. And he snored."

His wandering fingers moved to the neat venetian blinds. "Everything is so clean and so...anal. Shit, are you really a single man?"

"Yeah," I laughed. "I like a tidy house, that's all. So don't mess it up. You'll be in trouble if you do."

Tidy was a slight understatement. Immaculate would be closer to the truth. I almost trotted out 'a place for everything and everything in its place', but then I'd have sounded like a middle-aged wanker, so I kept my mouth shut. I adored a tidy house. When I lived out of the vans with Eggy, I used to dream of very little else. Eggy had mostly respected my need for order while we shared space, but lonely bachelorhood did have its advantages. Number one being my apartment remained exactly as I liked it.

Reaching into the fridge, I pulled out a few things for dinner. Having lived with Clem for a while before they bought their place, I'd picked up a few culinary ideas from him, and tonight was carbonara night. Perching on one of my bar stools, Otto made himself comfortable.

"Why didn't you want to go home, then? Have Clem and your brother gone out?"

"Nah," he said, almost sheepishly. "They...um...they appreciate their own space sometimes, I think."

I grinned. "I hear you, buddy."

Blushing, he fiddled with the hem of his T-shirt. "Hear *them*, more like. Odin's teeth! When people fall in love, how long until they can last five minutes without ripping each other's clothes off? I mean, Clem's hot and all, but Ragnar chases him around the house like a dog with two dicks!"

Horny was Eggy's default factory setting, I'd long ago deduced that. Probably not what Otto needed to hear. "They'll settle down. They haven't been together that long."

"It's coming up to a year, Christian!" Leaning closer, he whispered in a conspiratorial fashion. "From what I can work out, they do a lot of edging. And I mean a *lot*."

My puzzled frown must have given me away.

"You know what edging is, right?"

So this conversation had taken off at a tangent—I thought we'd been talking about Eggy's sex life. "Dude, I've been a painter and decorator since I left school. Of course I know what edging is. But Eggy certainly never had the patience for it. He always left the hard bits, like window frames, to me."

"Not that sort of edging, Christian! Odin's teeth! I thought you were a sophisticated man of the world! I mean when," his voice dropped to an even lower register, "you know, one person makes the other person nearly...er...you know...come. And then they stop and do it all over again. Bringing each other to the edge."

He laughed good-humouredly. "I'd be rubbish at it; I reckon if a hot bloke touched my dick, even through five pairs of trousers, I'd be jizzing all over the place."

How wonderful for you, I almost replied. How wonderful to be secure in the knowledge your dick would respond appropriately to the slightest provocation.

"Shit, I should engage my brain before I open my big mouth." He clapped a hand to his face dramatically. "Sorry."

I reddened but laughed it off. I was too old for blushing. "It's cool. But way too much oversharing, bro."

Otto giggled. "And sometimes..." Those wide grey eyes

sparkled with a mixture of awe and amusement. "And some-times...I swear Ragnar spanks Clem!"

Oh Lordy, that Eggy's innocent, youngest brother had to listen to all that bloody carry on. From my years in the vans, I could truly empathise. I might not have known the correct terminology for Eggy's sexual preferences, but I'd become exceedingly familiar with them. Sounded like Otto's innocence was being stripped away without even leaving the house.

He watched me fry the bacon lardons for a few minutes.

"Christian?" he began tentatively. He schooled his features into an uncharacteristic grave expression.

"Yes?"

He sounded deathly serious. *God, please, don't ask me about my sex life or make me talk about my trip to the doctor's; please don't bring it up.* Him knowing my worst secret was bad enough.

"Ragnar mentioned that you...um...that you had an Xbox? And FIFA?"

Relief flooded out of me. Okay, so now we'd got to the real reason for his visit. At twenty-nine, I sometimes felt I hadn't distanced myself much at all from my nineteen-year-old self. One minute swaggering with enough machismo to take on the world and win, the next trying to understand how to navigate the vast ocean between your big brother's sexual confidence and your own. And then wanting to clear all that adult crap from your head and lose yourself in what was basically a toy for grownups.

"Go on, then. The telly's in my bedroom. Don't mess with any of my stuff!"

As I cooked the pasta, I texted Clem to let them know Otto's whereabouts. No immediate answer, confirming Otto's assump-tions as to how they were spending their evening alone.

Once Clem became a permanent fixture in Eggy's life, I

finally accepted Eggy would never be mine. I didn't know if I'd ever stop having feelings for him, but these days I could park them on a high shelf. Like a box of faded photos, I'd periodically flick through them, remembering the good times, before carefully putting them back where they belonged. In the past.

People laughingly joked the best way to get over someone was to get under someone else, and I was increasingly of the same opinion. I wanted to test the theory. However, until my dick and brain reliably worked in tandem, I'd be somewhat hampered. Felipe would be a willing and able participant in my experimentation, but the thought of confessing my utter lack of sexual experience to a cool, knowledgeable guy like him filled me with anguish. Add unpredictable erectile dysfunction into the mix and god knew what fucking disastrous scenario I would be setting myself up for.

Maybe I should stick to playing FIFA with nineteen-year-olds.

With these gloomy thoughts, I balanced two glasses of water and two heaped plates of food on a tray and took them through into my bedroom. Otto sat up, cross-legged, in the middle of my bed, glued to the TV.

"Dinner is served."

"Can I finish this game first?" His gaze never left the football match he orchestrated with the handset.

"You can, but I might have eaten it all."

He made a teenage groaning sigh, expressing his unhappiness much more eloquently than any words possibly could, before throwing the handset onto the bed in disgust. "You've made me lose now, Christian."

"And the world didn't stop spinning, did it? If you don't spill your dinner on my duvet, I'll give you a game later. I'll show you how to do it properly."

He scooted up the bed until his head rested against the

wooden headboard, and I did the same. Halfway through my food, the thought struck me that being alone in my bedroom with another man, squashed next to him on my bed, was quite intimate. And also a first for me, excluding Eggy. If I'd extended this invitation to Felipe, or any of the other Felipes before him, then by now, my heart would be racing, my panicky dick would be up and down like a whore's drawers, and I'd hardly be able to swallow a mouthful. As it was, my dick snoozed, my heart thrummed at a steady rate, and I savoured the taste of my own cooking.

"Not bad." Otto hoovered up the pasta as only a teenage boy could. "I'll award you eight out of ten. Clem's is better, but giving me a massive portion earned you an extra point. And I haven't had to eat it with those two licking each other's lips clean afterwards. So maybe I'll bump you up to a nine."

Praise indeed. "Glad I could be of service."

In retrospect, inviting a nineteen-year-old to play FIFA against me was a dumb move. He effortlessly trounced me three times in succession, his delighted smile an older but no less sweet version on the ten-year-old boy proudly holding up a crab to the camera.

"Christian?"

"Yes?"

"How did you know you were gay?"

I huffed out a laugh. An easy question to answer. "I've been hanging around fit, tanned, half-naked men carrying surfboards practically since I could walk. I've known what I liked for as long as I can remember. How about you?"

"I dunno really," he mused. "Having a crush on Harry Styles maybe, since he was, like, sixteen? Fancying my brother's mates, who used to think I was sweet and let me crawl all over them and play-fight with me and let me snuggle into their laps when I pretended to be tired?"

I could easily imagine a cute, younger version of Otto manipulating those innocent young men. "You're a naughty boy, you know that?"

He nodded happily. "Yep. Do your parents know you are gay?"

A less pleasant question. If this was his strategy to thrash me at FIFA even more comprehensibly, then it worked. "I don't see much of my parents, mate. I don't know if they know, or not."

Or care, I could have added. After they'd divorced, both had gone on to build new families with their new partners. My dad certainly didn't give a shit. We'd not been in contact for years, not since the fateful night I'd met Eggy, on my way back from being refused entry into his new family home. My mum possibly wondered, but we weren't exactly close. We'd never talked about it.

Eyes fixed on the screen, Otto chewed his lip in concentration. "So how did you hide it, when you were my age?"

Pretty bloody easily, seeing as it had been a secret only shared with my left hand and my computer's private web browser. "Um...I don't know. I guess...er...I was discreet."

"I think that's the main reason why I left home, Christian. Yesss!" He hissed with satisfaction as he scored an absolute corker from outside the penalty area. "I don't want to have to spend the next few years hiding who I am or being discreet. I want to be gay as fuck."

I smirked, thinking of his skinny outfit and his seductive, uninhibited dancing from a few nights ago. "I think you've achieved that goal, buddy."

He risked a look at me during the replay, his appraising gaze sliding across my body, scanning my face before gluing back onto the screen. "I suppose it's easier for you. I mean, you don't really scream gay, do you? You know, with your hair and clothes and stuff. And your body."

Although I knew what he meant, I was fairly sure he hadn't said this entirely as a compliment. Young gay guys didn't have bodies like mine. They either aspired to be Eggy, with abs so grooved lovers used them as footholds on the long climb up to his mouth, or like Clem, the cool, slender, pale, and interesting type. Whereas I channelled a straight, aging surfer vibe, the kind of guy who enjoyed Friday-night beers and a curry a little more than was healthy for him. The kind of guy who'd given up on trying to impress. As long as I had a clean T-shirt and a pair of board shorts, I was good to go.

"What's wrong with my hair and clothes?"

His concentration was back on the game. "They're all right, I suppose. For a surfer dude stuck in the 1990s. But you really should invest in some conditioner for your hair. The sea salt makes it quite straw-like. You've got split ends."

"Charming."

"Your body is really nice, though. I love it."

I'd say one thing for the fluffball—he entertained me. "So I'm your brother's embarrassing best mate, and I've got split ends and a nice body, even though it's the wrong body for a gay guy. Anything else I should know?"

The tip of his wet tongue poked between his teeth as Otto concentrated on the game, both thumbs flying over the console. A sudden yelp of delight escaped him. "Yeah. You're shit at FIFA. I've scored a hat trick."

I'd become quite fond of the fluffball's company, tolerating him following me like an extra shadow as I cleared up. I decided to put him to some use, even if he did make a complete hash of washing up. So much so I insisted he redo half if he ever wanted to play on my Xbox again. Cue more teenage groans. You'd honestly think I'd asked him to lick everything clean with his tongue. When I wasn't looking, he retaliated by tipping one of my perfectly aligned yellow sofa cushions onto the floor. Little fucker.

And he never stopped bloody talking. "Christian, do you think I should get my eyebrow pierced?"

"I dunno, mate. It depends if you want to get it pierced."

"Have you got any piercings?"

"Nope. And you haven't rinsed those glasses properly. They'll look smeary when they're dry."

"What about tattoos?"

"Yeah." I chuckled; I'd almost forgotten about it. "I've got a little surfboard on my arse. I had it done by some random guy in France when I was stoned, years ago. Eggy says it looks more like a dick than a surfboard."

He giggled. "Let's have a peek."

"No," I replied firmly. "I'm not getting my arse out for you."

And so it went on.

Neither was he familiar with the concept of personal space, which I discovered when he trailed after me into the bathroom.

"I'm...um...I'm kind of doing something...um...private here?" I murmured, unzipping my fly.

"That's okay." He shrugged, narrowing his eyes at his reflection in the bathroom mirror. "You can carry on. Maybe I should get my nose pierced instead of my eyebrow. What do you think?"

Not used to pissing in company, I discovered rather too late that I had a shy bladder. Forcing myself to relax, my pee eventually trickled out, in dribs and drabs. "Um...yes, I guess? If you want to?"

"Mmm. I considered a tattoo of a devil on my neck, but I think Ragnar would kill me."

Christ, this was turning into the longest piss ever. And, with Otto actually quiet for once as he contemplated his perfectly straight nose and shapely eyebrows, one of the noisiest too. I glanced across at his reflection, only to notice his eyes on where I endeavoured to complete my business, his expression one of sympathy.

"That's an age problem, Christian," he pronounced sagely. "A poor stream. Comes to us all one day."

Little *fucker*.

Chapter Five

When Fifty widens his vocabulary

My date with Felipe fell on the same day as my follow-up appointment with Dr Marchena. This time, I managed not to disgrace myself in the waiting room and felt positively calm as she ushered me into her office, Otto hot on my heels. He'd told Eggy he needed a check-up on a few baseline tests after his epilepsy meds were issued.

"The good news is all your blood results have come back as normal." Dr Marchena smiled at me. "So you can rest assured there aren't any physical reasons for your erectile concerns."

As if personally responsible, Otto beamed at her. So, all that remained now was to sort out the madness inside my head. I should have felt relieved, yet I experienced a slight twinge of disappointment instead. The simplicity of having a hormone imbalance, cured by popping a daily pill, had held appeal.

"Last time, I think I mentioned the first steps we need to tackle. Ensure you follow simple advice, such as keeping slim and fit." She cast a quick professional eye over me, and I automatically sucked in my belly. "Which you clearly do."

"He is exceedingly fond of tapas," interrupted Otto, as

though they were discussing a particularly challenging toddler. "But I'll keep an eye on him."

Before carrying on, Dr Marchena threw him an approving look. "And you need to avoid excessive alcohol consumption and steer clear of drugs such as cannabis, which research has shown, time and time again, reduces a man's sexual drive and ability to perform."

Oh god, she'd used the 'p' word. Perform. My least favourite verb in the English language. Even voicing it out loud gave me performance anxiety. It always conjured up images of me on stage with my dick out, trying to bed an impossibly handsome young actor in front of an audience of thousands.

"He's not going to smoke any more weed ever again," my self-appointed minder vehemently assured her. News to me. He patted my arm. "Are you, Christian?"

"No."

I'd agreed in the reluctant, sulky tone of voice Otto himself might have used. My marriage to the pungent green plant had been the most enduring and happiest relationship of my life so far, but yeah, they were right. Time to initiate divorce proceedings.

"And from now on, he's going to limit alcohol to a couple of beers at the weekends."

The little fucker.

"Excellent," replied Dr Marchena brightly. "Seems like you have a good support network helping you, but if you do need the details of an organisation, then..."

"Thank you," said Otto smoothly. "If we need further assistance, we won't hesitate to get in contact."

I was both touched and amused by the 'we'.

"So, now I'll come onto how best to overcome your problem. There are several drugs I can offer you—erectile enhancers. Viagra is the popular one that you have no doubt heard of.

There are many others, all with slightly different profiles and pros and cons, but I'm reluctant to jump straight into that."

Now we'd got down to the nitty-gritty. Despite the air-con, my T-shirt suddenly felt damp on my back, and I shifted in the plastic chair, struggling to focus. Fortunately, Otto absorbed every word, his face a mask of concentration. I hoped we weren't going to be having too thorough a debrief afterwards.

"I'd be interested to know what you think the problem is, Christian, in your own words?"

Where did I start? Did I tell her I'd become convinced I was slowly going mad? That I wished I'd smoked less weed? Regretted not experimenting with other boys at Otto's age, instead of hiding in my room listening to my parents arguing? Been a less awkward and more sociable teenager? That I should have surfed less and explored my sexuality more? That I wished I'd got very drunk a few times and fucking gone for it, with random strangers? Popped my cherry, got it over with? Explored promiscuity? Not pined over Eggy for so many years, not lay in my van, night after night, listening to him enjoying glorious sex, while I wanked myself to death, wishing it was me?

Unfortunately, we only had a ten-minute appointment slot.

"Erm...I think that...I...erm...I think that I go on a date, then throughout the evening become more and more anxious about what will happen at the end. What he will expect...um...sexually, I mean. I'm petrified I won't...won't...get...hard if, and when, the time comes. So I get all worked up and make excuses to avoid anything...um...fun happening. Which usually ruins the date. I rarely meet up with that person again."

She steepled her hands and continued to stare at me, with a sympathetic listening face, nodding slightly but not speaking. So I felt obliged to carry on. Glancing to my left, I spied Otto had rediscovered his attraction for the white floor tile.

"And I...I...I...it's been so long since I...um, did anything more than only go on dates. I'm worried I'll be crap at it. That I won't be able to...um...perform. So now I don't really want to anyway anymore. Except...I must want to, as I wouldn't try to date otherwise."

Despite the wise nodding opposite me, I wasn't sure I made sense. But no way could I admit I was still a virgin to this terribly understanding doctor, and most definitely not to Otto. Pride stopped me; shame stopped me. God, I had my bloody thirtieth birthday in three months' time! So my answer hedged around it. I pretended to be out of practice, rather than utterly unpractised, and she continued pretending she didn't think I was an absolute moron. Otto nodded wisely too, as if discussing his brother's best mate's erectile dysfunction was an everyday occurrence.

Dr Marchena quizzed me about experiencing impotence with previous partners, and I truthfully denied it, as long as my faithful left hand didn't count. Which, strictly speaking, it didn't. It was my previous, current, and future partner, though, not enjoying much action at the moment.

When she had totally wrung me dry, she sat up straighter, evidently about to pronounce me insane. "Christian, let me tell you what I think, and you can tell me if you disagree."

Her gaze switched between Otto and me. "Developing and maintaining an erection is a complicated biological pathway, involving the circulatory system, hormones, erectile tissue, nervous tissue, and cognitive processes. Somewhere along the line, possibly a combination of excessive recreational drugs and life's hurdles, you have a disconnect between your cognitive processes and all the other components of that pathway."

Wow, a whole heap of medical jargon. What the fuck were my cognitive processes? I must have radiated incomprehension because she thankfully took it down a notch. "Basically, Christian, your brain and your penis aren't talking to each other. Or rather, your brain is talking far too much, and your penis has switched off."

When we were safely back in the car, Otto observed, "Gosh, she's rather good, isn't she? Very thorough."

I agreed heartily. I couldn't imagine old Dr Jones in Woolacombe being quite as conscientious. Or knowledgeable. We'd have had a minute of the most excruciating conversation ever; then he'd have told me to 'man up' or 'close my eyes and think of England' or something. And that would have been *without* revealing my homosexuality.

In her pithy assessment of my delicate issue, Dr Marchena was right on the money. Somehow, I needed to acquire a strategy to stop my brain overthinking and simply let the scenarios play out. She'd given me some tips how to best achieve this, links to a few useful websites, and an open appointment to return. I also had a prescription for Viagra in my pocket if, and when, I chose to use it, although she strongly encouraged me to give the non-medicinal route a try first.

We all agreed, Otto included, that I needed to focus on building a relationship with someone. To let the intimate times then follow naturally, instead of trying to force them, with or without a chemical erectile enhancer. Of course, much easier said than done. When you reached my age, the bit following a date was kind of expected, especially in the gay community. Felipe enjoyed our drink-and-dinner meetups, but he definitely pushed for more.

"You must think I'm an absolute fruit loop, Otto." I put the car into gear and drove away from the medical centre back towards the town.

"No." His lips curved in a smile. "Well, not entirely. Although to have a completely functioning willy and fail to get it up, even just thinking about going on a date with a hot guy, is hard to get my head 'round."

"Or, in my case, not hard at all."

Giggling, he turned slightly in his seat to face me. "I actually think you're really brave admitting you have this problem and wanting to address it. And even if this is the strangest experience of my life, Ragnar would want you to have support. He'd hate to think you were going through this on your own." As I smoothly joined the flow of traffic, he continued. "By the way, I've been doing some reading."

"Of course you have."

"I'm going to nursing college, remember? I love all this kind of stuff! Anyway, like the doctor said, erectile issues in young men are more common than you would imagine, and for all sorts of reasons. In this context, I'm classifying you as young, by the way."

"Thanks. You're all heart."

He ignored me. "There are biological reasons of course, like she said, but from the websites and blogs I've looked at, most men are like you—feeling anxious and under pressure to perform."

Christ, who blogged about their erectile dysfunction? Having the bottle to make the doctor's appointment took me almost a year, and I nearly did that under a false name. As Otto carried on, I found myself nodding at him anyhow. He sounded way older than his nineteen years. Someone like him would blog about it; he'd have no trouble sharing his woes with the world.

Otto Eggebraaten would become a wonderful nurse one day. I had no doubt. Something was incredibly refreshing and open about him. He'd make any patient feel one hundred percent at ease. Despite my embarrassment, him tagging along had been a good thing.

He laid a hand on my arm briefly. "Oh, and Christian,

didn't you hate it when she talked about performing? So judgy, a horrible word. It's enough to make anyone scared. I mean, I haven't even had sex yet, but being expected to perform feels like way too much pressure. It makes it sound like an X-rated, sex version of *Strictly Come Dancing*!"

I chuckled, glad I wasn't the only one who had picked up on that.

"I mean, I know I'm going to be shit at sex the first few times. I'm pretty rubbish at putting on a condom, for starters. And then, when I've achieved that minor miracle, I'll be too bloody excited to last more than three seconds. Maybe not that long!"

I laughed at his prattling. Who needed weed to relax, when they could listen to one of Otto's monologues?

Sniggering to himself, he gazed out the window. "Hey, Christian, do you reckon Ragnar considers sex a performance? It certainly sounds like it. From what I can make out, him and Clem have a first half, an interval, a second half, and an encore. Maybe I should offer them an ice cream at halftime."

"You know exactly what he'd do with that."

Otto snorted. "Ooh, cover me in mint chocolate chip, Ragnar! Lick me 'til *ice cream*, Ragnar!" he chortled, in a high-pitched voice that sounded absolutely nothing like Clem. He was still giggling at his own joke as we reached the top of his road.

"Thanks for being there today. The doc talked a lot of sense, didn't she?" I pulled into the overgrown drive in front of Eggy and Clem's sprawling villa. "And I think she's right. I'm someone who needs to know a person, be really comfortable with them before I can relax enough for the other stuff, you know? So I'm going to give that a try before I use my prescription."

"Totally," Otto agreed. "Viagra won't help in the long run. Especially as you're demisexual."

"I'm what?" This didn't sound good. I wasn't much of a scholar, but even I knew demi meant half of something.

"Odin's teeth, Christian! Do I have to explain everything to you?"

"Er, yes, quite possibly."

He tutted at me. "You've pretty much defined it yourself. It means you don't fancy anyone unless there is a strong emotional bond. That's why you aren't really a one-night-stand sort of person." Chewing his lip in thought, he frowned. "It's like...um...if being gay is having a door that swings one way, and being straight is a door that swings the other, then you've, like, got a locked door, and hardly anyone has a key. But when you finally meet a person holding one, it will be awesome."

How the hell did Otto know all this stuff, and I didn't? Demisexual. I rolled it over my tongue a few times. Seemed like a good fit. It maybe went part of the way to explaining my penis-related anxieties—although not all the way. Some of that was down to me being an introverted grump who'd spent too many years pining for someone unavailable. But the door thing worked for me. Although mine was barred with a five-gauge mortice lock and deadbolts at the top and the bottom. Now I needed to find a person with a key to unlock it.

Eggy had one, although he'd never wanted to use it. His door was well-oiled and swung both ways. I'd have to keep on searching until I found someone else.

Otto didn't seem in a hurry to get out of the car, and I wasn't in a hurry for him to go. The only man alive who could turn a trip to the doctor's to discuss my erectile dysfunction into a fun morning out. If I could find someone with whom I felt this relaxed, then maybe that emotional bond would strengthen, he'd miraculously produce the key to open my door, and sexy times would follow.

"Do you think your Felipe pal is the right man for the job?"

God knew. We'd been on plenty of dates, and he'd talked about his job, and I'd talked about mine. I knew stuff about Felipe's parents (still alive, happy, and loving), and he knew about mine (probably still alive, possibly happy, and totally uncaring), but I still felt like I hardly knew him. I'd exchanged deeper, more thoughtful conversations with the fluffball as we waited for FIFA to upload than I had with Felipe.

Smiling to myself, I remembered the conversation we'd shared in the car on the way to the medical centre. It hadn't been a conversation, really, just Otto rambling on, confiding he owned a razor blade but hadn't actually needed to use it. Not even on his upper lip. And then he'd followed that little anecdote with a monologue about trying to shave his balls with Erik's electric shaver aged sixteen. He somehow managed to tear his scrotal skin so badly he'd had to show it to Erik, who pissed himself laughing and told all the other brothers. But he'd totally taken my mind off the awkward appointment ahead. As we strolled into the waiting room, I'd found myself at ease and almost cheerful.

If only Felipe were so easy to talk to. Or if only I was better at talking to Felipe and all the other Felipes without feeling so threatened.

"I don't know." I shrugged. "But I think I'll continue to give him a chance anyway. He's a nice guy. One thing may lead to another."

Seemed my mini relationship expert agreed. "Yeah, and if he doesn't click with you, then you could always move on to the next. Maybe try someone completely different. Someone you wouldn't normally go for, perhaps?"

Which, as it happened, was kind of my plan, as much as I

had one. I didn't seem to have a problem finding men attracted to me. If Felipe turned out to be a dud, then I'd persevere.

Clem, who had a few shopping chores in town, took Otto's spot in my car. I had a couple of purchases to make of my own. With the sun high in the sky, I flipped down the windshield visor, glancing at myself in the mirror, then reversed out of their drive.

"Do you think I should get a haircut in town, Clem?" I shoved a clump of blond curls behind my ear. "Go a bit… neater?" Otto's blunt assessment was correct; the ends were a bit crispy.

"Christ, don't ask me. I'm not exactly a style guru." Clem tugged at his long-sleeved black T-shirt. "According to the fluff-ball, I'm still in my adolescent goth-lite phase. Your hair is fine—the shaggy surfer thing is your look."

"Hmm." I continued to study myself sceptically. "Maybe. Or maybe it's time for a makeover."

"Oooh! This is exciting! You're not trying to impress a certain Spanish history teacher are you, by any chance?"

I didn't know. Was I? Otto's face, critically examining my sun-bleached mop, flipped into my mind. Surely I wasn't trying to impress a nineteen-year-old?

"Nah, not really." I hummed, absently tucking another unruly lock behind my ear, only for it to spring forwards again. "It was…er…it was only something Otto said."

"Otto?" Clem laughed incredulously. "His favourite pyjamas have a picture of Spiderman on the front. Be wary of taking fashion advice from him." We drove a little further. "He thinks you're wonderful, by the way."

"Who does? Felipe?" I doubted that very much.

"No, not Felipe. Otto. All we ever hear is 'Christian said this' and 'Christian said that'. And of course, we've had the whole story about his night in Gators and how you bravely charged to his rescue."

"Oh yeah?" I said neutrally.

"Gosh, yes, you can expect your medal of valour through the post any day now. Singlehandedly fighting off a whole army of aging queens trying to steal his virtue. When all he wanted was a quiet little boogie with Alicia and Celine."

Otto's version of events and mine differed wildly. If that was a quiet little boogie, god help the gay libido of Corralejo if he decided to have a noisy one.

Ten minutes later found me in the changing rooms at the back of the huge Zara store on Corralejo high street, surrounded by several pairs of chinos. Clem slouched in a chair, doing an excellent impression of a bored husband dragged shopping with the wife. Despite his attitude, my introduction to Felipe was Clem's fault. He'd been in cahoots with Carlos from the start, since Carlos had introduced his cousin to Clem as a potential Spanish tutor. My self-appointed relationship brokers decided Felipe would be a perfect match for me and set us up on a date. He saw this shopping trip and my attempts to spruce myself up as very promising. And no doubt he'd be filing the experience away for book material. He'd begun his next novel, about a 1970s surfer struggling to find love. Since I'd gleaned that information, I'd felt like a specimen under a microscope, my every move studied and documented.

"This is the super-slim fit." I frowned doubtfully at my reflection in the mirror. "My thighs look like a pair of chicken drumsticks."

"Trust me, those trousers look great on you, Fifty," Clem disagreed, rolling his eyes at me. "Have you ever met a man who didn't enjoy chewing on a chicken drumstick?"

My cheeks flamed, and he laughed. Disappearing into the changing room, I re-emerged a minute later in the classic fit.

Clem shook his head. "Nope. Definitely not. They make you look like you work in IT and have three kids and a mortgage to worry about. And no penis."

The super-slim fit it was then. Chicken drumsticks, package hugging, and all.

"Which colour?" Self-consciously, I dithered in the changing-room doorway, holding up two pairs. "And don't automatically say the black ones because black's your favourite colour."

"Um...the black ones? But the navy looked good too." He raised his hands in a helpless gesture. "Fuck, I don't know."

Fat lot of help he was. "We're gay, Clem. We're supposed to be good at this stuff."

He sighed heavily. "Why don't you buy both pairs? They're in the sale."

Head tilted to the side, I examined myself in the floor-length mirror, trying to recall the last time I had worn something other than jeans or board shorts. It must have been at my grandfather's funeral, aged sixteen. Wearing a shirt felt odd too, the collar scratchy on my neck. Clem had picked out a nice, light-grey check with quite a fitted cut, a little tight around my broad shoulders, then narrowing at my waist. Standing sideways, I sucked my belly in for the second time that day.

"You don't think I should try the next size up?" I was so far out of my comfort zone I'd need a map and compass to find my way back.

"No, definitely not. That shirt fits perfectly. And shows off that gorgeous belly you hide under all those baggy T-shirts."

I must have given him an extremely sceptical look. He waved me away. "For goodness' sake, Fifty, men out there would donate their left testicle to get their hands on a body like yours. You could sell tickets letting them rub their faces through your chest hair alone. Haven't you read any daddy kink?"

I reddened again. "I must have missed that article in *Surfing World.*"

Letting out a quiet exhale, I focused on my midriff. I had grown way too fond of *patatas bravas.*

"Buy the shirt. And that other white one too, and both pairs of trousers. I'll start checking out the belts while you change."

Daddy kink. What the fuck was that? I bet Otto knew.

"Any...um...any need to make a few purchases here?" Clem suggested slyly, as we wandered through the underwear section on our way to the cash desks. "You know, maybe some tight white briefs to show off that rather fine package? Or a couple of pairs of lacy manties?"

Fine package? If my package was delivered through the letterbox, you'd sue the postal service for damaged goods. "Bloody hell, Clem," I muttered, colour once again rising in my cheeks. No way would me buying sexy underwear make it into his next novel. And tight white briefs? Why would I subject my block and tackle to those uncomfortable things when I had a neat drawerful of M&S's essential-range black boxers back home? And what the fuck 'lacy manties' could be was anybody's guess, but they didn't sound at all practical. And very itchy.

Later, soaping myself in the shower, I contentedly pondered my day and concluded I'd made progress. Having negotiated a follow-up trip to the doctor, I'd been reassured my condition wasn't terminal. I'd taken steps to smarten my image, even if my new trousers bordered on obscene. I'd googled lacy manties, then deleted my browsing history in case Eggy accidentally uncovered it. And I had a date lined up.

Even my wayward dick, sensing my good humour and in response to my googling, spontaneously rose. Deciding to put my recently acquired tips from Dr Marchena into practise, I closed my eyes, imaging myself and Felipe enjoying a romantic stroll along the beach. No pressure, merely a friendly meander, hand in hand, the evening sun warm on my face, his palm secure in mine, and my new shirt not chafing at my neck. Approving of this low-anxiety scenario, my dick stayed hard. Shutting my eyes tight, with my soapy hand, I indulged in a few satisfying pulls.

Cautiously, I moved my mental camera roll on a few reels, until Daydream Felipe and I reached a rocky cove. Tugging me down onto the dry, non-itchy sand, Daydream Felipe slipped an arm around my waist, his fingers resting well above my waistband. "I'd like to kiss you, Fifty," Daydream Felipe murmured in his lisping Spanish accent. With a hand gently on my shoulder, he brought his lips inches away from my own. My dick approved of this image too; I massaged my balls before forming a soapy tunnel around my shaft.

Daydream Felipe and I kissed, a gentle covering of my mouth with his. As our tongues brushed, I tasted the red wine we'd shared earlier over a romantic dinner. His hand travelled down, from my shoulder and across the front of my new grey shirt. His palm felt good there, a warm, low-stress, firm press over my heart. My dick enjoyed it too, lengthening and growing in my fist, my breath audible over the spattering of the shower.

Not content to stay over my heart, Daydream Felipe's hand roamed further south. I let it happen, his mouth pressing harder, his probing tongue playing Twister around mine. A tingling in my spine warned me I was close, and I chased it desperately, his hand on my belly so sure of itself.

"Just this, Fifty," perfect, non-threatening, Daydream Felipe whispered in my ear. "This kissing is enough for me, until we know each other better."

Bloody hell, that was an orgasm. Fortunate I was in the shower. Otherwise, I would have made a right mess of my bedsheets. Jizz everywhere, months of the stuff, mixing with the foamy water before disappearing down the plughole, my perfect fantasy Felipe disappearing with it.

Fuck, yes! I'd done it! The trick had worked. Guided imagery, she'd called it. Playing sexual encounters over in your mind, again and again, conning my brain into relaxing, tricking it into going with the flow, enjoying the show. I was a natural at this. Tonight's date would be a piece of piss.

Full of happy thoughts and basking in the afterglow of a tremendous and unexpected orgasm, I reached for my expensive new conditioner and gave my hair much-needed attention.

Chapter Six

When Fifty discovers daydreams and reality don't always collide

The first five minutes of my date with Felipe matched my excellent mood. Daydream Felipe and Real Felipe sang from the same hymn sheet. With classic, olive-skinned Mediterranean looks and a neatly trimmed beard, Real Felipe was undeniably a handsome man. He complimented me on my attire, cleared his throat in a way I'd started to notice, and then planted a chaste kiss on the cheek. My dick paid attention with a happy little response, before settling down again, another very positive sign.

The date veered slightly off course when our waiter turned out to be bloody Alejandro. Recognizing me as swiftly as I recognised him, he flounced away to hang up our jackets, then glared as he introduced himself and pouted his way through the list of the evening's specials. Bloody hell. Of all the gin joints in all the towns, or however the quote went. Strangely, I wasn't the only person displeased to see him. Felipe looked ready to vomit.

"Are you okay?" I asked as he took a seat opposite me. We had a romantic corner booth all to ourselves, which hopefully would steer our date back on track.

"Yes, thank you." Felipe gritted his teeth. "Only I wasn't expecting to see him here. I know his family own this restaurant and the hotel next door, but I assumed he'd be too high and mighty to wait tables."

"Perhaps someone called in sick," I suggested, and he grimaced.

"Or perhaps he saw my name on the booking and decided to spoil my night."

Obviously some history between these two, then. I was intrigued. "We could go somewhere else? It's not too late."

Felipe shook his head. "No, we'll stay. The food is great, and I...well...I'd looked forward to bringing you here tonight."

Sharing how much I'd dreaded it didn't feel fair. "Me too."

Alejandro glided back to our table. Alejandro and Felipe's knowledge of each other didn't surprise me. They were of a similar age, and Corralejo was not an especially large town. Notwithstanding, the animosity in Felipe's eyes threw me completely. Upholding social convention, they greeted each other with standard air kisses to each cheek and much back patting. Polite news updates on the wellbeing of each other's sisters, grandmothers, second cousins, and neighbour's cats were exchanged before Alejandro turned his ire and attention back to me.

"You are claiming all the attractive men in Corralejo, yes?" He tossed his head in Felipe's direction. "You are not leaving poor Alejandro any, is that it, mister?"

The drinks menu landed none too politely in my lap.

"Er...what's going on?" Felipe queried, not unreasonably. His dark eyes darted between Alejandro and me.

"Felipe. Your partner for this evening has several pokers in the fire," answered Alejandro on my behalf. "He has not informed you, no? Perhaps you have more than two pokers, mister? Yes? A different poker for tomorrow night, perhaps? Three pokers? You are playing games with my friend Felipe here?"

I'd never had my poker in any fire, but this indignant hot-tempered waiter didn't need to know that. Or the confused history teacher.

"Fifty, what's happening here? What are you hiding from me?"

With the alarming sensation my evening was running away from me, I held my hand up to a bemused and increasingly agitated Felipe. "Whoa, just a second. Hold on. Felipe, let me explain. Our delightful waiter here tried to have a crack at Eggy's younger brother recently, and I took it upon myself to warn him off."

"Is true! You say he is yours! You say back off, Alejandro, he is mine!" Alejandro flared his nostrils at me.

I shook my head. "Yes, I did say that, but no, he's not mine. He's not anybody's. He's only a kid."

"But you say he is yours! I hear with my own ears! I see you hold him like so!" Cue arms around his own waist accompanied by an obscene hip thrust. Most definitely an exaggeration. "If the blond boy is not yours, then surely, he can be mine, no? I can have my hands on him like this, I can show him a good time, no? You have this very nice señor Felipe, here. I have the very nice blond boy. We are all friends; we forget everything, and I tell you the best food on the menu tonight." He waved his arms around expansively, encompassing the entire restaurant in his proffered friendship.

I shook my head again. "Not happening, Alejandro. Sorry. The boy is nineteen. Trust me, you do not want him. Not unless you want to be messing with his big brother as well."

Felipe and Alejandro then conducted a rapid conversation in Spanish, most of which I followed. Felipe outlined Eggy's physical attributes, and Alejandro, by turn, described how very much they differed from Otto's. He wouldn't have forgotten Eggy in a hurry. Both thankfully concluded chasing Otto would be a dick move. I sensed Felipe enjoyed a quiet satisfaction in scaring Alejandro off.

"I say have the *osso buco* tonight," Alejandro begrudgingly offered. "Is good, the best in Fuerteventura. I would give you recipe, but then I have to kill you."

After this shaky interlude, Felipe and I both settled on *osso buco* and agreed on the wine choice, hopefully a promising sign of things to come. And it was, for at least our tapas starters and halfway through the delicious *osso buco*.

"So what's with you and our delightful waiter, then?" I enquired, after Felipe glowered for the umpteenth time at Alejandro's retreating rear view.

Felipe harrumphed. "It's old news."

Taking a leaf out of Dr Marchena's book, I stayed quiet, hoping for more.

"We've known each other since school. He was my older brother's friend and my first proper boyfriend." He stabbed his veal with more force than the beautifully tender meat required. "He was twenty to my eighteen. And a flash bastard, even then."

He chewed the meat, his eyes hazing over. "I was in love, and I thought we both were. I stayed on the island and started teacher training college, but Fuerte wasn't good enough for Alejandro. His papa sent him to business school in Tenerife so he could help run the hotel."

Sending young Alejandro off to business school had paid dividends, as the tapas, the *osso buco* and the wine were seriously top notch. In between delicious mouthfuls, I discovered Alejandro systematically shagged his way around the Canary Islands, all the while keeping young Felipe on the hook. For five whole years. The poor lad had so many hearts stuffed in his eyes he'd been too blind to spot the way our annoying waiter had been taking him for a ride all along—until Felipe surprised him at home one afternoon with his dick entrenched in someone else's arse. I let him bitch about it for a while and concentrated on my food. Unrequited love. I could relate.

"I know it happened ages ago," confessed Felipe bleakly, when he'd finally got it all off his chest. "I'm thirty-six. But it still fucking hurts, you know?"

Yep, I knew.

We devoured the remainder of the *osso buco* in silence. Having my date's ex-boyfriend and one true love hovering over my shoulder while I attempted a romantic dinner for two killed the mood. Felipe virtually singlehandedly polished off the first bottle of wine, and I helped him with the second. Otto would have been proud of my abstinence. Despite Felipe's increasing tipsiness and the worsening animosity between him and our increasingly annoying waiter, I held out hope to salvage our date. I'd endured worse.

In an attempt to get to know him better and to shift the focus of our evening as far away from Alejandro and sex as possible, per my guided imagery/performance anxiety/ demi-sexual revelation strategy, I quizzed Felipe on his job at the local school.

Big mistake. Don't get me wrong—it was great finding a teacher so passionate about kids' education. Indeed, he did an excellent job of convincing me the Spanish Civil War was a uniquely fascinating period of history. But for forty-five minutes straight, no interruptions? And drunk and repetitive? I began to wonder whether discussing my erectile dysfunction might have been a more pleasant option.

Not to mention the throat-clearing thing. Otto's observation had been absolutely on point. And once I'd noticed it, I couldn't un-notice it. By the time Alejandro swept our plates off the table, it sounded like chalk down a blackboard.

Bizarrely, my only saviour was Alejandro, who attentively replenished our wine scarcely before our glasses emptied, checked my food met with satisfaction, and generally loitered as if we were a pair of restaurant inspectors. The first time his fingertips brushed against my back, I waved it off as accidental. When he clumsily dropped a fork and lightly ran his hand up my thigh while retrieving it, I knew it wasn't.

Unfortunately, despite being drunk as a skunk, Felipe had the ability to both talk incessantly *and* clock his ex coming on to me. So he decided to bloody join in. Without pausing for breath, he swerved into a slurred analysis of General Franco's military strategy to the accompaniment of his shoeless foot running up and down my calf.

"Can I interest you in dessert, *señors?*" purred Alejandro, thrusting the menu under my nose. One of his hands rested lightly at my collar, his fingers tickling my hair. Ale-handsy was living up to his name. "I have an extremely special dessert for you, *señor* Fifty, if you are interested. Better than blond boy."

"No, he's not interested." Felipe's foot on my calf edged higher. "In your special dessert or any other dessert you have in mind." He glared at me. "And I'll have to take his word regarding the blond boy. If he wants dessert, it shall be me offering it. The bill please, Alejandro."

My phone pinged in my pocket, giving me a moment's respite. Making my excuses to Felipe, I fled to the gents. After relieving myself, I checked my messages. A missed call from Eggy and a text from Clem, asking me to casually check in on Otto at a bar a couple of streets away, if convenient. Bloody convenient, as it happened. Thumbing a quick reply, I braced myself and headed back to the table.

Alejandro blocked my path. His sly, foxy features had taken on a leer. "Are you done fucking with Felipe?"

Suffice to say I would not be leaving a generous tip. I'd been on some bad dates in my time, mostly centred around my dick worries. But this one definitely leap-frogged to the top of the league table. I was feeling positively sexually harassed. On the upside, I'd not dwelt on my dick problems once.

"That's not exactly any of your business." As a laid-back surfer dude, I preached peace, not war, but the guy had seriously started to piss me off.

"No? You not fucking Felipe? He is a good fuck. You want to do fucking with me instead? Later tonight, perhaps?"

I detested confrontation, but sometimes, it was unavoidable. Rolling my shoulders back, I stood straighter, as I'd seen Eggy do on countless occasions when he wanted to look threatening. "Listen, mate. Do you proposition all your diners? If you do, then it doesn't sound like the best of business plans. Now get out of my bloody way."

If Eggy had spoken to him like that, Alejandro would have scurried back to the kitchen. As it was, he smiled annoyingly, as if I'd laid down a challenge. "You play hard to get with Alejandro? You tease Alejandro? I like a man who likes to be chased, Mister Fifty. I like very much."

Out on the pavement, Felipe faced me accusingly. He hadn't looked at me or uttered a word as we grimly split the bill, waited for our jackets, and said our goodnights. I didn't blame him—our romantic dinner had been totally hijacked. At least after that farce, he wouldn't be in the mood to proposition me.

I felt sorry for him; none of this was his fault. And given a chance, maybe we could have swung the conversation down all sorts of fascinating avenues. We could have relaxed in each other's company. I could have developed an emotional attraction to him, despite him droning on about the failings of the *bachillerato* school examination system. Alejandro's antics had kind of put a halt to all that.

"Sorry about what happened in there, Felipe." We hovered

outside the restaurant, unsure what to do next. Convention dictated we'd move on to drinks or go back to his place or mine. But so far, nothing about this date followed convention.

"That makes two of us." He noisily cleared his throat. I tried not to notice.

"I had no idea Alejandro would be there, or that you and he had history. I'd never have agreed to that restaurant otherwise."

Felipe sighed heavily and fumbled in his pocket for a pack of fags. He put one to his lips, then produced a lighter. After taking a long puff, he blew the smoke away from me. "I'm trying to give up. I was doing okay this week, until now."

"Alejandro drove you to it?"

He nodded, sucking in another drag. "Yeah. That guy sure knows how to ruin a night out. And do you know what the fucking stupid thing is? I'm still not over him. Despite how he behaved. I still fucking want him."

God, and I thought I'd had it bad over Eggy. I understood it, though. Whereas Felipe was solid and dependable; Alejandro brushed his teeth with charisma. Not too dissimilar to myself and Eggy.

"Probably not the sort of thing you confess to the bloke you've invited out on a date."

He laughed softly. "No. And if I hadn't drunk so much, I probably wouldn't. I'm pretty shit at dating."

That made two of us. Recalling Clem's text, I glanced at my watch. "Fancy another drink? I'm buying."

I spied Otto in a dark corner of the pub before he spied me. A stack of empty cocktail glasses wobbled on the table beside him. His girlies were crowded around, and thank god, the boys in his party looked to be of a similar age. I'd report back to Eggy with good news.

Drinks ordered, Felipe and I awkwardly stood next to each other at the bar. We'd been silent on our walk from the restaurant. He'd smoked another cigarette, and the fresh air had sobered him up.

"Do you come here often?" he began, and I laughed at the cheesy chat-up line.

"No, the clientele is a bit young for me."

"Yes, I always wonder if I'll find myself in a shady corner of the back room with a young man, then realise a fraction too late, that I gave him detention five years earlier for smoking in the playground." Felipe scoured the packed bar. "Maybe I should suggest dropping by to Alejandro. He likes them young. You do too, according to him."

"It's all bullshit," I replied sourly. "He jerked both of our chains tonight. We should have left after one drink and gone somewhere else."

Without warning, Felipe's hand found mine down at our sides. I tried not to tense as he gave it a small squeeze. "We could make this a very quick drink, Fifty?"

And it landed, the moment I always hoped might never arrive. There was no mistaking the suggestiveness of his comment, nor could I find anything unreasonable about it. Nothing about Felipe was unreasonable. Despite all the odds, a handsome, intelligent, well-dressed, slightly dull teacher wanted to get inside my pants. If only to help him forget the man he really wanted to be with. So why did the thought of going back to his place make my insides clench and my dick shrivel even further into itself, recoiling like a snail in its shell?

"Yeah, sure." I took a gulp of Tropical, more to give me something to do with my hands and mouth than actually speed up my drinking.

"Your level of enthusiasm knocks me out," he responded sarcastically.

"Sorry, Felipe, I...I..."

"I was joking, honey. It's fine."

Turning to face me slightly, his hand released mine and tracked up my side. His fingers smoothed a path across my belly, only an inch above my belt. Daydream Felipe had made exactly the same move on the beach, and I'd lapped it up, leading to the finest orgasm I'd experienced since listening in on Eggy's exertions. Real Felipe's fingers regrettably did not elicit a similar response. My dick didn't so much as twitch.

I willed myself to relax, not to overthink it. I breathed deeply, then took another swig of beer. My glass was dangerously close to being empty; Felipe had drained his. Cold sweat broke out across my brow as my stomach flipped, but not in an anticipatory, excited way. More in a top-of-the-rollercoaster-wishing-I'd-stayed-at-home sort of way.

Clearing his throat, Felipe tugged on my belt, pulling us closer together. "Drink up, Fifty," he murmured in my ear. "I have an exceedingly comfortable bed not five minutes' walk from here."

Taking a small step closer, he discreetly rocked his groin up against my hipbone. Even with my inexperience, I knew what a hard dick through denim felt like. I also had a rough idea of the effect it should have on me. A paralysing fear gripped my insides, that his hand would stray lower, that he'd feel around and find...nothing. Real Felipe had deviated from the fantasy script.

Oh, fuck. I had to get it over with sometime. Felipe was as good a man as any. Tipping back my head, I gulped the last of the beer, then slapped my empty glass down on the bar. Like Marie Antoinette heading towards the guillotine, I trailed in his wake.

Three feet from the exit, a piercing squeal jolted me out of the maelstrom swirling around my head. "Christian!" A grinning, white-haired elf pounced on me and climbed his way up my body to plant a wet smacker at the corner of my mouth. "Oh my god! Christian, I'm having such a fun night! Let me show you Matthieu! Odin's teeth, he's gorgeous! He's on holiday here from Germany with his parents. Unfortunately, his flight back home is the day after tomorrow, but I am *so* going to get off with him before he goes."

Climbing back down my body, he quickly registered Felipe's hand in mine, his eyes rapidly darting from me to my date. Then, much to Felipe's chagrin, he hiked up my body again and hissed in my ear. "Do you want to go with him? Do you think you've found an emotional connection? Or would you prefer not to? You know, with your...problem and stuff? I'll back off if you're happy. Or I'll help if you aren't."

The mixture of panic and pleading in my eyes told Otto all he needed to know. Swinging off my arm, he proclaimed in a loud voice, "Please, please, *please*, Christian. At least join us for one drink. You must come and check out Matthieu. I'm not gonna lie—he's so hot. You can meet Alicia and Celine properly, too. I've told them all about you."

Not everything, I hoped.

Otto's delighted excitement was infectious. If his enthusiasm at bumping into me was only for show, then he did a very good job. As he tugged on my other hand, pleading for me to follow, I couldn't help smiling down at him. How could anyone resist those guileless, wide grey eyes? I'd been unable to resist them for years when Eggy had been the one persuading me to join him on one venture or another. And although I knew I should be heading with Felipe for the door, psyching myself up for kissing him and possibly more, Otto felt like a welcome reprieve.

"Is this the guy Alejandro was after?" Felipe asked, giving

Otto a disdainful once-over. "I thought you weren't into chasing kids."

Tonight, the fluffball had gone all out on 1980s pastels: white jeans accompanied by an oversized, baby-pink, vintage 'Frankie Says' T-shirt, almost reaching down to his knees. The abundance of leather strappy things looped around his slim wrists and neck could fully equip a bondage club. Smoky black eyeliner rimmed his grey eyes, no doubt pinched from Clem's bathroom cabinet.

"I'm not into 'kids'. This is Otto, Eggy's brother, and, yeah, I said I'd look out for him. For your info, he's nineteen—a full-grown adult."

Completely contradicting the lecture I'd given Otto about adulthood and age when I'd rescued him from Alejandro.

Felipe gave me a curious look before raking his eyes over Otto one last time.

"Fine," he said unsmilingly. "I'll call you." He followed his curt farewell with a swift peck on the cheek before turning on his heel. We watched him stomp off.

"God, I pissed him off, didn't I?" Otto said with alarm. Not that much alarm. He grinned wildly at me. "He walks funny, doesn't he? Maybe it's his flip-flops." He paused, beaming. "Or his felipe-filopes! Have one of the grapefruit mojitos. They're yummy. I've had two."

I'd deduced that bit myself; he weaved slightly as he dragged me to the bar.

"Don't worry." He pre-empted me. "I won't have any more. So there's no need to go telling tales to the big hairy Viking.

"Everybody, budge up! This is Christian, my minder. I know he's ancient, but he can be quite funny when he forgets to be all sensible and mature."

The cocktail tasted every bit as sickly as I expected, the cheap rum leaving a cloying layer on my tongue. But after the wine in the restaurant and the single beer, it took the edge off. I squashed onto the bench seat, Otto on one side and Alicia and Celine on the other.

"Love the shirt," cooed Alicia, fingering my sleeve.

"It's gorgeous," agreed Celine.

"Oh my god! Christian! You've done your hair too!" Otto's delicate fingers carded through my shaggy mess as he closely examined the ends. All the attention had me hot under the collar, but I had to admit, I kind of enjoyed it, too. "Wow, it feels so soft." He eyed me up and down, and I passed the inspection. "You scrub up okay, for a surfer, don't you?"

The boy sitting on Otto's far side—and most definitely a boy, not a man—placed his arm possessively around Otto's shoulders.

"This is Matthieu," Otto whispered in my ear. "He's only seventeen, but I think he looks older. He's got fake ID, which is how he managed to squeeze past the bouncers." His eyes twinkled at me. "Age appropriate enough for your approval, Christian?"

Frankly, Matthieu, with a hint of bumfluff on his chin and a smattering of angry red spots across his sunburnt nose, didn't look a day over fifteen. At least Otto's virtue would remain intact for the time being; Matthieu innocently gazed at him as if the sun shone out of his arse.

I spent more than an hour with the kids, until well past midnight. Much longer than I expected. Their excitable, tipsy chatter mostly washed over me and lost me entirely when they talked about a YouTuber they avidly followed. The girls tutted at the state of my bitten nails and lectured me on skincare routines after a day surfing. It was fun, ridiculous, and, most importantly, completely unthreatening.

In some ways, it reminded me of nights out with Eggy before Clem came on the scene. We'd be in a pub—the Red Barn mostly. Eggy would happily hold court, and I'd be next to him, sometimes joining in and sometimes quiet, relaxed and at ease. Squished next to Otto, the press of his lean thigh warm against mine, felt the same, although Otto wiggled in his seat like he'd got ants in his pants. Every now and again, to make his point, his hand rested on my arm, much the way Eggy's had done.

As I meandered back to my apartment a little while later, after Otto gave me a nudge and a wink, loudly whispering he would be walking Matthieu home, something occurred to me. My brain and dick were finally working in tandem. And they were both confused.

Chapter Seven

When winning at FIFA is not necessarily a good sign

Arriving back at the shop the following lunchtime, having waved goodbye to my morning surf class, I found Matthieu propping up the counter, deep in conversation with Otto. The fluffball leaned so far across towards him I'd have been surprised if his feet still touched the floor. Unfortunately for him, I wasn't alone. Eggy loomed at my shoulder.

Anybody who knew Eggy also knew the fierce Viking thing he had going wasn't entirely an act. Yes, he allowed Clem to roll him over and tickle his belly, but as Alejandro and many others like him could testify, the hairy Viking had bite. The glint of madness in his sharp grey eyes, born of hundreds of generations of marauding warriors, never truly disappeared.

Not that Otto cared, perhaps due to having four more Eggys back in Norway. So his opening gambit was certainly bolder than anyone else's would be. "Ragnar, say hello to Matthieu. He's flying back to Germany tomorrow, so I'm taking him clubbing tonight. Matthieu, this is my brother, Ragnar. He's now going to be really embarrassing and pretend to be scary, but when you get to know him, he's a big cuddly marshmallow."

Clem and I both concurred Norwegian was an odd

language. When, for example, Italians or Germans conversed, even if most of the words were incomprehensible, you could generally glean an idea of what they were discussing. Occasional words sounded similar to their English counterparts, only with added grunting (German), or a dramatic flourish (Italian).

This was not the case with Norwegian. Eggy and Otto could have been contemplating how best to build an atomic bomb for all I knew. After adding in the hurdy-gurdy intonation and utter lack of gesticulation, discerning whether Norwegians were declaring undying love for one another or outlining precisely how they'd like to remove each other's eye sockets with a wooden spoon was difficult. From the tic in Eggy's jaw and the clenching and unclenching of his huge fists, I deduced this particular conversation closer to the latter than the former.

The bizarrely unheated debate ended with Eggy marching into the back office and slamming the door. Unruffled, Otto gave his beau his full attention once more. "Matthieu, how about we have a few quiet drinks in Gators tonight and then maybe head to the beach afterwards?"

As far as Matthieu was concerned, Otto could have proposed a midnight yomp to the North Pole and he'd have been grabbing his hiking gear, such was the adoration in his puppyish eyes. After he left, Otto let out a long sigh.

"You okay?" I asked him.

Appearing distracted, he didn't answer for a minute. I wondered if he was experiencing one of those focals. "Mmm, yeah," he replied eventually, glancing at the closed door. "Count yourself lucky you don't have big brothers. They're a pain in the arse."

"He's only looking out for you, you know. This is all new to him, too."

He sighed. "Yeah, you're right. But how can he expect me to behave like a grown-up when he treats me like a child? One minute he's telling me to enrol in Spanish lessons, do some voluntary work, and write a CV, and the next he's forbidding me from going clubbing because he says I'm not old enough. How come I'm plenty old enough for the shitty stuff but too young for the fun stuff?"

I laughed, partly at his perceptive assessment of the situation and partly at his stance: legs apart, arms folded across his chest and the defiant jut of his chin. A scaled-down replica of a grumpy Eggy.

"I'll have a word with him, buddy," I promised. "When he's calmed down a bit. Fancy some FIFA later this afternoon, before you and young Matthieu paint the town red?"

Later, when he swung by my apartment, Otto's mood had switched yet again. He joined me in the kitchen as I fixed us a plate of roast chicken sandwiches. He seemed tired, which I attributed to his late night. Listlessly, he sauntered around the kitchen, picking objects up at random, firstly a mug and then a tea towel, before putting them down again. When I enquired, with a wink, how last night had ended with Matthieu, he appeared not to hear, lost in his own world, gazing out through the blinds into my little backyard.

"Hey, Otto, has someone taken the batteries out?" Jerking out of it, he turned and gave me a confused smile as I pointed to him. "You, you're very quiet for once. What's up?"

"Nothing. I'm good." He paused, a puzzled look crossing his face. "I think. A little hungry, maybe."

He followed me wordlessly when I carried our plates through to my bedroom. Once settled next to each other on the bed, and with the game loading, I probed him again about his night with Matthieu.

"He kissed me after I walked him home." He smiled faintly

at the memory. "It was a bit sloppy, to be honest; Matthieu was quite drunk. But it was all right. Maybe four out of ten for execution? Six for enthusiasm?"

I was sure poor Matthieu had no idea he'd been graded on his kissing technique. "Perhaps he'll improve tonight, now he's had some practice." I thought Otto had arrived in Fuerteventura without any prior experience. "What yardstick are you measuring him against?"

He took a bite out of his sandwich and chewed thoughtfully. "Miriam, mostly. Oh, and I did kiss a boy at the end of a maths lesson when I was fourteen, but I don't count that. It was a dare."

"Who the fuck is Miriam?"

He took another bite. In the time I'd eaten half a sandwich, he'd virtually polished off both of his. God knew where he put it all. "Oh, she's my older brother Erik's girlfriend. He's marrying her next year. She gave me kissing lessons. She's really good."

From his matter-of-fact manner, I wondered if kissing older brother's girlfriends was, like, normal for Norway. Delving further, I discovered not. Young Otto was an opportunist.

"It started one night a couple of years ago, Erik and I were at home, no one else. He's four years older than me. Miriam is too. She came over, and we watched a film. Erik drank too much beer, then fell asleep. Miriam and I were bored—there isn't much to do in our village in the winter—and so I asked her to teach me to kiss properly. I think she'd drunk quite a lot of beer too, as she said yes. We've done it a couple of times since. I haven't felt her boobs or anything, 'cos I'm not into girls, but she's great at kissing. Hey, the game's loaded. Do you want to choose your players first?"

Not only was this tale extraordinary, more so by Otto's flat delivery, but I even beat him for the first time at FIFA too. Something distracted him from his usual annoying brilliance—

maybe his date with Matthieu later. His mind wandered all over the place.

"It smells funny in here," he observed between games.

I sniffed. "I can't smell anything. Perhaps it's the leftovers on the plates."

"Mmm," he agreed vaguely. "Or your dodgy aftershave."

"Or your bloody stinky feet. Get them off my duvet."

I proceeded to beat him again.

Before the next game, I carried the plates through to the kitchen, returning with two glasses of water. Maybe his lingering hangover from the night before had him distractible and edgy. He sat exactly as I'd left him, staring at the frozen game on the screen.

"Are you sure you're okay, Otto?" I asked, mildly concerned.

He frowned up at me. "What? Oh, yeah, fine." He wrinkled his nose and then clambered off the bed, taking a glass of water with him. "I'll just... I'm just going to..."

Not finishing the sentence, he wandered into the hallway, I assumed heading for the bathroom. Two seconds later, a splintering of glass and a shockingly loud thump cut through the quiet of my flat.

I leapt off the bed, heart thudding in alarm. "Otto!"

I'd never witnessed anybody having a fit. Suffice to say it was much, much worse than a faint. So much fucking worse. Skidding into the hallway, I found Otto on the floor at the entrance to the sitting room, curled on his side. Every part of his body jerked violently—his head, his legs, his arms, even his back seemed to be seizing. With every rapid-fire spasm, the side of his face smacked on the cold white tiles. Rushing to his side, not considering the shards of broken glass sprayed around him, I yanked off my T-shirt and shoved it under his head.

"I'm here, Otto. Otto, baby, I'm here, it's okay. Oh god, it's okay. Otto, you're okay." I babbled like a fucking loony.

Bubbles of saliva formed at his mouth, mixing with fresh blood from a gash on his lip, the redness a sharp contrast to the hideous ashen grey of his face. Inhuman honking noises accompanied his every breath, through clamped, gritted teeth and a wave of panic surged through me. Was he dying? Was he going to fucking die? Horrified, I realised I had no idea of the phone number for emergency services on this bloody island.

"Shit, Otto, don't die, don't die. Please stop. You're fine, Otto, you're fine." Fumbling for my phone, I pressed the only number I knew. Thank god he answered quickly.

"Eggy, shit, Eggy, it's me. Otto's having a fit. He's having a fit, dude. I don't know what to do! I don't know what to fucking do!"

I couldn't tear my eyes away from Otto. The fitting hadn't slowed down at all, the spasms more aggressive if anything. My face wet with tears, I sobbed pathetically down the phone line.

"Fifty, listen to me. He'll be fine. Just calm the fuck down." Shit, I didn't think he understood, his voice steady and firm. Why wasn't he fucking panicking like me?

"Eggy, he's—his mouth, he's..."

"Fifty. Are you at home?"

"Yes, he's in the middle of my fucking lounge! His lips are blue!"

"Okay, I'm ten minutes away. Is he lying on his side?"

I nodded before realising Eggy couldn't see me. "Yes, he carried a glass into...and I heard it smash and then a bang and..."

"Okay." Eggy sounded breathless; he barked something to Clem in the background, and then a door slammed. "Listen to me. The fit should stop any second. If it lasts more than five minutes, call an ambulance."

"I can't remember the fucking emergency number," I sobbed hysterically.

"One-one-two," Clem shouted in the background. "Stay on

the phone, Fifty. I'll keep talking to you. Eggy's driving. Eggy says he'll be fine. Take big breaths. Everything is going to be okay. Try to calm down."

Otto made an agonised grunting noise. I made a not dissimilar one myself as the spasms thankfully gentled. The acrid scent of urine filled the air as a puddle of liquid rapidly spread underneath his arse and thighs.

"I...I...I think it's stopping," I breathed. "Oh thank god, thank god, it's stopping."

"Start talking to him," Eggy instructed. "Keep him on his side, in case he needs to puke. Let him know you're there. He'll be very sleepy. We're two minutes away, max."

Disconnecting the call, I shuffled closer on my knees and gingerly lifted Otto's head so it lay in my lap. To my indescribable relief, his face and lips returned to a more normal colour, and his breathing pattern settled into a normal, regular snore.

Wiping the blood and drool from his mouth with my T-shirt, I pushed his damp hair off his forehead. "Ragnar's coming, Otto. He'll be here in a minute. It's okay, baby. Everything is okay."

He made another strange grunting noise and smacked his bloodied lips together. His eyes flickered open and slid around, unfocussed, before closing again. The grunting, lip-smacking, eye-opening cycle repeated itself three more times before his breathing settled into a heavy rhythm. Disconcerting to say the least, but not as fucking disconcerting as the fitting. Christ, I never needed to go through that again.

I had never been as pleased to see anyone in my life as when Eggy and Clem barrelled through the door. They quickly surveyed the scene of devastation: the broken glass, the piss, the bloodied T-shirt, and me, a gibbering wreck. Clem turned as pasty as I felt; Eggy looked concerned but in control.

He squatted next to me and ruffled Otto's hair. *"Kom, lille venn*, let's get you into bed." Sliding his arms underneath his brother, he effortlessly scooped him up and rose to his feet. Otto's lifeless limbs dangled, his head lolling back. "Bloody hell, he's heavier than the last time I had to do this." He smiled tenderly, giving his brother's face a nuzzle with his nose. "All right if I put him in your bed for a while, Fifty?"

"Of course. Erm...yeah, go right ahead. Clem and I will clear up here."

Eggy lapsed into Norwegian, the sounds of him sorting out his brother emanating faintly from my bedroom. I inhaled deeply before standing and clasping at my neck.

"Are you okay?" Clem asked, rubbing my bare arm.

"Yeah. Yeah. I'm...Christ...that was bloody awful. I thought...I..."

"I know what you thought. Eggy says it's horrible if you've never seen it before. But you handled it fine. Eggy says the only thing you can do is prevent him from hurting himself, like stopping his head from banging on the floor, and wait for the fit to stop. And then have him in the recovery position afterwards. You did all that."

I nodded. The adrenaline rush ebbed away, and I felt bloody knackered.

"Come on," he said. "Let's get this mess cleared up."

I found Eggy perched on the edge of my bed, softly stroking his brother's hair. Curled into a ball under the covers, Otto's slight frame hardly made a dent.

"I've dressed him in one of your old T-shirts and a pair of shorts," Eggy said, his voice low so as not to disturb. He indicated to the balled-up pile of Otto's wet and bloodied clothes on the floor. "Hope you don't mind."

"Of course not. How long does he normally sleep afterwards?"

"I don't know." A gentle smile tugged at Eggy's lips as he regarded his brother. "It's been a few years since I did this. When he was younger, he sometimes had another fit in the night. But he says his meds control it better now, so hopefully that won't happen. I should probably stay with him though, in case he has another one. Or, if you want us out of your hair, I'll wake him up and take him home."

"God, no, you don't need to do that. He should stay here."

I hesitated, wondering what I'd let myself in for. Hopefully not another fit. My poor heart couldn't take it. I ploughed on. "Why don't you go home? I'll sleep in here with him to keep an eye. The bed's plenty big enough. I can always phone you if I'm worried about anything. And you've got classes scheduled in the morning, and I haven't."

The most obvious solution, even though I regretted volunteering already. I really didn't fancy witnessing another of those fits in a hurry, which made me feel all kinds of selfish. God knew how dreadful it must be to actually suffer one.

"Are you sure?" Eggy glanced down at his brother.

"I'm very sure. Don't worry. I'll be fine. I'm an expert now." I sounded a hell of a lot more confident than I felt.

Eggy grinned. "Thanks. It feels mean to move him. It's nicer if he can be allowed to sleep it off. Usually, he's thirsty when he wakes. I used to make him a hot chocolate—the sugar helps. He'll feel a bit rubbish for a while."

Leaning in, he brushed Otto's fine hair off his face. "This is why I worry so much about him." He gave his cheek a gentle stroke. "The fits. I worry it will happen when he's out and about, and there's no one there to look after him. On the beach, or in a club."

Sighing, he carried on. "Maybe I should send him back

home. Everyone knows him there. As a kid, if ever he had a fit, someone would phone my dad, and one of us would be sent 'round to scoop him up. There was always someone looking out for him."

"He doesn't want to go home; he wants to be here with you. Go to nursing college."

"I know," Eggy replied sadly. "He says he's old enough to make his own decisions. But you can see now why I'm so protective."

"I can," I agreed. "But he can't let this rule his life. He doesn't have fits very often, does he?"

Eggy shrugged. "I don't think so. I guess I also feel really guilty for not being there when he was growing up. Clem says I should step back and let him live his own life, make his own mistakes, but it's hard, you know? He's either going to hang around with young lads who won't look after him properly, or some old guy will take advantage of him. And it's not only his epilepsy. He still has medication for his heart problem, and he gets so tired and..."

"You're going to have to let go at some point," I observed. "Clem's right. He'll make his own choices. At least you'll be there to pick up the pieces if he fucks up."

"If someone does take advantage of him, and not treat him properly, they'll be answering to me." His voice was grim and determined.

"Toenails and rusty pliers. Yes, I know."

We carried on chatting in muted voices, so as not to wake Otto, and discussed logistics for tomorrow.

Finally, Eggy stood and gave me a hug. "You're about the only person, apart from Clem, that I'd ever trust to look after him properly. I know he's safe with you. You're like another big brother for him."

Why the hell did that give me a twinge in my gut? Since I'd

joined him and his friends for a drink, my feelings for the fluff-ball hadn't been entirely brotherly. I squashed them down. "That's what mates are for. And you're at the end of the phone if I get worried."

"I feel so dreadful. For falling out with him earlier over his little friend, Matthieu. I should have let him have his fun. God knows I did a lot more at his age. I wish I hadn't said anything. Stress can bring on a fit."

I had no idea if that was true or not, so I said nothing and hugged him back.

"What was he doing here, anyway?"

I felt bizarrely defensive, almost as though I had something to hide. "Playing FIFA." I smirked. "He comes over every now and again. To give you and Clem some space. But mostly to scoff my food and play on the Xbox. He's a demon at both of those activities."

Eggy took one last look at his brother. "He really likes you. He's always telling me how nice you are to him. Thank you for putting up with him."

"He's no trouble at all. I like having him over."

"Yeah, but I don't want him to become a nuisance, always hanging around here after work. Kick him out and send him back to me if he starts getting on your nerves. I know you like your privacy."

The shape in the bed made a soft sighing sound, blond hair sticking up in every direction, the only visible part. "Nah, he's no bother. No bother at all."

In the dead of night, I woke to the warm body next to me huffing and shuffling around. He then startled and sat bolt upright. For a tense moment, I thought he might be starting another seizure, before his hand patted around under the covers, found mine, and clutched it.

"Ragnar!" he hissed from somewhere above my head.

"It's me," I whispered. "Fif...Christian. Ragnar's gone home. You're still at my place. We decided to let you sleep it off here."

In the dark I felt rather than saw him slump back down. He released my hand. Neither of us spoke. My phone informed me it was a few minutes after one in the morning.

"How are you feeling?"

He sniffed and pulled the covers up higher. "Pretty shitty. Fuzzy. My head hurts. The usual." His voice was slightly slurred, thick with sleep. "I guess I missed my date with Matthieu. He's flying back home tomorrow."

"Sorry, a night in bed with me is a poor substitute."

He chuckled softly and groaned. "You're not that bad. At least one of us lost our virginity, anyway."

"Uh...sorry? What did you say?" Suddenly, I was wide awake.

What the fuck? How the hell did he know? Was it that obvious, simply from playing FIFA with me? Or did I talk in my sleep?

"Your epilepsy cherry," he continued sleepily. "It's been well and truly popped."

Christ, this boy would be the death of me. I let out a sigh of relief. "You can say that again. You gave me a right bloody fright."

Fidgeting again, he pulled the covers back down. "I'm thirsty. And I bloody stink of piss. Can I take a shower?"

I fumbled for the light switch. In the dim glow of the bedside lamp, he seemed thin and wan in my extra-large T-shirt. Dark shadows circled his eyes. He sat up, his arms hugging his knees. "Sorry you had to deal with all that," he muttered, not meeting my eye. "At least it didn't happen in the middle of the pub, in front of all my mates. And Matthieu. God, that would have been even more embarrassing."

I waved it off. "Don't worry, mate. You can't help it. And if you want to talk embarrassing, you're sleeping next to a man who fainted in the middle of the doctor's waiting room in front of about twenty people a couple of weeks ago."

"Yeah, how could I forget?" He sniffed again, rubbing his face tiredly. "I meant to ask you—what was with the other night anyway? With your date, Felipe? He's quite hot. Didn't you want to go home with him due to your...um...problem?"

To avoid facing him, I swung my legs out of bed and busied myself with my bath robe. "Yeah. It's like I explained to the doctor. I...um...I started to feel panicky, that he would try and kiss me or something, then try to do more, and I wouldn't...erm... respond appropriately. And that made my panicking worse, and...fuck, you were at the doctor's when I talked about it. That night with Felipe was yet another fucking example."

I stood, turning to face him. "You've already heard all that shit once. We don't need to go through it again. Go take a shower and I'll make you a hot chocolate."

He emerged from the bathroom, dressed once more in my oversized clothing, and shuffled into bed, clearly still wiped out. Granted, it was the middle of the night. He sipped at his drink, resting back against the headboard.

"How often do you have episodes as major as that?" I asked curiously.

He made a face. "Much less than when I was a kid. Maybe around two or three times a year?"

"And do you know when you are going to have them?"

A dumb question, I realised as soon as the words flew out of my mouth. If he knew the seizure was coming, he'd probably lie down on the nearest comfortable surface, or at least empty his bladder first. But his answer surprised me.

"Sort of." He frowned slightly. "It's...it's like I know I start acting peculiarly. I smell a strange smell and feel a bit...off. But I can't do anything about it. It's like I'm watching myself becoming weird but can't tell anyone or prepare for it."

His shoulder twitched in a casual shrug. "My family got used to the signs and made sure I stayed at home or put me to bed. If Eggy had been around, he might have picked up on it, although occasionally I don't get any warning."

At least I had an explanation for his dazed behaviour earlier. I wouldn't be able to hold the FIFA wins over him. "How do you feel now?"

"Knackered." He ran a finger experimentally across his bottom lip. "And my tongue hurts. I must have bitten it. Do you want me to kip on the sofa for the rest of the night? I've taken over your bedroom."

I shook my head. I kind of liked having him with me in a way I hadn't expected, which both frightened me and filled me with an odd sensation in my belly. He was a kid, though, Eggy's baby brother. Tomorrow, I would text Felipe, apologise, and arrange to meet up. "No, it's fine. Stay here with me. I promised Eggy I'd keep watch over you all night. He feels guilty for bringing this on—he says arguing with you triggered it."

Otto grinned, the grin of a normal, mischievous nineteen-year-old. "I'll milk that for as long as possible."

"I thought you might."

After a while, he finished his drink and snuggled back down again. I switched off the light and lay in the dark next to him.

"Christian?"

"Yeah?"

"Does me being here make you nervous, you know, like Felipe would?"

"No," I chuckled. "Of course not, unless you start having another fit, in which case I'll be absolutely bloody petrified."

"I don't suppose you fancy a game of FIFA?"

"Jesus, Otto. It's two in the morning, and I'm an old man. Go the fuck to sleep."

Chapter Eight

When Fifty scores a perfect ten

After our early-hours chat and totally unused to sharing my bed with anybody, I imagined settling down to sleep again would be awkward. But, too shattered from his seizure to stay awake for more than five minutes, Otto's regular deep breathing soon had me slumbering too. With any other bloke, I'd have lain there as taut as cheese wire, frozen in an uncomfortable position, acutely aware of every centimetre of mattress separating our two bodies. Somehow, being with this brave, funny man-child felt different. An unfamiliar tenderness washed over me as he sprawled in his sleep, his shin slung across my thigh.

After spending most of the morning watching Otto sleep, in that carefree, untroubled way of teenage boys while real adults went about their day, I passed the baton to Clem and headed off to work. With Eggy out taking lessons, I manned the shop—a poor substitute for Otto—and caught up on tedious admin.

Paperwork and I weren't the best of pals. Barely on speaking terms, in fact, but at least we hadn't declared all-out war, unlike Eggy, who could scarcely be in the same room. So anyone who walked through the shop door to distract me was practically guaranteed a warm welcome, unless...

"Here to book a surf lesson, Alejandro?" I enquired sarcastically as he sashayed up to the counter. Not our usual clientele, in his tan linen suit and crisp white shirt. Keys to a luxury car jangled in his hand, and a pair of stupidly expensive Oakley's topped his slicked-back hair.

"Depends who is available." He ran his eyes down my front and back up again, lingering uncomfortably on my mouth. "If it's big scary fucker with long red hair, then no. If it's you or blond boy, then yes."

"We're fully booked. And blond boy will never, ever be available." I regarded him coolly. "Can I help you with anything else?"

"Are you doing my friend Felipe yet?"

Bloody hell, this man had a nerve. "Is it any of your business?"

"No, but I ask anyway. You like my friend Felipe?"

"Yes. I like Felipe. What's it to you?"

Alejandro leaned casually across the counter, his spicy, strong aftershave a tad overwhelming. "He talk about me, yes? On your dinner date? He talk about Alejandro?"

I barked out a short laugh. "He told me how you strung him along and were an utter bastard, yes."

A pained look fleetingly crossed his foxy features before he gave me what I thought he imagined was a beguiling smile. "You want do it with me? You want night with Alejandro? I show you a good time, yes?"

Paperwork suddenly looked so much more attractive. "Listen, Alejandro. I don't know what you're playing at, but you can bloody leave me alone. And the same goes for Otto too, unless you want a surf lesson to remember, with the big scary fucker. I'm not interested in your games with Felipe, or anyone else. I'm not interested in you. And if Felipe has any sense, he won't be either."

.   .   .

Every Sunday evening, the hotel hosted a beach party welcoming new guests, which Eggy and I generally attended. Good for business, apparently. Eggy usually followed Carlos's effusive greetings at the start of the event with a charming little speech about surf lessons and surfboard hire. Invariably, a queue of ladies formed, hoping to sign up. I tended to loiter in the background and leave him to get on with it. If we were a rock band, I'd be the drummer or the bass guitarist, and he'd be the preening, strutting lead singer.

A plentiful buffet and free beer. Nothing not to like. The evening never felt like a chore. Not even when Felipe turned up as a guest of Clem's, and not even when Alejandro glided out of nowhere as a guest of Carlos's, keeping well out of Eggy's range. Otto and his girls also tagged along, no doubt to scope out potential new friends amongst the guests—and to scoff the free food.

"You're developing quite the harem, Fifty," Clem observed mildly, sipping a sparkling water and nudging my arm. Against my better judgement, I'd related the story of my horrendous, hijacked date with Felipe to him and Eggy. Clem didn't bother pretending he wouldn't be using it for book material; he even asked me to clarify a few points.

A small stage, where Eggy would hold court, squatted at one end of the hotel's cordoned-off section of beach, the sand in front of it dotted with benches and tables. Clem and I had sneaked into our usual shadowy corner near the back, from which to observe the proceedings. Following the direction of his gaze, I caught Felipe surreptitiously watching me from the fringes of a gathering and felt myself blush.

"Felipe and Alejandro hardly count as a harem," I protested. "More like they're each trying to piss the other off by coming on to me. Felipe is still in love with Alejandro, and

Alejandro seems to take a perverse pleasure in winding him up. He tracked me down to the shop yesterday to ask me out. I'm trapped in the middle of a bizarre love triangle."

"Gosh, is *ménage à trois* your thing? You are a dark horse."

More fuel for his next novel. "Pack it in, Clem. Anyway, if you really want to discuss harems, you should keep a closer eye on your boyfriend."

A gaggle of young female holidaymakers clamoured for Eggy's attention. As usual, he lapped it up. While attempting to paw my surfing buddy, none of them had any idea they had totally overlooked his boyfriend quietly sitting next to me, the creative brain behind one of the most popular paperbacks sold this year. All things considered, Clem was a pretty cool guy.

"God," he groaned, "as if his ego isn't already big enough to fill the spare room." He turned back to me. "Don't look, but one of your admirers is on his way over. I'll leave you to it and rescue Eggy. You can fill me in on the details later."

Otto must have been mistaken; Felipe had a perfectly normal walk, even in flip-flops. I automatically tensed as he approached, holding a drink for himself and one for me. The throat clearing was definitely a thing, however, although if Otto hadn't helpfully pointed it out, I probably wouldn't have noticed.

"Hi," he said, passing me the beer. "*Salud.*"

"Hi. Cheers."

Dark straight jeans topped with a plain white shirt suited him—a man who knew how to maximise his Spanish good looks. He was gentle and kind, too. Honestly, if I had to confess my naiveté to any prospective lover, then he would be an ideal choice.

"Eggy's on form tonight." His dark eyes roamed over the groups milling around my friend.

"Yeah."

"My impression is he enjoys that sort of thing."

"Yeah."

"You should be up there too, Fifty. Ladies always appreciate a handsome blond surfer."

I squirmed slightly. "Um...thanks, I guess?"

Flirting with me must have felt like wading through treacle. As if summoning up the courage to say something important, he hesitated, then cleared his throat—again. "You know, we don't have to label ourselves as a big romance or anything, but when you've finished your drink, if you wanted, we could head over to my..."

"What, seeing as Alejandro's here and it will piss him off?"

"It wouldn't piss him off," Felipe replied calmly.

"I wouldn't be so sure."

"He'd scarcely notice, and he certainly wouldn't care."

Despite what Felipe thought, I'd spotted Alejandro eyeing us with interest, only pretending to pay attention to Carlos.

"Whatever," I said lightly. "But you're wrong."

"Fifty, listen. I'm done with that man. And he's...he's not the reason I'm asking."

His cool fingers unexpectedly interlaced with mine. I tried not to jerk away. "So," he murmured softly, "As I said, how about we..."

It was now or never. I could do this nice man a favour by making Alejandro jealous and earn something myself in return. Something I desperately needed to get over and done with. I had Felipe here, in front of me. A willing, patient, kind, and very attractive man, asking me for sex in the nicest possible way. No strings attached. He'd be understanding—hell, he'd been the very definition so far. And perhaps, if I plucked up the courage to tell him I'd never done anything like this before, if I laid out all my anxieties, then we'd kiss and...fuck.

Maybe we would turn into a big romance. Maybe finding

the balls to confess the whole story would be the last hurdle to overcome whatever held me back. I liked the demisexual idea, but perhaps it wasn't me. Once I overcame this bloody mental obstacle, maybe, overnight, I would transform into the old Eggy, or an English version of Alejandro, rampantly chasing tourists. Felipe's key would unlock an entirely different door altogether.

I broke out in a cold sweat. I had only one way to find out. "Um...yes. Yes, Felipe, I...um...I'd like that. Very much."

Tied up in the internal battle raging in my head, I hadn't noticed he'd stepped closer, very close in fact. His hand found my hip and rested there, only a soft touch, but enough to send an involuntary shiver up my spine. I caught a whiff of his fresh, lemony fragrance. This was it; it was really happening. My first proper kiss.

"Thank you," he whispered. As his lips grazed mine, he sighed softly into the kiss. Warm breath, with a slight hint of garlic, gusted across my cheek. Dark stubble lightly scratched my chin.

"Christian! Yay, Christian! Over here!" Otto, in manic pixie mode, cheerfully dragging two slightly abashed, sunburnt English lads behind him.

Felipe and I leapt apart, Felipe more from the shock of Otto's piercing cry than having been seen kissing another man.

Quickly taking in the scene, Otto mischievously grinned up at me, clinging onto my arm. "Goodness, Christian, I didn't interrupt anything, did I? Hello, Felipe. How's that tickly cough of yours?" His grey eyes darted between the two of us. The bugger knew exactly what he'd interrupted. Felipe looked bemused, as well as irritated.

Exhaling deeply, I shook my head, possibly with relief, and ran sweaty palms down my jeans. "Er...no, it's all good, Otto. Felipe and I were just...you know, talking."

Otto's unexpected arrival killed the moment entirely. On

the one hand, after psyching myself up, failing to progress beyond a chaste kiss was a let-down. On the other, that dry sweep of Felipe's lips over mine elicited nothing apart from sheer terror. Truly, I was a fucking nutcase. I briefly shut my eyes; no way could I meet Felipe's gaze. Squeezing my arm and totally ignoring my pissed-off companion, Otto wheeled me around.

"Christian, meet Tommy and George. They're from Cornwall and are kind of surf obsessed. They were on the beach when you won at Boardmasters a couple of years ago, and they've seen that YouTube video when you won the Rip Curl challenge, so I promised I'd introduce you."

Okay, so I didn't shout about it, but I was quite a decent surfer. Not as good as I used to be, as I had to earn a living these days. Nevertheless, seeing how the other Christian Grey was kind of popular, searching my full name on the internet yielded about a hundred pages of adverts for handcuffs and ball gags. My surfing videos were buried deep. Either these two young lads were less innocent than they appeared, or they knew where to search. I guessed the latter.

Back on solid, familiar territory, I shook the boys' hands; we talked surf shit for a few minutes, and I agreed to take them out later in the week. Otto seemed thrilled that my name meant something in professional surfing circles, which was pretty cute. Felipe? Not so much.

"Sorry about that," I began after they'd wandered off, back to the buffet station. "Otto is...er...excitable. And I think he's sort of adopted me as another one of his older brothers."

Felipe huffed a short laugh. "He's definitely taken a shine to you, but I'm not convinced it's an entirely brotherly fashion."

What did that mean?

I didn't have time to ponder. The hand once again landed at

my waist. He cleared his throat, and I stifled a wince. "Now, where were we?"

Another dry brush of his mouth against mine. From his point of view, it must have felt like kissing warm concrete. I scarcely moved a muscle. I might have even stopped breathing. He persisted anyway, even trying to waggle his tongue through the line of my lips. Or that's how it seemed.

Sensing my lack of participation, he broke away, his deep brown eyes studying mine speculatively. "If you want, you can kiss me back," he remarked, mostly amused, although I detected a hint of frustration. "I like you, Fifty. A lot. But if you don't think we're working, then you must tell me. Is it something I've done or said or...?"

"No, Felipe, it's not you. It's me. I'm...I'm..."

"Honestly, if you were any younger, I'd think this was your first time. If I've upset you, or if all that shit with Alejandro has upset you, or I'm misreading your signals, then please tell me so I can put it right."

Oh god. If I ignored his teacherly tone of voice, he couldn't possibly be any more considerate. He said he liked me a lot, and I believed him. So I would spill it all. Everything. Right here, in this quiet corner of the beach, I would explain about my erectile dysfunction, my virginity, my terror, my total mind-fuckery. And then—if he didn't run away screaming with laughter—we'd go back to his place, and I'd let him tear me apart, do anything and everything, get it done, get it over with. If my dick stayed soft, then...then...I'd just have to fucking deal with it.

"Felipe, it's not you. You're great, honestly. There is something I need to..."

"Mister Fifty, *buena noches!*"

"Fuck!"

Alejandro's fingers firmly goosed my arse, sending me jumping about three feet into the air, beer flying everywhere.

"Fuck!" I swore again, trying to rescue my drink. "Sorry. Gosh, Felipe, I'm so sorry. Let me wipe that off."

If a bloke Clem hardly knew had run his fingers down his crack, he'd have called him out, then come up with a witty put-down. Eggy would have thumped him. But me being me, I merely stood, rooted to the spot, trying to salvage my sodden shirt, clean up Felipe's, and apologised for my clumsy spillage.

"Ah, and Felipe is here, too. *Buena noches.*"

They did a stiff, cheek-kissy thing and exchanged a few civil words in Spanish while I dabbed ineffectually at my clothing with a paper napkin. From the grim expression on Felipe's face, he was even less pleased to see Alejandro. I had the distinct feeling Ale-handsy had timed his intervention deliberately.

Pretending to study us both, Alejandro gave a wicked grin. "I disturb something, yes?"

"Yes. As a matter of fact, you did," snarled Felipe, before giving me a hurt look. "But you know what? I think we were done here, anyway. Am I right?"

We stared silently at each other, Alejandro curiously watching to see which way I'd jump. But whatever game he'd been playing had worked. The spell had been broken; my moment of bravado had passed.

"Um...maybe. I'll...er...I'll call you, Felipe, okay?"

Silently nodding, Felipe backed away, deliberately shoulder barging Alejandro as he walked off. A brief, muted exchange in Spanish ensued. I didn't have to hear it to understand.

Alejandro shrugged elegantly. "He's always cross with me. We ignore him, yes?" He beamed. "Now I have you to myself. Much better."

Jesus, never in my life had I been the focus of so much atten-tion. Home and bed—alone—felt like an extremely attractive proposition right now. Just bloody Alejandro to escape from.

"You should leave Felipe alone," I commented. "He's a good

guy. You seem hellbent on pissing him off. Why can't you stay away? It upsets him."

"He tell you why?"

I nodded, watching Felipe's retreating back and wondering why I didn't feel an urge to chase after him. "Most of it. You treated him really badly when you were younger. You were together a few years—at least he thought you were, anyhow."

"And I tell him we still could be, but he is...how do you say in English? *Obstinado.*"

"Obstinate?" I offered. "No, wait, stubborn."

"Yes, exactly. He is stubborn. And has long memory. I say sorry. He say not forgiven. What can Alejandro do?" He raised his hands up in a typical Mediterranean questioning gesture.

Stop being a dick? Stop trying to bed every bloke in Fuerteventura, including me, the focus of Felipe's current attentions?

Felipe had re-joined some of the hotel staff chatting around the buffet table. From his body language alone, his misery was obvious. Necking the nearest glass of white wine in one gulp gave him away, too.

Alejandro also observed him, and his usually sharp features softened. "So, Mister Fifty, you and my Felipe, you should be together. If he won't have me, then he needs a nice man like you."

We weren't going to be together, even if Felipe wasn't interested in anyone else. Aside from the dickhead standing next to me. As Eggy and Otto would say, the gods weren't favouring us. Felipe had been pushed as far as we could go. If Alejandro wasn't preventing our relationship from developing, then it was Otto. That boy always appeared at exactly the wrong moment.

"Christian!" Speak of the devil. Otto bounded over again, bouncing on his toes. "Ragnar sent me to talk to you. He said that, seeing as most of your beer spilled down your shirt, you will be well under the legal limit, and so could you drive me home later? He doesn't want me to walk home alone because he's fucking paranoid. And him and Clem want to go via the beach, for a moonlit walk, AKA a moonlit shag."

I doubted Eggy had added the last part to the message, nor the gagging sound.

"Not good, not good." Tutting, Alejandro shook his head. "Sand everywhere. I try it once. I not like."

Upon recognising Alejandro, Otto, the little fucker, flipped from sulky teenage mode to cool, sophisticated twink. I swear he did it to wind me up. His grey eyes glittered with teasing promise as he ran his fingers through his hair. Full lips formed into a generous pout. Alejandro audibly swallowed. There was scarcely a gay man on the island whose blood wouldn't have pumped straight to his cock. Aside from mine, obviously, with my mislaid satnav.

"Well, hello again, Alejandro!" He covered his mouth with his hand. "Oops! I'm not supposed to be talking to you. My minder here," light fingers tripped up my arm, "says you are too old for me. What do you think?"

"I think I need a closer look, *mi querido*. Mister Fifty, if it suits, I give Otto a lift home, yes?" Alejandro eyed Otto lasciviously.

Bile rose in my throat, along with a surprising level of anger at the Spaniard. How dare he fucking have a crack at Otto? In front of me? A surge of brotherly protectiveness filled my chest.

That's how I chose to interpret it, anyhow. "No."

"But I insist. It is no trouble. Seeing Otto safely to his door would be my pleasure."

I bet it would. And through the door. And up the stairs. "I said no. Or do you want me to go and run that idea past Eggy?"

I witnessed a rare event for Alejandro. Thwarted and weighing up the odds. I almost felt sorry for him. But with Eggy in shouting distance, he wasn't going to take any chances. "Perhaps this time, I change my mind. You need to listen to your minder. But another time, blond boy?"

"No," I interjected again firmly. "Absolutely not."

Alejandro grinned wickedly. "He is still yours, yes?"

"No! He's not mine. But he's not yours either, so bloody back off!"

Otto gawped at our exchange, his wide eyes flicking between the two of us.

I groaned internally. Bed. That's what I needed. Bed, with maybe a film or my latest surf mag. I turned to Otto. "Otto, tell your brother I'll give you a lift and that we are leaving now."

"Omg, Christian, you are so embarrassing! I could have managed Ale-handsy; I didn't need you weighing in! I wanted to lead him on a bit, that's all."

"Bloody rein it in, Otto!" I shouted, as we marched to where I'd parked the jeep. "You need putting on a leash!"

"Ooh, kinky!" He laughed, which only served to irritate me even further. "I only wanted a bit of fun. Why are you so bothered?"

"I'm bothered because...because...because I just am, okay?"

Fuck, I didn't understand why I cared so much. Or why Alejandro flirting with Otto made me so angry. The whole evening had made me angry—fucking up my kiss with Felipe, bloody Alejandro, and now Otto trotting along beside me, all cheery and full of mischief. Being his bloody taxi service so his older brother could fuck his boyfriend on the beach.

"So, what happened with Felipe earlier, then?" Otto stood patiently next to the passenger side of the jeep, leaning across the bonnet as I fumbled my keys out of my pocket.

"Nothing happened." I kicked the tyre. "Nothing happened

because I'm so bloody shit at this. I was about to tell him about my, you know, my bloody problem, as I think he'll understand, when bloody Alejandro turned up. And then I lost my nerve. God knows when I'll summon up the bloody balls to go through it all again."

I accompanied the last part with an angry thump on the bonnet. I imagined Otto would be taken aback by my outburst, but he merely smiled sadly at me, then laughed. "My god, you are so useless, Christian!"

"Thanks for the show of support," I snapped. I knew; I didn't need a snotty kid to point it out. I climbed into the driver's seat and slammed the door closed before revving the engine, louder than necessary. Otto slumped down next to me. "I should be back at Felipe's place right now with his tongue down my throat, not bloody giving you a lift home so Eggy can clear off for the night."

Lips a tense, angry line, my companion stared straight ahead and said nothing. A mad dandelion clock of white hair framed his features; aside from that, he was the spitting image of Eggy. Actually, no, a slightly softer, prettier version, even though suffering the blunt end of my frustrations twisted his face into a hurt frown.

I swore loudly. He couldn't be blamed for any of this. The fuck-ups were all mine. I took a deep breath, trying to calm myself. "I'm sorry, Otto. I don't mean to take it out on you."

"Is that what you'd rather be doing?" he asked in a small voice. "Getting off with Felipe?"

I banged hard on the steering wheel with my fist. "I don't bloody know, do I? I don't know what I fucking want anymore." I banged down hard again.

"It's not the car's fault," he observed calmly. "Nor mine, for that matter. I'm only trying to help."

"How the hell are you trying to help?" I roughly reached for my seatbelt and cursed as the clasp refused to slot into the bloody hole.

A warm hand landed on my bare arm. "Like this," he murmured.

Still seatbelt-less, he swiftly reached across, cupped my grumpy face in both of his small hands, and covered my mouth with his. The touch of his lips was fleeting; I could almost imagine it never happened, aside from his hands still resting either side of my face, holding me in place. His mouth stayed inches from mine. I heard, rather than felt, the seatbelt slither back across my body. That first kiss shook me to the core.

"I hope you don't mind. I've been building up to doing that all evening." His grey eyes appeared wide and dark in the receding light. A small frown line dipped between them. "But in my head, I have to admit, you responded a little more positively."

"I'm...I'm stunned," was about all I could muster. I breathed in a heady whiff of Clem's expensive aftershave. "Trust me, this is much more of a response than Felipe got."

"Good."

For a few seconds, Otto stared at me intently, before closing his eyes and doing it again. The second kiss also shook me to the core. I steadied myself with my hands on the steering wheel as the press of his soft, full lips over mine rocked my world. One of his hands left my face, sliding around my neck and into my hair, firmly pulling me down closer to him.

Stricken, I remained motionless, until he laughed against my mouth. "If you like, you can kiss me back."

Not twenty minutes ago, Felipe had used the exact same phrase, and I'd almost recoiled in fear. Otto transformed it into the most beautiful sentence in the English language.

Pulling away, his eyes blinked open again, searching my face for clues. "Unless you don't want to, in which case I'll stop now and avoid you for, like, the next six months until we can have a conversation without me cringing and you feeling sorry for me."

"I want to," I blurted, more certain than I'd ever felt about anything, ever. I couldn't begin to describe how much I wanted to kiss him back. My pulse thudded in my neck, the temperature of the car stifling, the hotel guests a background buzz from very far away. "But I've never kissed anyone before."

Fuck, I'd said it. There was no swallowing it back down. My words hung in the humid air between us. I swayed forward dizzily, the edge of the steering wheel rising up to meet me. Squeezing my eyes tightly shut, I braced myself for that sickening rush of nausea and sideways tilt. I didn't know if you could faint from a sitting position, but I had a dreadful feeling I was about to find out.

Otto's voice, almost dreamlike, told me to calm down. His arms clutched my sides, holding me up. The dizziness gradually receded; the world reasserted itself on its axis. I inhaled deeply, then blew the breath out slowly as he wound down a window, letting in a rush of cool air.

"Wha-a-t?" he screeched, in a tone so shrill I'm surprised the glass in the windscreen didn't shatter. That noise drew me back from the brink of fainting as effectively as any smelling salts. A brief lull descended in the chatter on the beach.

"You've never kissed anyone?" he hissed, incredulously. "What the fuck, Christian?"

A pressing need to escape enveloped me. I wanted neither his pity nor his astonishment nor his piss-taking. I wanted to be alone.

Unfortunately, we were both in the car. After groping yet again at my seatbelt, this time more successfully, I gunned the engine and screeched out of the car park.

"It's nothing to be ashamed of, Christian. I've hardly kissed anyone either."

Prudently, Otto fastened his seatbelt too. I drove recklessly, with no clue where I headed. "Yes, but you're nineteen, Otto," I snapped. "I'm nearly thirty."

"Oh fuck." Now comprehension dawned. "Shit, are you a virgin? Oh my god, Christian, you are, aren't you?"

The car windows were still open, and I was forced to halt at a set of traffic lights. "Do you want to say that any louder, mate? I'm not sure the couple dining in that restaurant over there heard you."

He clamped a hand over his mouth in astonishment. "Oh my god, you're a virgin. I'm right, aren't I?"

A dogwalker on the other side of the road looked up, studying us curiously.

"Yep, they'll have heard you that time. Anyone else you want to share with?"

The lights flipped to green, and I sped off, eyes fixed on the road ahead. Sensibly, for his own safety, Otto kept quiet as we headed out of town. At random, I'd taken the route to the small coastal resort of El Cotillo, a road not that familiar to me, as the beaches weren't renowned for decent surf. At this time of night, traffic was sparse. I calmed somewhat.

My other big secret was out. No longer a burden I carried around with me, hidden from my best friends. The sole reason behind my disastrous attempts at dating, my panic attacks, probably my current erection problems and my fucking useless existence. And I'd shared it with this funny kid, sometimes as old and wise as the Himmeltindan mountains surrounding his home in Norway and sometimes as dumb and idiotic as a Labrador puppy.

"Why did you kiss me?" I asked into the silence.

"Er...because I wanted to? Duh! Along with all the other single gay men at that party? It's no biggie. I thought you looked hot tonight and fancied finding out what your lips tasted like.

That's all. Pretty good, as it happens. Seven out of ten, maybe, on the Miriam scale?"

He peered out into the darkness. "I didn't think it would get me kidnapped, though. Where the hell are we going?"

A sign leered out of the gloom on the road ahead, indicating a carpark. I signalled and pulled in. Unsurprisingly, the carpark was empty; this stretch of road didn't have any tourist attractions for miles. After killing the engine, I unfastened my seatbelt.

"Do it again," I ordered. "Quickly, before my brain thinks of all the reasons why you shouldn't and tells me it's a really bad idea."

I expected him to lean between the seats as before, delicately brushing his lips against mine. Otto had other ideas. Nimbly leaping across the gear stick, he straddled my lap, with his arms around my neck before I could stop him.

"It's not a bad idea at all." He pressed his mouth to mine before I had the chance to disagree. "It's the best idea I've heard in ages."

I couldn't describe that kiss. Not very well, anyway. But it lit a fire in my bones, like the first sip of a cold beer on a hot sunny day. Or that magical moment when the simmering energy of a powerful wave surges under your surfboard, and you know, you simply know, that if you hold it together, you're headed on the ride of your life. Its impulse shimmered through my bloodstream, pulsed through my veins, heating me up from the inside out.

Otto's fingers wound tightly in my hair. Pinning my head to the headrest, he hungrily attacked my mouth. I clutched the car seat uselessly, the lightning strike of his tongue licking across mine, wet, rough, and so fucking possessive. A fierce kiss, the kiss of a man, not a boy; he gripped my hair so tightly a soft whimper escaped my throat.

At some point I kissed him back.

I knew the moment I responded, as he groaned and smiled against my mouth, retreating briefly before determinedly advancing again.

"You're wrong," I gasped as eventually he let me up for air. "This is a very bad idea." His lips glistened, swollen and red in the dim light before he wiped his wet mouth on the sleeve of his shirt, then rubbed the sleeve against my own.

He flashed me a grin and dove down again, this time unclamping my hands from the seat and firmly positioning them on his arse, where they stayed rigidly fixed in position. It felt like that coordination game when kids patted their heads and rubbed their bellies simultaneously. I'd always been shit at it; the crazy sensations of Otto's mouth alone occupied every single brain cell.

When I felt on the verge of passing out from asphyxiation and sheer sensory overload, he pulled back again. "God, kissing you is so fucking lovely, Christian." That wicked smirk again. "Nine out of ten."

I chuckled; Otto ranked everything and everybody. It was fucking adorable.

"How do we make it a perfect ten?" I whispered, running my nose along his smooth jaw. Reaching the tender hollow under his ear, I pressed my lips against the warm skin, and he groaned again.

"You just did." He rubbed his groin, rearranging himself in his jeans. His reddened lips were half parted, his eyes dark pools in the dim light. So fucking pretty.

I tipped my head up for more, but he held me back. "If it's so good, Otto, then why have we stopped?"

"I had to. Otherwise, I would have jizzed in my pants."

A bubble of laughter burst out of me, slightly hysterically, both at his wonderful honesty and from the insane high of his kiss. He gave me a sheepish look, then grinned stupidly.

And what effect did kissing him have on my dick?

Well, the good news was I hadn't thought of it once. Not once. He'd captured my mouth so thoroughly; I'd been focused on nothing except the firing of every nerve ending in my lips, my gums, my teeth, my tongue, even in that dangly bit hanging at the back. I had no idea how my dick had responded to the whole interlude. It was soft now, but how it had spent the intervening few minutes would forever remain a mystery.

My hands suddenly felt huge and awkward covering his arse, and I let go, as if burnt. He made no move to get off my lap. I liked the weight of him there.

"Now what?" I asked softly.

He shrugged. "I dunno. We could kiss again, maybe? You've got a few years to make up."

"Cheeky sod. That's not what I meant."

"I know."

We kissed again anyway. More gently this time, more exploratory, but equally as nice. My dick stayed disappointingly soft, but hey, it was one less thing to worry about. And I had started worrying. Eggy's baby brother sat in my lap; my thirtieth birthday approached; Eggy would most likely kill me if he ever found out.

Sensing my lack of commitment, Otto pulled away, eyeing me speculatively before clambering back into his own seat.

"This was a mistake," I said blandly.

"It wasn't a mistake, Christian. And we only kissed. You're overthinking it." Those lips, full and swollen only seconds ago, were once more drawn in a thin tense line.

I started the engine. "No, Otto, I liked it, but we shouldn't have done it." My voice sounded harsh, brutally so.

"Fine," he huffed and folded his arms, staring out into the

inky blackness. "Call it a mistake. You're right. But maybe now you'll be more confident kissing Felipe or Alejandro or any other *age-appropriate* hot Spanish bloke who appears out of the woodwork. You seem to have acquired quite an entourage."

He sounded hurt, and I didn't know what to say or do. I pondered his words on the drive back to Corralejo. From the unbelievable high of him squirming in my lap and kissing me senseless, I'd fallen horribly flat. But kissing him had been wrong. And it meant nothing to him. Otto was perpetually horny and felt sorry for me, helping me out by giving me some kissing practice, exactly like Miriam. 'No biggie', that's what he'd said. 'Just kissing', he'd said. Such a casual dismissal. He wasn't hurt at all. It was only me, misinterpreting the intonation in his Scandi accent.

As I drove through the quiet streets, he turned on the radio to fill the silence. We didn't talk, not once. Dropping him off back at Eggy's couldn't come soon enough. Without a backward glance, he tersely thanked me for the lift.

Safely ensconced in a bed too big these days for one man, I tossed and turned, sleep refusing to come. I ran my tongue over my lips, still slightly bruised, but the lingering taste of him had vanished. What was it with me and bloody Eggebraatens? Flat on my back, a pillow bunched behind my head, I stared at the ceiling, seeing a pair of dancing grey eyes laughingly awarding me a perfect ten, as I tried to recapture the warm weight of him in my lap.

My Spanish entourage could go to hell. The only person I wanted to kiss again, and to rest his blond head on the pillow next to me, was Otto.

Chapter Nine

When Fifty converses in the language of love

"Thanks for taking Otto home the other night," remarked Eggy as we headed out to meet our class.

"No worries, bro. How was the moonlit walk along the beach? Get any sand in places sand shouldn't congregate?"

He clapped me on the shoulder, smirking. "Christ, yeah, bloody stupid idea. Especially when we've got a big comfy bed at home. Clem thought it was romantic, though, and that's what counts."

Vikings were such big softies at heart.

"How did Otto seem to you on Sunday? I worry his meds make him tired. He does too much."

Eggy had expressed this concern before. Personally, I didn't share it. As far as I could see, Otto worked hard and played hard. He took his Spanish classes conscientiously, and Clem helped him wade through all the paperwork for nursing college enrolment.

"Oh, he was...um...fine. You know, lively. Stop worrying about him so much. You burned the candle at both ends when you were nineteen."

"Yeah, I know," Eggy conceded. "But I don't want him to be

like me. I want him to achieve more. And god knows what he gets up to when he's out at night. I'd be much more relaxed if he settled down and found himself a nice, harmless, little boyfriend. Like that Matthieu boy who was on holiday here."

How about a nice, harmless, big boyfriend? Like, maybe, ten years older? I had a feeling that would go down with Eggy like a cup of cold sick.

"At least I know when he's playing FIFA at your place, he can't get into trouble. He's in extremely safe hands. Clem says he's imprinting on you."

I looked at him blankly.

"Yeah, I had to ask him too. It's what baby ducklings do. They follow their mummy's around everywhere." He chuckled. "He's definitely taken a shine to you. It's like he's found himself another big brother. But as I've said before, kick him out when he starts to get on your nerves."

Big brother? Get on my nerves? I couldn't get him off them. Otto filled my head as if constructing a permanent home there. And there was nothing brotherly about the effect he had on me. This morning, I'd awoke lying on my belly with my hand on my dick and soggy wet boxers. Even conversing about him with Eggy made me semi-hard. On the one hand, I should have been rejoicing, but it chafed like sandpaper inside a dry wetsuit. Let alone the fact that the fluffball who had ravaged my face so competently was Eggy's fucking precious baby brother.

"Mind you, he might be tired, but he's very perky. Something has put him in an excellent mood. He even brought all the mugs down from his room this morning, without being nagged! Some of them were ready to walk down the stairs themselves!"

Eggy continued to happily rabbit on about his brother, unwittingly torturing me. Second only to Clem, his beloved Otto was his favourite topic of conversation. Christ, I needed to keep my distance before things got out of hand. As Otto said in the car, we only shared a kiss. No biggie. I needed to focus on my classes, the shop, and perhaps phone Felipe to apologise (for the millionth time) for messing up. And go for yet another drink with him.

My phone buzzed with an incoming call, saving me from more of Eggy's Otto chat. An unknown number, a lesson booking most likely. I flicked it onto loudspeaker.

"Hola," I answered politely, and then in English, "Hi, Chris Grey speaking."

I hated referring to myself as Chris—I'd never been a Chris —but much preferred it to the sniggers from random strangers whenever I used the alternative.

"Señor Fifty, *finalemente.* I have found you!" Fuck. I'd recognise that Spanglish anywhere. Bloody Alejandro again. With an obscene grabby gesture of my fingers, I mouthed "Ale-handsy" to Eggy. He rolled his eyes in disgust.

"Are you phoning to book a surf lesson, Alejandro?" I responded politely, and Eggy grinned. "I think I already told you, my classes are full. Eggy's free, though. He'd be delighted to give you a private one-to-one."

"You play games with me, Señor Fifty. You funny man. I phone to see if you want night out with Alejandro, no? Like I ask before. Proper night. We drink, I take you for good paella, we—how do you say? We have had a bad start, but now we come to know each other, yes?"

Eggy snorted against the steering wheel. Endeavouring to suppress a snort of my own, I tried to come up with a polite way of refusing him again. Reason one: the man had admitted he played mind games with Felipe and made me part of them. Reason two: Felipe still held a torch for him, and Felipe was a nice guy. Reason three: he annoyed me like hell.

Reason four: I couldn't stop thinking about how much I

wanted to kiss the one person on the whole fucking island I should have stayed away from.

"Say yes!" Eggy hissed. "Even though he's a knob. Having him on our side is good for business. He bloody knows everybody. Say yes!"

I flicked him the 'v' sign even as I knew what my answer would be. Corralejo was a small town, even smaller in the winter months, and we were outsiders building up a name for ourselves here. We'd joined a 'you scratch my back, I'll scratch yours' sort of place. We couldn't afford to make enemies. Felipe's family were hoteliers, and hotels meant holidaymakers, which meant more business for us.

"Erm...that's...um...nice of you to think of me," I stalled.

"I speak with my old friend Felipe. He say you keep him dingling. Always dingling. You start dingling Alejandro too, okay?"

Eggy nearly crashed the car. Dingling? Was this some euphemism innocents like me had yet to discover? I hadn't done any dingling with anyone.

"He means dangling," Eggy whispered with a smirk. "You're keeping Felipe *dangling*."

"So, Mister Fifty, we go out, *si*?"

I felt tempted to say yes, and not merely as a shrewd business move. Thanks to Otto, I'd been inducted into the kissing hall of fame. I felt bolder. Otto and I could never be a thing, so maybe I should roll with it. Alejandro's blatant come-ons were somehow easier to manage than Felipe's earnestness and the disappointment in his soulful eyes every time I avoided taking our relationship further.

Did I find Alejandro attractive? Objectively, yes. Admittedly, his presence had never perked my dick up, but then it never perked up anyway. Thus, it made an unreliable barometer of my feelings for him. And if Eggy overheard me arranging to meet up with Alejandro, he'd never in a million years imagine I cultivated inappropriate thoughts regarding baby bro.

I should have a few drinks, throw caution to the wind. Allow him to take me back to his place, do whatever he wanted with me, get this fucking virginity out of my life for good. Assuming my dick played ball, obviously. Which could never be taken for granted. That prescription for Viagra still lay tucked inside my wallet, though. Simply the security of the tablet might help.

Taking an enormous breath in, I steeled myself. "Okay, Alejandro. I'll dingle you. Where shall we meet?"

Eggy shook his head in bewilderment when I signed off. "You're a strange one, Fifty. Eight years I share a bloody tent with you, and you live like a hermit. And now you're dingling left, right and centre!"

"Making up for lost time." I smiled at him, recalling Otto's laughing words. Weirdly, this was the closest Eggy had ever alluded to my lack of sexual activity over the preceding years. But despite everything we'd done together, the chasm of our different experiences with sex stretched wide. Contemplating confessing all to Eggy filled me with shame. The truth? I never wanted his pity. I never wanted him to understand how pathetic I was in a sphere where he excelled.

As he drove, I covertly admired his strong profile, the muscular, tanned forearm gripping the steering wheel, his mane of bronze hair piled loosely in a bun. Christ, the effect that flaming hair used to have on me, the hundreds of times I stifled the urge to run my fingers through it. All gone now. Just bitter-sweet memories remained, years wasted fruitlessly waiting for him to want me back. Still my best mate, though; he'd always be that.

. . .

I'd been home all of five minutes when there was a brisk knock at the door. I knew who it would be, of course, the knowledge accompanied by an extremely immature flutter in my belly. A nineteen-year-old comes over to play FIFA, and I'm checking my hair and wishing I'd worn a cleaner sweater? *Odin's toenails*, as said nineteen-year-old would put it. *Get a grip, Fifty.*

He swept through the door without so much as a hello. If I expected a debrief on our episode in the car, followed by a mature discussion about how his feelings were a teenage crush and mine were born of years of sexual frustration, and that we'd made a single foolish mistake never to be repeated, then I was set for disappointment. Much more important issues topped his agenda.

"Bloody hell, Christian, I am so done with my oldest brother! He needs chemical castration! And Clem's equally as bad."

I followed him into the kitchen, bemused.

"By my calculations, Ragnar ejaculated three times last night, and Clem four. I'd suggest they put one of those slip hazard signs in the bedroom, but it wasn't in the bedroom, was it? On no, they used the kitchen, the lounge, the hallway *and* the bedroom."

Way, way too much information. "I assume Clem is flying back to the UK for a few days?"

"How did you know?"

I shrugged. I'd seen it all before. "Lucky guess? Eggy's marking his territory before Clem goes, making sure he remembers what he's leaving behind."

"A trail of spunk all over the carpet is what he's leaving behind!" Otto grumbled, making a disgusted face. "It's gross. Honestly, I don't know how I'm supposed to sleep with that racket."

"Try playing Shakira through your headphones. She's about

the right pitch." I held up a baguette. "Ham-and-cheese sandwich?"

As I made our snack, I mused over how I experienced zero anxiety around Otto. If I'd kissed one of the Felipes the day before, like I had Otto, I'd be in a state of panic, petrified I'd be manhandled against the fridge and they'd discover my disinterested dick. Otto behaved as if nothing had happened.

"Oh, I forgot to say. That Spanish bloke that you've been dating, with the funny walk and the coughy thing, dropped by the shop while you were giving a lesson."

"He hasn't got a funny walk!"

Watching me butter the bread, Otto hoisted himself onto the kitchen counter and happily swung his legs. He'd stuck up his blond hair in what was no doubt considered a cool style with the effect of making him more elfin than ever.

"What did he have to say?"

"I think he was cross he missed you. He's going to phone you later."

"Okay."

Otto relayed the message neutrally, making it difficult to interpret. Was he pleased on my behalf that Felipe wanted to get in touch or disappointed? Had Otto completely blanked our sensational kissing on the front seat of the jeep from his mind? Was I merely a big brother substitute and a handy owner of an Xbox? I didn't fucking know. This relationship stuff was a bloody minefield.

"He's definitely knock-kneed. I watched him walk out of the shop. And he wasn't wearing his felipe-filopes. Very peculiar walk," he mused, intently examining his nails.

I suppressed a grin. "I'm sure he speaks highly of you too."

"I don't think he does, actually," replied Otto cheerfully. "I think he's decided I'm a cockblocker."

"A what?"

"Odin's teeth, Christian! Don't you know anything? You know, someone who gets in the way when you're trying to make your move."

"Oh." I busied myself with grating some cheese. Neither of us said anything until I had two identical half baguettes filled. I held one up. "Do you want to eat this here or in front of the telly?"

"Said the actress to the bishop." He sniggered. Trust a teenage boy to make a joke out of a vaguely penis-shaped sandwich. "I'm starving. I want to eat it here."

I handed the sandwich over, and he accepted with one hand. With the other, he grabbed my wrist. I took a sharp intake of breath.

"I want you here, too," he murmured, his eyes on my mouth.

He placed the sandwich down on the counter next to him and tugged me close by my belt loops, manoeuvring me into the V of his legs as he swung them.

"Kissing first, sandwich second, FIFA third."

We were roughly at equal height when our lips met. He slid his arms around my neck at the same time as he wrapped his legs around my thighs, pinning me closer to him. Kissing was as good, if not better, than I remembered. Otto tasted of peppermint toothpaste and smelled faintly of Clem's expensive coconut shower gel. Boldly, I ran a hand up the outside of his denim-clad thigh. He moaned into my mouth, so I did it again with the other hand, my thumbs coming to a stop at the crease of his groin. A snug place to rest my hands instead of hanging uselessly at my sides, like a pair of hams.

"You're getting into the swing of this kissing business," Otto observed around my mouth. "Quite the little expert."

Trust Otto to be able to talk *and* kiss. He rocked his narrow hips against me, against my thumbs now massaging that sensitive area, my fingers gripping tight.

"Touch my dick," he ordered in an urgent whisper, his mouth working its way along my jaw. Ensuring no misunderstanding, he shoved one of my hands around to the button fly of his jeans and rubbed it across the hard bulge grinding against my palm. A lurching sensation filled my lower belly, and, hallelujah, my own dick grew semi-hard. The sound of heavy breathing filled the kitchen.

"Undo the buttons, Christian!" he commanded, his words muffled against my neck. God knew what he did with his lips and teeth in the warm patch behind my earlobe, but it sure as hell felt amazing. With a shock, I realised the heavy breathing emanated from me. Fumbling awkwardly, I attempted to loosen the top button of his fly as he thrust against my hand.

"It would be a lot bloody easier if you sat still," I panted. I stepped back, away from the delicious sensation of his tongue, so I could see what I was doing. Unfastening someone else's trousers proved a lot trickier than unfastening your own.

"I can't! Jesus, Christian, get on with it!"

As the trouser fly burst open, my hand found his hard shaft, dripping with precum. He almost yelped at my touch, biting down on my neck, then sucking hard. His hips jerked off the countertop, and a rush of hot wetness filled my palm. I jumped back with alarm.

"Oh god, oh fuck," Otto breathed, before lifting his head away. Looking down at the creamy spunk coating my hand and the thigh of his jeans he half laughed and half groaned. "I think I may have broken Fuerteventura's quickest handjob record."

"That wasn't a handjob, dude. I scarcely touched you!"

"Yeah, all right, Christian, don't rub it in."

We were both in semi-shock—me at the novel experience of someone else's dick in my hand, albeit incredibly briefly, and him at coming in such a rush. I mean, the whole thing, from him kissing me, had lasted literally less than thirty seconds. I'd have been mortified, but Otto simply laughed it off, staring down at his still-semi-erect dick as if it were one of the seven wonders of the world.

"You know you reckoned you wouldn't be very good at edging, Otto? I think you were right."

He roared again as if I'd cracked the funniest gag ever and flicked his eyes down to my flat groin. "You'd be a bloody Jedi master." Leaping down off the counter, he chuckled with delight. "Who cares? It was fucking awesome anyway."

He put his clothing back together, then reached for his sandwich, waving it around. "That's made me even more starving. I'll eat this penis now and then maybe yours afterwards, if you play your cards right. Come on, last one into the bedroom gets the old handset."

"Is it okay if I stay tonight?" he asked later, eyes fixed on the football game. I'd lost every match so far, as my eyes had mostly been fixed on him. "I've brought my meds with me."

I wondered if he'd eventually tire of FIFA and move on to something else. Or someone else.

"I feel like a third wheel hanging around with Ragnar and Clem, especially on Clem's last night before he goes back to the UK. So I told them I'd be spending the night at Alicia's. Which I could do, but I'd rather stay here with you."

He side-eyed me briefly, shooting me a cheeky grin and giggling. "Shit, I've given you a massive love bite on your neck. You're going to have to come up with an explanation for that in the morning. Ragnar will want to know all the gory details. There's no way you'll be able to hide it."

I put my hand to the side of my neck, running my finger over the vaguely tender skin. Another first experience.

Otto frowned slightly at the game. "I've just remembered. I should have, you know, touched your dick too. Sorry, I forgot."

I'd had lots of daydreams—fantasies, really—about my first sexual experience. Mostly of the Daydream-Felipe-romantic variety, often involving a dark, lonely beach, since beaches were my favourite places. Or on a thick rug in front of a roaring open fire, the only light an enchanting glow from a dozen candles. Both naked, my faceless partner and I would tenderly kiss one another, whisper sweet nothings. There would be a lot of—for want of a better description—heavy petting, the whole scene suffused with love.

Needless to say, an Xbox, a phallic baguette, and a fluffball who forgot to touch me in return never featured. If I'd blinked, I might have missed the whole episode.

"It's okay." And I really meant it. Not having to worry about whether I stood at full mast, half-mast, or completely flaccid was liberating.

"I could touch it after this game, though, if you like?"

Candles and moonlit beaches were overrated. This was the most sexually exciting night of my life.

"You do know, don't you, Otto, that if your brother found out about this, he'd definitely kill me?"

"He loves you!" Otto responded. "He's always singing your praises. He even said you are better at surfing than him. So, no, in his eyes I don't think you could do anything wrong."

I filed away that piece of surprising information about the surfing for next time I wiped out and Eggy relentlessly took the piss.

"Dude, I'm ten years older than you. He'd think I'd taken advantage. I'm not exactly what he wants for you. Honestly, I know your brother very well indeed. He'd never forgive me."

"Mmm." His forehead wrinkled again; this had clearly not occurred to him.

"It's fine," he said after a few moments, smiling across at me. "In that case, we'll have to make sure he doesn't find out. And you're not taking advantage of me."

That I did know. If anything, it was the other way around.

"So when your Spanish men get in touch," he continued, "you should arrange to go out with them, so no one suspects anything."

He'd confused me. Did Otto want me to see other men? Were we going to embark on an open relationship? Were we a casual, liberal, Norwegian thing?

"But you'd better not fucking do anything with either of them. Otherwise, I'll kill you myself. I won't wait for Ragnar."

Cleared that question up then.

"I know I said in the car that it wasn't a big deal, kissing you," he continued earnestly. "I was trying to be cool. FYI, it's a very big deal. I don't want you being with anyone else." That look of determination again, the familiar proud jut of his chin. "So now we've got that straight, Christian, we can do some more of this."

Until he actually dropped the handset on the bed, I was unsure whether 'this' meant FIFA or the kissing stuff. It became clearer when he whipped off his T-shirt, revealing a pale, hairless chest. A faint vertical scar, starting at the dip of his collarbones, tracked down to the bottom of his ribcage.

He saw me looking and ran a finger down it. "This is from my heart surgery. I don't remember it, as I was a baby. But I nearly died, apparently."

Despite not exercising much and being small and skinny, Otto had inherited Eggebraaten genes. So he had the good fortune of a naturally athletic shape, with square shoulders and elegant posture. The scar attracted my attention, but the overall sight of him—bare-chested and cross-legged on my bed, in belt-less, baggy blue denim, with the white waistband of his boxers peeking over the top—grabbed bits of my insides and shook them around.

I hesitated before reaching for him, a familiar anxiety rising. My horny brain desperately wanted to kiss him again. My dick, however, hadn't received the memo. If Otto looked at or touched it, he'd discover that for himself. Humiliating beyond belief. Instead of leaping onto the bed to join him, I stood paralysed with indecision next to it.

I need not have concerned myself. The decision wasn't mine to make. In addition to Eggebraaten genes, Otto had bucketloads of Eggebraaten swagger, too. Sensing my uncertainty, he shot me a wicked smile and indicated with his chin. "Come on then, Christian. Get your kit off and get into bed. If I'm showing you my puny body, then we're definitely having a gander at yours."

In the end, we both climbed into bed wearing our boxer shorts. Otto was too busy with his back to me, folding his jeans or maybe being kind, to notice my lack of showing in the groin region, enabling me to slip under the covers unnoticed.

"I'm sorting my meds so I don't forget to take them in the morning," he explained.

Having arranged them to his satisfaction, he dived under the duvet to join me and took a deep breath in. "Mmm, lovely. Smells like you in here." He beamed, then pushed the duvet down to our waists. "Let the dog see the rabbit, then."

Knowing you had a decent, tanned, and muscly physique, which received covert, admiring glances on the beach, was very different to a man leaning up on their elbow in bed next to you, studying your body at close range. Especially when you knew you were too fond of tapas. Judging from his expression, Otto was ranking me, exactly like he ranked everything else. As he laid a cool palm over my chest and gently rubbed with his thumb, I awaited his verdict.

"Your skin is softer than Ragnar's and the other brothers'," he pronounced, apparently satisfied. "Smoother. It's nice. And I love your chest rug."

To demonstrate, he nuzzled his nose into it, sighing with pleasure. I frequently debated in front of the mirror whether to manscape my chest hair or leave it be, since even I knew chest bushes like mine had gone out of fashion along with Burt Reynolds and chunky gold medallions sometime during the 1980s. As Otto breathed me in, I decided I'd keep it.

His eyes swept critically down to the trail of blond, curling hair below my navel, disappearing under the duvet, and travelled back up again to my chest. "The brothers are vainer than you, though. Their six-packs are better defined. You're broader and chunkier around the shoulders. With more padding. Much cuddlier, Christian."

What he gives with one hand he takes with the other, I thought to myself and couldn't help smiling up at him, relaxing. Never knowing what he would say next was definitely part of his charm.

A teasing smile curled at his lips; faux-innocent grey eyes stared intently into mine. Then, leaning over me, he leisurely claimed a kiss. I sighed through my nose as his tongue slipped inside. Automatically, my arms snaked around his neck, pulling him closer. My pulse climbed when his bare chest landed on mine, warm flesh against warm flesh and I trailed a hand down the swoop of his spine, my palm caressing the small of his back, the hairless, marble perfection of his youthful skin.

I must have been doing something right. With a groan of pleasure, Otto shifted, flinging one thigh over mine so he half lay on top of me, his kisses more heated. The warm length of his lean frame nestled against mine, the firm, lithe weight of him sending sparks to my groin.

My dick stirred—my fucking dick actually stirred, thickening rapidly as his hand trailed from my chest down my side, pausing to rest lightly at my hip. I gasped, his palm sizzling against tender flesh only inches from my shaft. Shit, if he moved his fingers, if they inched across even a tiny bit, I couldn't predict if my dick would beat a hasty retreat or behave appropriately and stay firm. Fuck, I had no clue.

Granted, I was scared he'd find it soft, but even worse, I feared he'd find it hard and then play with it, and it would soften, and then...

I tensed under him, and, sensing it, he pulled away.

"Just chill, Christian, okay?" he murmured breathlessly. "I promise I'm not going to touch your cock. Mostly because I'll come if I do, and I don't want to come yet."

Laughing, he pressed his nose into my neck, almost shyly considering his surname was Eggebraaten. Reticence had not been embedded in their genetic makeup. "I'm trying to make this last, Christian, although it's fucking impossible. Like, your body feels amazing, and you might be, like, a virgin and everything, but you're a bloody great kisser. And your hand on my arse is...fuck."

Otto was almost as useless at this as me. We made quite a pair—me in agony, wanting to enjoy it but fretting about my lack of ability to come, and Otto on a hair trigger, trying to do the exact opposite.

Just like that, my nerves ebbed away. I was horny and needy and wanted, and I fucking loved it. So we kissed some more, and I stroked his lower back some more, until Otto humped my leg. Small movements at first, his shaft hot granite against my thigh. Moving my hand lower, I covered one of the tight mounds of his arse, loving the flexing and unflexing through the fabric of his underwear.

He announced he was coming in a breathy gasp and an urgent fumbling at his waistband. As hot seed splashed across my thigh, he clamped down onto my neck, and his biting kisses ignited my flesh and my soul.

"You need to invest in a packet of baby wipes," he declared as he hopped off the bed, returning from the bathroom with a roll of toilet paper. "That's what Eggy and Clem use. Eggy even bought Clem a plug-in electric wipe warmer."

Bloody Viking softie.

"And you need to keep the wipes by the bed for next time. Well, actually, not next time, as I reckon that's going to be in about ten minutes when I've got my breath back. Which doesn't leave you enough time to go wipe shopping."

I shook my head. He was like a kid at Christmas with a new toy. And the new toy was me. I could live with that. Although, at the back of my mind, I remembered all kids tired of new toys eventually. "Ten minutes?"

Tearing off a strip of toilet roll, he rubbed at the mess on my leg and pouted. "Yeah, give or take. I'm a high achiever. Maybe I'll stretch it to fifteen, given that I'm hungry and need to eat something before we go again. I've been reading, by the way."

"Of course you have."

He ignored me. "As I said, I've been reading. I've been looking at statistics for recovery time between ejaculations. Did you know the average refractory period for an eighteen-year-old man is only fifteen minutes? I reckon I can beat that, especially with you helping."

My personal refractory time currently averaged around four weeks, but I kept that to myself. No doubt I'd soon be informed of the normal range for a man of my age. Flicking the balled-up tissue onto the floor, Otto dived back into bed and propped himself up on his side, looking at me. "Don't panic, mate, I'll pick it up later. God forbid we muss your bloody tidy house."

Grinning, he made a face. "Your refractory time, old man, in case you were wondering, is about thirty-six minutes. Once you get into your stride, we're going to shave a few off. More of a target than a guideline."

Good to know.

I'd always believed sex made men sleepy. If humping my thigh could be classified as sex, then this didn't apply to Otto, as he bounced around the bed like the Duracell bunny. After warning me for the third time about his imminent death from starvation, I took the hint and heated up a couple of frozen pizzas. We ate them perched next to each other on stools at the kitchen counter. I didn't trust his greasy hands on my sofa.

"So, you know you told the doctor that your...um...problem down below is a newish thing?"

He'd thrown on one of my old grey T-shirts, which drowned him. His hair stood up in little devil horns, reminding me of a mischievous pixie, especially when he tossed out such alarming questions.

With a careful nod, I braced myself for what came next. Knowing Otto, it would be direct. "Yeah, it's been about a year or so," I answered, reddening slightly.

He waited until he'd swallowed his next mouthful before speaking, not embarrassed at all. "So, here's what I want to know, Christian. If this is a fairly new problem, and you are, like, nearly thirty, why are you still a virgin? I mean, what the hell were you doing for the, like, ten years before your dick decided to have its midlife crisis?"

I most definitely required alcoholic sustenance to answer that question. Plucking two Tropicals out of the fridge, I passed one to Otto.

"Because, you're really hot," he carried on, rolling a shoulder in a light shrug. "I'd get it if you were, you know, fuck-ugly."

"Beauty is more than skin deep, Otto," I reproved him, trying to hide my amusement.

"I know, I know, and ugly goes straight to the bone, blah blah blah. Thanks for the lecture. But I meant on the inside, duh." He threw me a quick grin, almost self-conscious. "Although the outside isn't too bad either."

Looking back, I think that was the moment I could, and perhaps should, have disentangled myself from becoming any more involved with Otto. To protect my heart. Our newfound relationship didn't include romance or loving gestures, no flirting really, and certainly no easy labelling. Otto didn't seduce me, not knowingly anyway, but he could be so unbelievably and unexpectedly sweet, like now. It took my breath away.

"I don't know why, to be honest," I confessed. "At your age, I was obsessed with surfing. I lived for it, so I didn't have space in my life for anything else. And my folks split up—my dad ran off with another woman—so my head only had room for all the shit going on at home. Hitting the surf became a way to escape."

I paused, thinking back to that miserable time. I couldn't blame every failing on my parents. "And I'm not sociable anyway, as you've probably noticed. I never discovered the Woolacombe gay scene—if there is one – so...so I think instead I concentrated on my surfing."

"Use it or lose it." He bobbed his head wisely. "You know, the less sex you have, the less you want it."

"Yeah, I guess an element of that happened."

"And you smoked too much dope. Ragnar told me. Way too much. Which is one of the reasons, according to Dr Marchena, that..."

"Yep, I know. I attended the consultation, too, remember?" I took a swig of my beer and carried on, before the inevitable weed nagging started. "Anyway, and then I met someone, and...I fell in love."

Now I had his attention. His eyes lit up. "A man, I'm assuming? What happened? Did something dreadful happen to him?"

"No," I chuckled. "He's perfectly fine. It's only that he didn't love me back, not in that way. And I wasted far too many years hoping he would."

"Are you over him now?"

"Yeah, I am," I responded. "One hundred percent."

Especially since you crash landed into my world, I nearly added. "He's in an exceedingly happy, long-term relationship with someone really nice."

I had no idea if Otto had joined the dots or not regarding the object of my unrequited love; he was too busy demolishing his pizza. "Is he the kind of guy who buys his partner a wipe warmer?"

I laughed. "Yeah, exactly that sort of person. Although if you only knew him superficially, you wouldn't expect him to be so thoughtful."

"Relationship goals," replied Otto around a mouthful of pizza. "I bet he's rubbish at FIFA, though."

I'm not sure Eggy would recognise an Xbox if I threw one at him. "Yeah, I'd have beaten him every time. In retrospect, I have no idea what I saw in him." I gave Otto a soft shoulder nudge, and he nudged me back. I hesitated, then added, "Actually, I recently learned he did buy his partner a wipe warmer."

My words hung between us, the only sound Otto chewing through his pizza crust. His face gave nothing away. Maybe I shouldn't have told him.

Finally, he finished chewing, swallowed, and then took a gulp of his beer. Pushing his plate to one side, he eyed me thoughtfully. "Yeah, Ragnar's a good-looking guy. I can see the attraction. He's not your type, though. It's a shame it took you so long to work it out, but if you had, then you might be shacked up with some other cute Scandi boy, instead of me."

I didn't think the world was big enough for two Otto Egge-braatens. I'd confessed I'd once been hopelessly in love with his older brother, and he literally didn't seem to give a shit.

"When you finally sort your dick problems out, it's going to be one hell of a party." He licked his greasy lips with relish. "You'll have enough jizz inside you to fill a beer barrel."

"I'm not sure it works like that, dude."

"We're gonna have fun finding out, won't we?"

Although sex didn't wear him out, filling Otto up with food did. He'd accompanied his late-night feast with one of his epilepsy pills, which he admitted made him dozy, especially combined with a single can of beer. So after we'd tidied the kitchen to my exacting standards, we took turns in the bathroom and toddled back to bed.

"Big spoon or little spoon?" he eventually queried when we were lying on our backs side by side. A gulf of about six inches of mattress spanned between us—even Otto had lost some of his usual bravado. I felt like a kid having a sleepover. Being entirely new to me, it took me a second to get his meaning. Perhaps in the sleepover spirit, he expected a shared dish of ice cream.

"Oh...um..." I considered our comparative sizes. "Big spoon, I guess?"

"Okay," he agreed happily. "We can always swap if that doesn't work."

Otto was more of a fidgety fork. Or one of those many-pronged spaghetti spoons. At any rate, there were no curved, smooth edges. Having thrutched about, trying several positions to get comfy, we settled back at the beginning with me as the big spoon, which he concluded was the most comfortable after all. I agreed.

"We can't turn up at work tomorrow together," he said drowsily, wriggling back into me. "Ragnar will spot us."

"That's okay," I yawned. "I'll drop you off at the corner, and you can walk the last five minutes."

My eyelids felt leaden. I'd had a busy day of kids' classes in the water, followed by an even busier evening.

"I'd like to spend tomorrow night with you too, but Ragnar wants me home now Clem's away. And it would seem weird for me to spend two evenings at Alicia's."

"Mmm." Wrapping myself around him like this felt bloody marvellous. I could stay in this position forever.

"Alicia is very sweet letting me pretend to be at her place."

"Mmm."

"And it will be nice to have Ragnar all to myself. I mean, I love Clem—he's so kind to me—but Ragnar and I have so much time to make up from when he was..."

"Otto?" I interrupted.

"Yeah?"

"Go the fuck to sleep, sweetheart."

Chapter Ten

Keeping up appearances

I slept straight through my alarm the next morning, which must have had something to do with the comfiness of the fluffball snuggled into me. After jerking awake and swearing loudly, I barely had time for a piss before pelting out the door, let alone any meaningful conversation.

Otto was not a morning person, I discovered; not entirely awake when I manhandled him into the jeep, and in a sleepy daze when I manhandled him out again a hundred metres or so from the surf shop.

As I burst into the store, Eggy was waking up the coffee machine in the back office. "Dude, you can chill for five. Your class is running late—their minibus has only this minute arrived at the hotel."

He wandered out into the shop, balancing three steaming mugs in one hand and what I prayed was a bag of cinnamon rolls in the other. Otto pushed open the shop door. Thankfully, the short walk had revived him.

Eggy's face immediately softened. "*Hei, lille venn,* did you have a fun night with the girls?"

My mug of coffee became the most interesting object in the

room as Otto nodded. "I had an excellent night, Ragnar." He shot me a meaningful look. "We're going to do it again very soon."

"Good." Handing him a coffee, Eggy hugged him close and planted a light kiss in his hair, evidently content his brother had kept out of mischief.

"Did you take your tablets this morning?"

"Yes, Dad."

Eggy wrinkled his nose. "Does Alicia not have shower facilities at her house?"

"We...I...overslept," Otto mumbled, pushing his brother away. "I'll have one later here when you've gone."

Eggy turned to me, flicking through the message pad on the counter. "You're not the only one who looks like he overslept, little friend. You two are a right pair!" He did a double take. "Whoa, dude! Otto, take a look at this! I'm not sure our pal Fifty did much sleeping. What the fuck is that on your neck, bro?"

Oh dear Lord. I'd completely forgotten.

Eggy crowded round me, whooping with delight, and Otto, the little fucker, did the same, even lightly fingering the tender patch below my ear.

"I thought only teenagers got those," he cackled. "Christian must have found himself a hot young lover."

"Dudes." I batted him away. "It's wetsuit rash, okay?"

Eggy didn't buy it. "Mate, I've been surfing long enough to know what wetsuit rash looks like, and that ain't it. Looks like old Ale-handsy is living up to his name, you dirty bugger."

The good-natured ragging continued until my class poured into the shop, relieving me of my inner turmoil. I now had dates lined up with both Alejandro and Felipe, thanks to a late-night text from the latter. Neither of which I wanted. What I wanted stood not two metres away from me, greeting and high-fiving all the kiddies milling round the counter like long-lost friends as he checked them off the list. And two metres away from him hovered his enormous, overprotective big brother, beaming at his youngest sibling with joy in his heart.

I was totally screwed.

Otto didn't come over that week. Probably for the best. With Clem back in the UK for a few days, Eggy wanted him around at home. From the brief updates in the shop between surf lessons, Eggy kept little brother busy sanding down and painting the outside window frames. My own assistance would have been welcomed, but I thought a little space from Otto might give me some perspective on my growing attachment to him. And anyway, I had a couple of dates to negotiate, neither of which I anticipated would be straightforward.

First up, a daytime coffee with Felipe. Confident our encounter wouldn't be sexually threatening—even his nemesis Alejandro wouldn't try and jump a date in the middle of a busy pavement café—anxiety plagued me, nonetheless. Without the diverting props of alcohol, dinner, and a crowded noisy bar, we were going to have to do some talking. And that wasn't my forte either.

I arrived first and perused the menu. I'd only eaten breakfast an hour or so earlier, but a plate of mini *roscos fritos* wouldn't have gone amiss. Regretfully, I pushed the menu to one side and stuck to an americano. Nicely padded was Otto's description of my belly. Felipe strolled towards me, waving hello at some passing friends. Nope, nothing wrong with his gait at all. He had a perfectly normal walk.

"I'm surprised you came." Either of us could have opened with that line, but I got it in first.

"I nearly didn't," he confessed.

We didn't talk about anything much until the waiter took

our drinks orders and delivered them to the table. Surrounded by happy holidaymakers, our table was by far the quietest. Possibly since neither of us wanted to confirm what we both suspected.

"It's...um...it's not working, is it?" Again, that line could have been me or him. This time it was him.

"No," I agreed. "But through no fault of yours. I'm to blame."

Felipe sipped his espresso. "Don't be so sure about that. Sometimes I think I walk around with a sign on my back, reading 'doomed from the start, don't bother'." He stared forlornly into his coffee cup, fiddling with a sugar sachet.

"Or maybe you have one saying, 'I'm in love with Alejandro, although I'm trying desperately not to be'?"

He gave a short laugh, showing even white teeth. Extremely attractive. "Yes. That as well."

"Are you going to do anything about it?" I ventured. "Or continue to torture yourself?"

He made a flapping, helpless motion. The two elderly ladies at the table next to us oohed and aahed over a heaped mound of *roscos fritos* placed in front of them. I eyed it wistfully.

"People change, Felipe." I manfully turned my attention back to my companion. "Alejandro was very young when he cheated on you. And young gay guys aren't exactly well known for their...um...restraint."

"He's not exactly well known for it now."

"Yes, but I suspect you've both grown up a lot since. And the way he behaves, doesn't it make you think he's perhaps looking for something missing? I don't know that he'll be happy, deep down, chasing tourists for the rest of his life."

From the sex noises emanating from the table adjacent to ours, the women appeared to be enjoying their *roscos fritos.* As one of them licked stray sugar from her lips, my belly rumbled.

"Would you like me to order you some of those?" Felipe asked with a small smile. "I have a feeling I won't have your full attention until I do."

I sighed heavily. "Nah, I'm watching my figure."

"As are most of the women in this place, apart from those two," he chuckled, jerking his head in the direction of the two women practically drooling. "And me, of course." Raising an arm, he signalled to the waiter. I gave myself a mental reminder to punish myself with a hundred sit-ups later.

"Look, Felipe. Let me tell you something. I was besotted with Eggy for a long time. Years and years. We lived together, which made it even worse. And worked together too. Everywhere I looked, there he was, reminding me how much I wanted him. And he was exactly like Alejandro back then—he shagged anything with a pulse, aside from me, which made it tougher still."

Felipe's eyes widened. "Does Clem know?"

"About me being in love with Eggy? Yes." I nodded. "They both know." I let Felipe digest that. "A couple of years ago, I plucked up the courage to do something about it—this was before he met Clem. I tried to kiss him. It was fucking awful."

I cringed, recalling the dreadful night I lunged for Eggy and he pushed me away. Even now, the look of horror on his face had me squirming.

"But, although it was excruciatingly bad, it helped me get over him. From that moment, I knew for sure I needed to move on. He didn't want me. He made that very clear. It took me a while, but seeing how right him and Clem are—"

"So, what are you saying? Do you think I should have it out with Alejandro?"

"God knows, but why not? You have nothing to lose, and it might help you sort your own feelings. As currently, you're miserable and neither moving forwards or backwards."

Felipe nodded. The *roscos fritos* arrived, and we both dived in. Pretty soon, I was stifling sex noises of my own. Felipe, of course, as an elegant, sophisticated European, daintily nibbled a corner as if he could take it or leave it.

"Alejandro and I never talked about what happened all those years ago." He swallowed down the tiniest mouthful. "Not properly. When I went to his house to surprise him and found him with this other guy, I basically walked straight out again. He broke my heart. He tried calling me and everything, but I never spoke to him, not for about three years. I couldn't. It hurt too much. The only time I ever do now is if I bump into him out and about, like at the restaurant."

At least I'd known Eggy shagged lots of other people. I stole the last *roscos fritos,* and Felipe pretended not to notice. "As I said, Alejandro might have changed. Why don't you give him the opportunity to apologise? It might help you move on. Or offer him a second chance?"

"I don't know if he wants a second chance," said Felipe gloomily. He swiped a streak of sugar off the plate with the tip of his finger, then sucked on it thoughtfully.

"Do you want to give him one?"

"In a heartbeat," he replied sadly. "I'm fucked, aren't I?"

This conversation had turned into the most interesting and forthright one we'd ever shared. I still didn't sense a developing emotional attraction to him. Despite him looking very hot in his chino shorts and tailored polo shirt, he did absolutely nothing sexually for me. Whereas a certain cute blond twink, gripping an Xbox handset, in a ragged pair of denim cut-offs, his boxers poking out of the top, had my belly turning somersaults.

We could become friends, though, Felipe and me. Like me, he'd not had much success in the relationship department.

Of course, I totally recognised the irony of me offering relationship advice to anyone, but I blundered on anyway. "Alejandro will be in Gators bar on Friday night, if you're interested. No time like the present."

"How on earth do you know?"

"Um…he's got a hot date, except his hot date isn't interested. And I can assure you, the hot date won't mind in the slightest if you muscle in."

Felipe shook his head at me over the rim of his coffee cup. "Bloody hell, he's got a nerve. He knows you and I have been out a few times. But no way could I see you and Alejandro together. Or you and Eggy, for that matter." Felipe shook his head. "Definitely not Eggy. You are so not his type. Clem suits him perfectly."

"Yes, he made that abundantly clear." I grinned at him, and he smiled back.

"So what about you, Fifty?" he asked gently. "You're a difficult man to work out. We could have had, I don't know, a casual thing, couldn't we? We still could. I'm not that terrible a proposition, am I?"

How much time did we have? Not enough—I had to get back to the shop. "Nah, you're great, Felipe. Alejandro's a fucking idiot if he can't see that. It's me. I've not been myself over the last year or so; I won't bore you with the details."

"You know you could tell me about it sometime?" His eyes were kind, gentle, and he reached across the table to give my hand a quick squeeze.

"I will," I promised, and I meant it.

An unexpected lull in surf lessons on Friday afternoon found me, Eggy and Otto all in the shop together. Five days without Clem made Eggy grumpy. He was also twitchy beyond belief, as Otto had two focal episodes over lunch, which occasionally heralded an all-out seizure. The focals were easy to miss, and if you weren't in the know, they could be misconstrued as plain bad manners. Otto's unusual quietness was the first sign, sometimes accompanied by lip smacking. During a focal at Eggy's house, he'd stared into space, ignoring me, and then been uncharacteristically sharp when I repeated myself more loudly. Today's lasted only a few seconds, a little lip smacking supplemented by vacantly staring into space.

Otto had a real-time awareness of his focal seizures, in a vague sort of way, and today's left him frustrated and snappy. Afterward, he slumped miserably over the desk in the back office. With no sign of the weird behaviour preceding his big fit, thank god, I crossed my fingers that everything would settle down.

"How are you feeling?" I asked him, perching on the edge of the desk. Eggy was busy next door, fitting out a customer for a new longboard.

"Fine," he muttered, then groaned. "God, I fucking hate my epilepsy."

I didn't have much to say. He was so bright and cheerful most of the time; forgetting he lived with a chronic health condition was easy.

"I'll probably never be allowed to drive. I can't go surfing or swimming. I can't even have a fucking bath! And I hate, hate, *hate* having focals in front of Ragnar! He'll be watching me like a hawk from now on."

He slammed his hand down on the table with frustration. "I'd organised going out with Celine and Alicia tonight—he's going to knock that on the head for sure. I bet he'll make me accompany him to collect Clem from the airport instead, and I'll have to put up with Clem practically going down on him in the car on the way home. Fuck my life!"

Otto buried his head in his hands again, and I gave him a gentle nudge, at a loss to make things better. "Listen, sweetheart,

I've got a plan. I'm going out tonight with Alejandro. You text me from Gators with Alicia and Celine, and we'll join you there. Eggy will be happy I'm checking up on you, especially after your focal, and it will stop Alejandro being...well, Ale-handsy. Two birds with one stone, okay?"

Three birds with one stone, actually, as I hoped Felipe would pitch up too.

"Do you think he'll go for it?" Otto asked doubtfully.

Checking Eggy remained occupied, I leant down and pecked him on the cheek. Such a little thing, but I'd sure as hell never done that before. Despite what we'd enjoyed in bed, I think Otto was surprised himself.

"I've got an ace to play with Eggy." I threw him a wink. Winking—not something I did either. "Remember, I've lived with him for years. Watch and learn, buddy, watch and learn."

"Another satisfied customer," announced Eggy cheerfully, bustling through into the back office. "He bought the Wave Bandit in the end. Good choice for him. And he's sending his mate over to get kitted out for one too. How are you feeling now, *lille venn*? You look brighter."

"Tickety-boo," replied Otto, with as much cheer as he could muster. "I definitely don't think that focal is leading to anything more. I think we've scared it off."

"Good," Eggy replied. "Make sure you take it easy today, okay?"

"I hear Clem's back tonight?" I casually enquired. "You've missed him, I bet."

"Yes, but he is always here in my heart." He gave his broad chest a dramatic Viking thump. "Always. We're two halves of one whole, you know that."

Otto pretended to retch. "Two halves of one whole idiot. I suppose you are going to be showing Clem tonight exactly how much you've missed him?"

When he grinned at me, I realised Otto had caught on. I hurriedly continued. "It might be nice for you and Clem if Otto stayed at my place tonight. I don't mind. You know, so you can have a bit of romantic time together."

Otto gagged again. "Romantic time being a euphemism for ripping his clothes off and shagging him on the lounge rug."

Eggy swatted him, and I laughed before outlining my plan for meeting Otto and his girls later in town. Eggy wavered. The pull of having Clem all to himself was strong. "Won't having Otto hanging around cramp your style, dude? I don't know if old Handsy will be very pleased to have my kid brother trailing after you."

"Um...nah... I'll...um...I'll square it with him, it will be good," I hedged. "Can't appear too keen. And we'll...erm...we'll have plenty of other nights on our own. If Otto's tired, I'll have an excuse to go home early. I'm fairly knackered myself."

Yep, definitely wavering.

"Clem will be the tired one after all those important meetings and dashing about in London, without your wonderful support," Otto interjected. "And travelling is so exhausting. When he finally arrives, he'll want nothing more than to snuggle up to his big hairy ginger Viking and..."

"All right, *lille venn*, don't push it."

Chapter Eleven

When Fifty discovers he has things in common with smoked fish

"I'm going to make one thing very clear before we go any further," I informed Alejandro, firmly kicking his leg away. He'd been attempting a game of footsie with me under the table.

Amused, he raised his furry black eyebrows at me. Taken individually, his features were desperately ordinary—nose too big, eyes too close together, and snaggly canines making his smile wolfish—but all combined, his face worked. Clem would be able to define it so much better than me, but sex appeal was how my mum would have described it. Good old-fashioned sex appeal.

"You and me, Alejandro, it's not happening. Not tonight, and not any another night either. Ever. This is not a date."

I played a high-risk strategy, laying out my cards this early in the evening. He might choose to cut his losses and bugger off while the night was still young. As he contemplated me, clever eyes narrowed, I took a long sup on my beer.

We had elected to meet at a tapas bar around the corner from Gators, a low-key place more popular with locals than tourists. At an outside table, a sharing plate of *chopitos* accompanied by a platter of tasty morsels of *manchego*, olives and chorizo lay between us. Alejandro had the wiry Mediterranean physique of a guy who existed on a diet of espresso and fags. Thus, I endeavoured to show some restraint. If I'd been alone, I'd have scoffed the lot by now.

"You spend evening with Alejandro, you change your mind, Mister Fifty. You forget all about your blond boy." Heat rose in my cheeks, and he spotted it immediately. "I was right, yes? Blond boy, he is yours after all? You playing with fire now?"

Shit, it was that obvious? The sooner we broke the news to Eggy, the better. Him finding out from another source would be disastrous. It would be bloody disastrous anyhow; I didn't need to make it any worse.

"We're very good friends, that's all," I lied, and he waggled his finger at me.

"I understand. I keep the secret under my hair, no?"

"Under your hat," I corrected, and he laughed.

"So, you tell me why we are here, and you dingle with me, or is that a secret too?"

I snagged a *chopito*, washing it down with the last of my beer. Hands down, this place produced the best tapas on the island. Alejandro raised his arm to attract the waiter's attention and ordered us a couple more beers. One *chopito* remained, and I eyed it lovingly. I had a problem with sharing plates. Although participants politely pretended they didn't keep a tally, we could both probably list exactly who'd eaten what, down to the last olive. Or perhaps that was just me. Disappointingly, I knew the remaining delicious morsel on this particular sharing plate didn't have my name on it.

"We're here," I began carefully, "as it's a nice way to spend a warm summer evening. You know, chatting with a new friend, sharing some great food, having a few drinks. And maybe we could, perhaps randomly hit Gators Bar later, which happens to be only around the corner? And who knows? Maybe we'll bump into a very attractive, single, lonely old friend. One whom you treated rather badly in the past but still have feelings for. A friend who happened to choose tonight to drop by a bar he rarely visits, on the off chance that a certain, equally attractive old friend decided to recognise the error of his ways and apologise to him for being an unfeeling bastard?"

Alejandro's command of English wasn't as good as Felipe's, but it was enough. "You are talking about my Felipe, yes?"

His Felipe. Taking that as a good sign, I pressed on. "Yes, your Felipe. Think about it, Alejandro."

"And while this is taking place, Mister Fifty, you could, I don't know, hang around the dance floor, yes? And definitely not watch a certain beautiful young blond man party with his friends? Is that a plan, Fifty?"

Sharp as a tack, Alejandro. I rested forwards on my elbows, staring at him intently. "You're what? Thirty-five, thirty-six? How many more summers are you going to spend having one-night stands with tourists? Until you become an embarrassment? Until you're old enough to be their dad? You know, you're not far off already."

"I'm thirty-eight." Grimacing, he downed half of his drink. Okay, so easily old enough to be Otto's dad. The thought made me squirm. I had nothing against age-gap romance—it would have been rather hypocritical—but romance didn't come into Alejandro's dealings with the tourists.

"Felipe hates me." He picked up the last *chopito*, absent-mindedly chewing on it. Bugger, I had planned on allowing him about another thirty seconds and then pinching it for myself. He didn't give it the attention it deserved.

"No, he doesn't," I replied emphatically. "He's scared, but he's prepared to give it another go. He hasn't moved on from you —not for lack of trying, but he hasn't. You really hurt him."

"Once a man has a taste of Alejandro, he never moves on."

Christ, with that ego, this man could be related to Eggy. Had Viking raiders ever reached as far south as Spain?

Alejandro gave me a rueful smile. "My Felipe, when he felt nervous, he used to do this very cute cough thing before he spoke. He still does it, yes?"

One man's meat was another man's poison and all that. "Yes. It's very...cute."

Alejandro washed down the *chopito* with the remains of his beer and reached for his wallet. I did the same, but he waved me away. "You pay next time, *mi amigo*. Maybe we go out and there are four of us, yes?"

I scanned the heads in the packed Gators bar. Alejandro topped the age range in there, and I wasn't far behind him. No sign of Felipe, but I felt quietly confident. Alejandro spotted Otto before I did, squashed around a corner table with a pile of friends. I looked over at the same moment that he looked up, his eyes searching for mine. The joyous kiss he blew in my direction, the unspoken promise in his eyes before turning back to his mates, settled around my heart like an electric blanket.

Alejandro and I chewed the cud at the bar for over an hour, while the holidaymakers and the tempo of the music heated up around us. When not flirting or eye-fucking almost every bloke in the vicinity, Alejandro proved great company. We talked about work, soccer, Clem's books—we even discussed mortgages and life insurance, being proper grown-ups. He knew all the locals of course, and soon, quite a large group of us propped up the bar.

Since Eggy hooked up with Clem, I'd missed this blokey camaraderie. Don't get me wrong. Eggy and I still enjoyed the occasional beer together after work—Clem wasn't much of a pubgoer or a beer-drinker—and I spent scores of nights socializing at their place, cadging dinner off them. I had never been made to feel unwelcome. But a proper, chilled night out with mates, like I used to have in Woolacombe? Definitely been missing from my life over the past year. I was in no rush to go over to Otto. He had his circle of friends, and, hopefully, I'd begun to find mine.

A couple of beers in, added to the couple we'd had at the restaurant, and Alejandro tapped my arm, jerking his chin in the direction of the packed dance floor. "We show these kiddies how to dance, yes?"

What Clem disdainfully referred to as Euro Trash pounded from the speakers, a relentless, dominant, cheesy drumbeat bursting with a wild excess of synths and catchy vocals. For a classical music lover like Clem, it didn't get much worse. Tonight, with booze running around in my veins and the knowledge my man danced only a few feet away, I fucking loved it.

As we made our way through the crowd, we caught the eye of a group of German girls barely out of their teens, hogging a section of floor space. They beckoned us to join them and I revised my earlier opinion of Alejandro's oily glide onto the dance floor. With Otto no longer the object of his attentions, I recognised it for what it was: a fucking sexy, finger-clicking, hip-rolling masterclass in how to show you'd still got it. Shaking my head in disbelief, I followed him.

And how did Christian Grey make his entrance onto the dance floor? Exactly how his namesake would have done. Like he fucking owned it. With his head held high and strutting, secure in the knowledge at the end of the evening, he'd be going home with the prettiest boy in the entire bloody club.

"You never told me you could dance!" screeched a voice in my ear. Said prettiest boy in the entire club flung his arms around my neck.

"You never asked."

Okay, so I couldn't manage the booty-shaking, provocative manner of Otto, or even emulate Alejandro's smooth, sinuous moves. But yeah, I could follow a beat well enough, much better than the gang of British lads hurling themselves drunkenly around the other end of the dance floor, and significantly more rhythmically than the German dad-dancing going on behind us. Perhaps it was down to a good sense of balance, achieved from all those years spent on a surfboard, or, more likely, from all the years spent surreptitiously watching and wanking to old One Direction videos. Otto didn't have a monopoly on Harry Styles fantasies.

Whatever. I'd impressed Otto, and so, for the first time ever, I threw some shapes with my hot man, and it felt bloody marvellous.

Alejandro had disappeared. I took a while to notice, not surprising with Otto grinding his skinny tush up against me. When Alicia, Celine and the rest of his crew joined us, he slacked off, although the hedonistic clientele of Gators most likely didn't give a stuff what we were up to.

As we formed a group and danced in a more sedate manner, I searched over the heads of Otto's friends for Felipe and Alejandro. And found them, dark heads together at the far end of the bar, deep in conversation. From this distance, who knew which way the encounter headed? I turned my attention back to my man, who pushed up against me once more.

"I'm tired, Christian," he yelled in my ear, looking as bright-eyed and bushy-tailed as ever. "*So* tired. And Ragnar said I must be taken home when I'm tired."

His hand slipped under the waistband of my jeans, and he gave my arse a squeeze.

"Heaven forbid we disobey Ragnar." I smiled at him, and he pushed his groin up against mine, making his need all too apparent.

"Odin would be very disappointed," he agreed gravely.

Tourists jammed the streets of Corralejo, which was bloody irritating because I suddenly needed to kiss my man like I needed oxygen to live. Hand in hand, we half ran, half walked home, dodging groups of holidaymakers until we turned off the main drag and onto the quieter side streets. The only sound became the pounding of our feet on warm tarmac.

Otto breathed heavily next to me. "Odin's teeth, Christian! What's the rush?"

"You know what the rush is," I panted, not slowing. "I want...I want..."

My body had finally remembered how fucking awesome it felt to be horny.

We barely made it through the door before Otto had me pushed up against the wall, his mouth glued to mine, his groin grinding up against my thigh. And, my god, I ground right back at him. He'd grown an extra pair of hands. They landed everywhere—knotting in my hair, grabbing my face and at my fly, making quick work of my clothing.

And then one of those extra hands curled around my knob.

If not for the wall behind me, I'd have collapsed boneless to the floor, from the unbelievable thrill of thrusting into the channel of his fist and from the exhilaration and sheer fucking relief of knowing I had a cock hard enough to smash concrete.

"Shit, Otto, I'm going to...I'm..."

My belly tensed; my balls tightened. I was close, so close, and Otto sensed it, his hand frantically flying, his thumb dipping into my slit, each pull exactly the right pressure, exactly the right speed.

"Yes, Christian, I've got you, Christian."

I came. Hard and fast and joyous. Fucking hell, I *came*.

I must have slid down the wall afterwards, since I found myself in a panting, inelegant sprawl on the floor. Otto stood over me, tutting. My knob still hung out of my jeans, and I didn't give a shit.

"You're making the place look untidy, Christian."

Catching hold of his shins, I wrestled him down too. With a squeal, he landed in my lap and covered my mouth with his.

"Thank you for that," I whispered against his lips.

"You're welcome. Anytime."

Resting my head against the wall, getting my breath back, I drank him in; crazy wild hair, dancing grey eyes, reddened, swollen lips quirked in an amused smile. Somehow this ridiculous boy, with his endless chatter and his Xbox expertise, had done the impossible. He'd brushed aside my hang-ups and insecurities as easily as sweeping autumn leaves into the gutter. Ploughing on regardless, he'd afforded them the attention they deserved, amounting to absolutely none at all.

He wriggled in my lap and tentatively licked his palm, coated in my spunk. "Mmm. It tastes okay. A bit salty. But better than smoked herring."

"I shall have that written on my gravestone—his spunk tasted better than smoked herring."

"Nah, on your gravestone they are going to write, 'he was shit at FIFA but made great post-sex sandwiches'."

Not the most subtle of hints. Otto had two modes: horny or hungry. Having satisfied the first, he'd switched to the second. Something puzzled me, though.

"Don't you need to, you know..." I jerked my chin down to his groin and then back up again. We'd concentrated on my pleasure—and fuck me, it had been bloody pleasurable, but Otto wasn't one to ignore his own needs.

He waved me off, clambering to his feet and offering me a hand up. "Oh no, Christian, I'm fine. I jizzed in my boxers the second I touched your cock. It was fucking awesome."

• • •

Otto showered while I prepared a stack of ham sandwiches and brought them to bed. Deliberately making a show of dropping his damp towel untidily onto the floor, he paraded bare-arsed around my bedroom, sorting out his meds and toiletries from his rucksack and lining them up neatly next to the bed.

"You look like you're moving in." I tried not to stare at his long, pale dick or his peachy, perfect arse. He was semi-hard, and, astonishingly, my dick plumped up again too. I surreptitiously fondled it under the covers, revelling in the novel experience, imagining those two delicious firm mounds cupped in my hands.

I'd never seen him totally naked before. Jutting hipbones and pointy elbows, he was all sharp angles, yet moved with the confident grace of someone totally at ease with himself. Quite an impressive skill to master at the age of nineteen. At a decade older, I was way off accomplishing it.

With everything arranged to his satisfaction, he yanked back the bedclothes, regarded me critically, and shook his head. "No, Christian, absolutely not. Those pants are coming off. Now. No excuses."

No one likes a show-off, but, you know, one time, maybe. And I felt pretty pleased with the way my night had panned out so far. Face heating, I wriggled out of my boxers, then stretched out, lacing my hands behind my head.

"Gosh, hello! Look who's finally decided to come out of hibernation!" Eyes gleaming, he kneeled up next to me, studying me like he was preparing for an exam.

I squirmed a little under his scrutiny, hoping he hadn't spotted me sucking my belly in. My full erection softened slightly. "Haven't you seen another bloke's dick before?"

He laughed. "I've got five brothers! Of course I have. All hung like moose."

"Moose? Is that the Norwegian equivalent of hung like a donkey?"

Shrugging, he carried on staring. "I don't know, but once, when we were on holiday over in Senja, we saw this one moose that—"

"Christ, now you're giving me a complex." My dick wilted; I regretted not leaving my boxers on. Pride comes before a fall and all that.

Otto grinned wickedly at my discomfort. "Don't worry, Christian, your cock is a decent size too."

That was me damned with faint praise.

"No really, it's very nice—the nicest one I've ever had in my mouth, that's for sure."

I frowned. "Well, that's easy to say! You've never had one in your—oh."

A famous surfing quote said the best surfer out there was the one having the most fun. In much the same way, it probably wasn't the Rolls Royce of blowjobs. But, from where I lay, Otto's mouth clamped around my dick was the sexual equivalent of every European supercar rolled into one.

Surprisingly for him, he took it slowly, exploring with his tongue, planting soft, wet kisses down my length and back up again. Which felt pretty fucking sensational. Every now and again, he flicked his eyes up to me, gauging my reactions. I shifted onto my elbows, all the better to watch him.

His hands weren't idle, either. One steadied my dick at the base—not that it needed much support. It stood up ramrod straight quite happily on its own. The fingertips of his other hand trailed up and down my bare inner thigh, and I spread myself wider.

"You like that, don't you?" he murmured.

No answer required or expected, fortunately, because as he swallowed me down, the only utterances within my capability were incomprehensible moans of absolute fucking delight. Otto's mouth, hot and wet, his cheeks hollowing as though he'd done it hundreds of times before, not stumbling even when I helplessly arched my hips higher, even when I tugged his hair.

I should have kept my eyes shut. If I'd not been watching, I'd have lasted longer, eking out every drop of pleasure his tongue, lips and throat had to offer. But, as it was, that last look down at my shiny, glistening dick as it disappeared into the tunnel of his mouth, his lips stretched tight, and my orgasm pistoned through me, out of control, catching me by surprise.

And Otto too. As ropes of my spunk hit the back of his throat, they equally swiftly shot out again onto my belly, accompanied by a retch. Eyes watering, Otto clapped a hand over his mouth, blinking rapidly.

"Bloody hell, Christian!" he panted, grimacing and wiping at his mouth. "A bit of warning next time! I know I said it tasted okay, that didn't mean I wanted to neck a gallon of the stuff!"

A snort of laughter escaped me. I couldn't help it. He was so indignant as he kneeled between my spread legs, wrinkling up his nose and giving me the evil eye. Despite nearly vomiting, his dick was still hard.

He shook his head at me, trying not to smile. "Come here, you idiot."

Spreading my arms wide in welcome, he flopped down onto my belly, not caring about the cooling, sticky mess he'd deposited there, and I held him close. "We're pretty sophisticated, aren't we?"

He giggled. "I'd say so. We should produce videos for Pornhub. Or for one of those funny home video shows. An X-rated version, though. People would pay good money to watch us making a complete hash of things."

"Sorry I didn't give you a warning, sweetheart. It sort of happened out of nowhere."

"I'm that good, eh?"

"No complaints here."

"Oh my god, Christian, your sex face. Not gonna lie, it's hilarious; exactly like your *patatas bravas* face but, like, on steroids."

"I don't have a *patatas bravas* face!" I would never eat *patatas bravas* in front of him again.

"Yes you do. It's like this." He proceeded with the most undignified facial expression known to mankind. To think I'd eaten out with Felipe looking like that, on many occasions.

Wrestling Otto onto his back, I pinned him down and tickled him until he screeched with laughter and begged me to stop. And then I kissed him senseless, because if I didn't occupy my mouth, then I would come out with something stupid, like how fucking adorable he was or some such shit.

Eventually, we calmed down. My brain stopped conjuring up crazy words he would never be ready to hear, and I wasn't ready to say. I rolled him over, so he once again lay spread-eagled across my belly. Yawning, he wriggled against me. "Odin's teeth, it's comfy lying on your tummy. All squishy and warm. Like being cuddled by a bear. A friendly bear, not, like, a hungry polar bear or anything."

He prattled about hungry polar bears in the Arctic Circle, about icebergs melting, about the sandwiches we'd forgotten, about the best sandwich he'd ever eaten (ham, hummus, and gouda cheese on seeded bread), about how his knob was still hard and I needed to do something about it, about Eggy and Clem, about nursing college, about...well, everything and nothing. After a while, I switched off, my attention drifting in and out, enjoying the lilt of his singsong accent and the press of his warm body against mine.

All the time he chattered, he rubbed himself along the length of my thigh, unashamedly getting himself off. My hand gently massaged his rounded buttock as he rocked against me. Moaning happily, he brought himself to completion, adding to the stickiness between us.

"That's better," he chuckled, easing himself onto my other, dry thigh and smearing the mess around a little more. He gently bit down onto my shoulder, licking, and nibbling at my skin. "I want to lie here every night. I'd like to move in. I think I'd be very happy living here with you in your tidy apartment."

A vision of waking up every morning with Otto chattering in my ear flitted through my head. Yeah, I could cope. Saying yes would be so easy. "I think we're a bit early in our relationship to be moving in together, don't you? Not to mention your brother..."

A teenage boy once more, he groaned and huffed a sigh against me. "God, Christian, don't remind me. He'll never let me move out. I'll be stuck listening to him and Clem having brilliantly smooth, mutually fulfilling, choreographed sex forever."

"We should tell him, you know. About us. Before he guesses or finds out from someone else."

Raising himself up, so his chin rested on his steepled hands, and his pointy elbows dug into my chest, Otto regarded me seriously. "Not yet," he pleaded. "Not if he's going to be as pissed off about us as you think he is. Let's have a little longer."

I agreed too easily. As the mature adult in our relationship, I ought to take the lead. Eggy was my oldest mate. It should have never got even this far without telling him something. Right now, cuddled up in bed with Clem, at the back of Eggy's mind sat the reassuring knowledge: his loyal best friend was closely guarding his favourite, youngest sibling.

Which he did, after a fashion. Extremely closely.

"Okay, until the end of the month. We'll tell him then." I hesitated before I half-jokingly added, "You might become bored of me by then, anyway. So we won't have to worry."

That stubborn, familiar vee of a frown line between his eyes appeared. Sometimes, he reminded me so much of his brother. Or maybe it had become the other way around—Eggy's mannerisms made me think of Otto. "No, I won't! That's a crazy thing to say!"

He sat up straighter, straddling me, and thumped hard on his chest, over his heart, another gesture so reminiscent of Eggy. Otto might have stood knee-high to a grasshopper and weighed not much more, but he had as much Viking blood coursing through his veins as any of his strapping, bronze-haired siblings. "You're in here, Christian," he fiercely declared. "And don't you dare tell me I'm only nineteen and I don't know anything. You'll be wrong. I am Bjørn Otto Sigurdson Eggebraaten of the Vestvågøy Eggebraatens, and I know my own heart."

He slumped back down dramatically, huffing, and fidgeting until he made himself comfy once more. "And that's the last I'm going to say on the matter," he added imperiously.

Which kind of put me in my place.

Chapter Twelve

Factor Fifty all over

The next day, I had a surprise lined up for Otto. I'd secretly planned it for weeks, ever since he first came over to mine in the doldrums after his girlfriends had gone surfing without him. It was a Saturday, the second in the month, which meant Eggy, Otto, and I had a day off. The summer tourist season could be a long old slog, so we had a quid pro quo agreement with another surf shop in Corralejo to cover each other's businesses once a month.

Otto had woken pretty much in exactly the same position as he'd fallen asleep, starfished across me. The first sign he stirred was a contented purr. The second was

him lazily rubbing his nether regions against mine.

I hadn't watched much porn for years. When I lived with Eggy in the vans, I made do with a tiny phone screen, but our signal was fairly hit and miss. And since I'd had a big telly installed in my apartment, porn only served to remind me of my erectile problems, so I'd abandoned watching it all together. The odd bits I had seen always zoomed in on slick, acrobatic oral or penetrative sex. Horribly intimidating, especially for someone with my levels of performance anxiety.

So I had no idea, and Otto most likely didn't either, that sex could also mean this, the simple sleepy rubbing of one dick against another. I guessed we weren't the first men to discover the easy joy of it. Neither of us felt the need to speak. Even Otto stayed silent, the only sounds the rustling of the bedclothes mingling with our gently puffing breaths.

And just like that, in the cool, dim haze of an early morning, with his lithe, warm body tightly cocooned against mine, I fell head over heels in love.

Afterwards, curled up against me, he announced, "I've been reading."

Dawn light loved Otto. Soft orangey rays poured through the cracks in my drawn blinds, dappling the exposed pale skin of his shoulders in an almost shimmery glow.

I ran my stubbly jaw lightly across one of them, causing him to squirm against me. "Should I be worried?"

"Did you know your testosterone levels are highest at about eight in the morning?"

"What, mine in particular?"

"No, Christian." He rolled his eyes at me. "Duh. Men in general."

"Good to know. And I'm supposed to do what, exactly, with this information?"

"So, it's a good time for us to have lots of sex." He put a finger to my mouth, tracing along the line of my lips, his own lips pursed as if deep in thought.

I had an insane urge to blurt out 'I love you', but held back, as it would most likely send him running for the hills. Which was precisely why falling for a teenager was a dick move.

"I want to have proper sex with you soon, Christian. You know, like, proper."

Yeah. Like, I knew.

The sentence hung there between us, mostly because I couldn't think of a suitable response. My answer was a yes, obviously. Looking back, it had been a huge fucking yes since we first kissed, but, me being me, that yes came with enough baggage to fill the hold of a jumbo jet. It felt like no time at all since I confessed my humiliating erectile problems to a kindly female doctor. Now, I lay in bed with my eager young lover, post-orgasm, and about to discuss future orgasms.

And, knowing Otto, we'd be discussing in some detail.

"So, you need to familiarise yourself with the location of your prostate if you haven't already. That was the other thing I've been reading about. And whether we use condoms or not."

I couldn't remember the name of the dude who invented the internet, but he had a hell of a lot to answer for.

"Um...condoms?" I homed in on the latter part since I figured that was a whole lot easier than discussing my prostate. To be brutally honest, I wasn't entirely sure of my prostate's location or function, and I didn't want Otto to discover I was a complete imbecile. I'd get back to him after accomplishing some quiet reading of my own.

"Yeah, you know, those slimy rubbery things men put on their willies to stop catching diseases and making babies? Although the 'making babies' part isn't of grave concern. Condoms are really embarrassing to buy at the pharmacy, by the way, especially when you look about twelve. So that will be your job."

"I know what condoms are." Sarcastic little fucker.

Condoms. Aspirational items I'd never found a use for. I made a mental note to throw out the old, out-of-date packet in my drawer before Otto came across them.

He gave me a kiss. "The one's in your drawer are out of date, by the way. But I don't want to use them, anyhow."

So much for throwing them out.

"Neither of us has ever been with anyone else," he continued earnestly. "I know they might make it easier the first time, but I want to know what it feels like to be deep inside you without anything separating us."

While I digested that bewildering piece of information, he kissed me again.

"Now, what was that surprise you were going to tell me about?"

This boy systematically slayed me.

A deep-seated need had taken root without me noticing, a need to give Otto everything he wished for. Which included fucking me. But that was only the beginning, as I had an over-powering desire to tend to all his other needs, too. I wanted to feed my hungry man decent dinners every night. I wanted to make sure he took his tablets on time and accompany him to his doctor's appointments (without fainting). I wanted to help him choose his nursing course and drop him off at college with a packed lunch on his first day. I wanted to be close by when he did that sexy dancing thing with his friends, shielding him from predatory eyes, all mean and moody and making it one hundred percent clear he was mine. I wanted him to move in. I wanted to be thrashed at FIFA by him at three in the morning.

I didn't know whether Otto wanted all these things too.

So, yes, I'd had a quick look online at the daddy thing Clem had jokingly thrown my way when we were out shopping, and yes again, I possibly ticked most of the boxes. Apart from the bottoming during sex one, but then, most daddies weren't in relationships with assertive young Viking descendants who liked to be top dog (literally) in all aspects of their lives. And on a more practical level, if we did it the other way around, my unpredictable dick might balk halfway through, a worry I could frankly do without.

Before leaving my apartment for our secret little excursion, I presented Otto with a gift. One pair of flowery red-and-blue board shorts, which he'd admired in the shop earlier in the week. After he put them on and modelled them to my satisfaction, I began coating his pale flawless skin in the highest factor sun cream available in the town pharmacy.

"Yay! Are we going to the beach?"

"Partly," I explained. "Stop dancing around! It will end up in your eyes otherwise."

Okay, so what started as innocent sunscreen application took a little longer than I anticipated. Because my god did circling my hands over his chest and lean belly give me an astonishing desire to ensure coverage of every inch of him, including parts that wouldn't be exposed to UV rays. Slipping my greased hands down the back of his new shorts, my finger ghosted over the crease of his arse as I cupped those two delicious globes. He leaned up on tiptoe, delivering an open-mouthed kiss, his hands already tangled in my hair. He tasted of toast and coffee.

"You like that, don't you?" I murmured.

"Ugh," he replied with a moan, rubbing his hard shaft up against me.

"Is that Norwegian for 'yes please, Christian'?"

Feeling braver, I ran my finger along his crease again with a little more pressure, this time down to the back of his balls, and then skimmed his tight little hole. We hadn't touched each other there, but from the high-pitched moan into my mouth and the quickening of his breath, it met with his approval. Unashamedly, he spread his legs wider, a silent request for more.

"Do you want me to…?"

"Yeah, fuck yeah. Like that, fuck."

With the pad of my slicked middle finger, I massaged the bud of his entrance. The noises escaping from his throat as I teased him hit me right in the gut. Frantically rubbing himself up against my thigh, only seconds later, he came with a growl.

"You're quite...ah...thorough with the sunscreen, Christian," he gasped, clinging onto me. "I'm going to have to develop a fondness for sunbathing. Chances of me burning my arsehole today are precisely zero."

"You've developed a fondness for humping my thigh." I kissed the tip of his nose.

He grinned up at me wickedly before sliding down to his knees. "These thighs of yours keep me awake at night," he murmured. He pulled the fabric of my shorts aside, then licked along the inside of one.

"Babe, nothing keeps you awake at night."

I canted my hips forward into him as he pulled my board shorts down to my knees. My beach surprise could wait a while longer. Otto's tongue laved up and down my shaft, and his cool hand cupped my balls, giving a gentle squeeze. I'd gone from erections being merely a distant memory to a permanent state of arousal. I swore, if Otto accidentally brushed against my big toe, I'd get a hard-on.

As he sucked one of my balls into his mouth, my legs buckled, threatening to give way and I wildly grabbed at the countertop behind me for support. Worrying about staying hard felt like a faraway nightmare, a hideous dystopian universe this boy with his funny ways and his sweet tongue pulled me out from. As my spine numbed and my belly tingled, his lips moved from my balls to my dick, the wet heat of his mouth licking and sucking and...

"I'm gonna come," I panted, possibly a fraction of a second later than Otto would have liked. But bloody hell, did he look fabulous with my spunk dripping from his chin and splashed across his cheek. The pink tip of his tongue darted out, swiping a drop from his upper lip. He swallowed, and I almost came all over again.

Delicately, he wiped his mouth with his thumb, then gave me a solemn look. "I might be risking my gay credentials here, Christian, but I'm still not sure about the taste."

Like bees on nectar, holidaymakers swarmed over the beach immediately next to the hotel. Waiters sweated in the heat of the day, serving drinks directly to the occupants of sun loungers. Children squealed from the trampolines down at the kid's club and overheated toddlers mithered to their mothers. Yet, a mere hundred metres away in either direction, the stretches of sand were practically deserted, save for a few couples seeking a little privacy and occasional local families making the most of the sea breeze and the sunshine.

Although fun, a trip to the beach wasn't what I had in mind, which registered with Otto when I picked up the widest, longest, chunkiest bodyboard we had in stock.

"Christian." He eyed the board anxiously. "You know I'm not supposed to go in the sea. Ragnar will go crazy if he finds out."

"He's not going to find out. He's probably still in bed with Clem, and then he planned on spending the rest of the day painting their downstairs bathroom. We've discussed colours."

"Okay, but even though it pisses me off, he's right about this. I once had a focal attack in the swimming pool, when Dag took me, and my head went underwater for a minute when he stopped paying attention. I nearly drowned."

Smiling at him, I also picked up a plastic bag I'd hidden under the counter. He eyed it with distaste. "And I'd rather drown than wear a big, puffy orange lifejacket. Someone I know might see me."

I wasn't so old I couldn't remember what wanting to fit in with the crowd felt like. My mum once bought me a cheap, knock-off version of a surf hoodie when everyone else had the Rip Curl one. I chose mild hypothermia instead.

But no harm would ever come to Otto on my watch. How could I admit keeping him safe and happy had become my number-one priority in life, without confessing how deeply I'd fallen? I gave him a hug. "I'm not going to make you wear a life-jacket, sweetheart. Trust me, okay?"

Dumping our towels and Otto's rucksack at the bottom of a sand dune, we made our way to the water's edge. I'd picked a fairly quiet stretch of beach away from the hotel, and no one paid us any attention. I slipped the bodyboard leash around my left ankle, before kneeling in the shallows and tying the collar of a second, longer leash around my right ankle. Thanks to one of the seamstresses at the hotel, this leash wasn't attached to the board; the other end had a second ankle loop. I firmly secured this loop around Otto's pale left ankle. Giving it a tug to ensure it was secure, I looked up at him. "Joined together forever now, mate."

Though he still seemed dubious, we waded out, me attached to the board and Otto attached to me. I suggested he lie on the board and paddle with his feet, while I swam ahead, pulling him along behind. With a brisk onshore wind, we didn't need to go much more than six feet deep to reach a suitable point beyond the break. When we did, I turned the board around, facing the shore once more, and held it steady.

Otto lay on his belly, his big eyes fearful. "Promise me you know what you're doing? I can't swim very well, and I'm defi-nitely out of my depth here."

I'd swum out of my depth too, in so many ways, but not here, not in the water. The sea was one of the few places on earth I felt in control. I looked towards the horizon.

"Okay, stay exactly as you are. There's a corker of a wave coming, and it's got your name all over it."

As the swell surged underneath us, I paddled swiftly, choosing my moment to heave myself up onto the board. I sprawled on top of Otto, flattening him, and laughing out loud at his surprised *oomph*. I had chosen well; the wave was a beauty. Picking up speed, it rolled to shore, lifting the nose of the surfboard and sweeping us ahead of it.

All Otto's fear evaporated in the thrill of the ride. He shrieked with delight as we flew towards the beach. Head up and arms outstretched, his blond hair streamed out behind him, as if shooting down from the crest of a rollercoaster for the very first time.

"Bloody hell, Christian! That was ace!" he screamed, as we tumbled sideways into the shallows. Tethered together, I hauled him up, the board bobbing behind me. "Why the hell did Ragnar and the brothers never think of doing this?"

I shrugged modestly. Being appreciated, especially by Otto, felt nice.

"Can we do it again?"

"If it swells, ride it, dude!" I laughed back at him. "Of course we can. Climb aboard, Lord Eggebraaten."

I lost count of how many waves we rode that afternoon. Enough to know I would ache like crazy tomorrow, from pulling him out beyond the breaks and then heaving myself back up onto the board again. I hadn't spent this much time body-boarding since I was a kid. Way more exhausting than hanging around on a shortboard in deeper waters, chewing the cud with Eggy, waiting for the perfect drop.

My eyes never strayed from the fluffball, not for even a second. Not a chore. During one of our many paddles back into the water, I think he had a brief focal spell. He definitely had a hazy moment, but no way would he have acknowledged it for fear I'd put an end to his fun.

And the best part? Otto's slippery, wriggly, wet body securely under my own, safely tethered to me. His squeals of joy. The wet, open-mouthed, salty kisses we exchanged as he lay on the board, waiting impatiently for the next wave.

"Oh my god, Christian, this is so cool. I love you so much!" he shouted after a particularly swift run in.

His words resonated deep in the pit of my stomach and hot tears pricked at my eyelids. I hoped he couldn't sense the effect they had on me. Those words meant nothing to him. He declared he loved me the way he might have declared his love for a particular flavour of ice cream or his favourite footballer on FIFA.

Even around the Canary Islands in the height of summer, the coolness of the Atlantic Ocean crept up on you, and we hadn't worn wetsuits. With blue lips and pruny skin, Otto was tiring, although he'd have been the last to admit it. Despite the attentive sunscreen, his nose had turned pink. Promising each other we'd do it again soon, we headed for shore.

"Last one to the sand dunes carries everything back!" he shouted, fucking ridiculous, seeing as we were tied together. We raced anyway, the most ungainly, lopsided three-legged team in history—me lugging the surfboard and clumsily tagging after my much nippier, shorter partner. Our strides were stupidly incompatible. Giggling, we collapsed breathlessly down onto the warm sand, Otto tumbling into my arms.

We didn't notice the quiet man sitting a few metres away, tucked in against a small sand dune. Not until he spoke. "That looked like a whole heap of fun. Well, fun for people who actually enjoy splashing around in cold, salty water."

Clem, dressed for winter as usual, an ancient straw hat perched on his head.

Grateful for small mercies, he was alone.

"Hi, Clem!" Otto flashed him a grin, still panting. "Oh, my, did you see us? Odin's teeth, that was fantastic!"

Letting out a whoosh of air and disentangling himself, he flopped onto his back in the sand, shielding his eyes against the sun. "Christ, I'm knackered."

Clem regarded me with narrowed eyes, his head slightly tilted to one side, a small smile playing on his lips. With a lurching sensation, I wondered how much he'd seen. Not the kissing, I hoped. We'd been a long way from shore, with me treading water at the front of the bodyboard, shielding Otto from prying eyes on the beach.

"Hi, Clem." I nodded at him pleasantly, my heart jackhammering in my chest. "Have you been here long?"

"Only a half hour or so." He indicated the notepad next to him. "Eggy's painting, so I decided to go for a walk. Thinking time, you know?"

I did. If he could, he took himself off every day for a short period alone. He said his best ideas came when he was driving or walking, plotting chapters in his head, revising paragraphs.

Otto and I were still tethered together. Awkwardly, I reached down to separate us. "I...um...I thought Otto might like to try body boarding. Seeing as he spends his days sending everyone else off for a good time in the waves." I held up my homemade double leash. "I...er...I tied him to me, so he's been perfectly safe."

"I have." Otto lifted his head up. "Completely safe. Even if I'd had a proper seizure, I was attached to Christian. No way could I have drowned."

"You've obviously put some thought into it," Clem observed calmly, directing his statement to me.

"Yeah, he did." Otto smiled at us both. "It was a fabulous

surprise. Don't tell Ragnar, will you, Clem? I don't want Christian to get into trouble. He was only being nice."

Clem gravely regarded us both, taking in Otto's pleading face and my no doubt shifty one. Even if Otto hadn't yet picked up on it, I'd bet the surf shop Clem had guessed about us. Slightly nauseous, I shivered, despite the heat of the afternoon sun radiating down from an endless blue sky. I wasn't ready to face Eggy yet, and I wanted to be the one to tell him myself, however dreadful that conversation might be. Focused on the sand running between my fingers, I couldn't meet Clem's eye.

"I won't say anything," Clem agreed eventually, and I let out the breath I didn't realise I'd been holding. "I can see Fifty is taking great care of you."

And there it was. What he hadn't said more powerful than what he had.

We chatted about Clem's trip back to the UK, about the bathroom being painted, about the weather, the beach, the screaming kids on his packed flight. When he glanced at his watch before standing up to leave, we stood up too.

"I've got the car, if you want a lift home," he suggested to Otto.

It would have appeared odd if Otto had declined, although it irritated the hell out of me, nonetheless. We were both adults. We should have been able to thank him, then explain we were heading back to my place, for a shower, food, and bed. Together.

Instead, we stood around awkwardly before Otto politely thanked me for the bodyboarding, Clem hovering like a proud parent collecting his son after a playdate. Except I didn't want Otto's gratitude. I wanted to grab him and kiss him and whisper that the pleasure had all been mine.

He gathered his belongings as I separately gathered mine, and I watched, alone, as he walked away from me towards

Clem's car. My mood suddenly flattened. Bleakly, I wondered if soon he'd be walking away from me for good.

After a few paces, however, Otto spun around, shooting me his wicked grin. "Don't forget your homework, Christian!"

What? I must have looked as puzzled as I felt. Cupping his hand so Clem couldn't see, he mouthed, "Your prostate! Find it!"

Chapter Thirteen

When Fifty enjoys an early-morning cup
of tea

A cursory browse of the internet reassured me I'd found my prostate years ago. I was merely too uneducated to know the name for the sensitive little nubbin hidden up my arse that turned a common-or-garden wank into what Eggy humorously referred to as a posh one. So no homework required, thank goodness, because we were bloody busy, flat-out with surf lessons. A quick dinner then crashing on the sofa was all I could manage at the end of most days,

With work on a never-ending loop of surf lessons and board servicing, Otto didn't manage to come over to mine for another three days. We had to endure a barbecue at Eggy and Clem's place first. Usually one of my favourite ways of passing a warm evening, but not when the love of my life sat a couple of feet away and I couldn't touch him. At least Clem's fabulous cooking kept my hands and mouth occupied.

"How's it going with old Handsy, then?" Eggy enquired with a cheeky grin. "You've been keeping a very low profile recently, mate. He giving you a night off to recover?"

I felt rather than saw Otto stiffen next to me.

"Uh, yeah," I mumbled. "Something like that."

"Come on then, spill the beans, dude!"

"We're...um...we're taking it slowly."

"Handsy doesn't do anything slowly," Eggy crowed. "If I know him, I bet he's been giving you a right—"

"Otto?" Clem interrupted. "Come and help me carry these plates into the kitchen."

I threw Clem a grateful look. Otto couldn't follow him fast enough. Eggy watched them both go and then handed us another beer each and settled back in his chair. He'd already polished off a few in the afternoon and was in an expansive mood. We clinked bottles.

"Just like old times," he declared happily. "You, me, a beer each, watching the sun go down. We've come a hell of a long way, haven't we?"

"We certainly have, dude." I sighed contentedly in the gorgeous teak lounger. It formed part of a set Clem had arranged to have shipped from the UK. "This is a damn sight better for my back than those deckchairs we had at the vans."

"Who would've thought," he mused, stretching out his long legs, "that we'd be living here and still working together. And me, with a bloke like Clem." He shook his head in amazement. "I still think he's going to wake up one morning and wonder what the hell he's doing with an illiterate grimy surfer, when he could, literally, take his pick."

"We're all wondering that, dude."

He rewarded me with a soft punch to my upper arm. Soft for a Viking, anyway. "And you seem to have that side of things sorted now, with your little team of Spaniards."

"Yeah," I began doubtfully. "I...um...there's probably something I..."

Otto and Clem laughing over something in the kitchen wafted through into the garden.

"Listen to them." Eggy jerked his head over in their direction. "They get on so well. When Otto first arrived, I worried he'd be quite the handful, but he's settled down a lot. Clem's very happy to have him around."

"Mm," I agreed, not sure what else to say.

"The gods are smiling on me. I've got my favourite brother, the love of my life, and my best mate all together. Perfect." He belched and leaned forwards, resting his elbows on his knees. "What's really impressed me about Otto is his focus on learning Spanish and getting into college. He's got his priorities right. Fuck, I wish I'd been half as savvy at his age. The other stuff, relationships and everything, can all come later. There's no rush."

Clem and Otto returned, bearing more trays of meat for the barbecue. Eggy stood to give Clem a hand, swaying a little. "Are you going out later, Otto?" he asked.

"Nah." Otto threw me a quick glance. "I'm happy to hang around with you guys."

"See?" A look of pride stretched across Eggy's face. "So sensible. Proud of you, little bro."

God, I needed to tell him soon. Maybe it wouldn't be so bad.

"That was fucking torture." Otto pushed me up against the fridge. We'd escaped and were back at my apartment. "Not gonna lie, if he tells me once more to stop pestering you, I swear I'm going to kill him."

An hour earlier, over a plate of peri-peri spareribs (Clem's amazing homemade sauce), Otto had politely asked me if he could come to mine for an Xbox session after we'd helped clear away the barbecue. Naturally, I had reassured him that would be no problem at all, trying to behave as nonchalantly as possible while simultaneously avoiding Clem's arched eyebrow.

"I might stay over if it gets late," Otto had carelessly added, "if that's okay with you, Christian? And, as you know, Ragnar doesn't like me wandering the streets alone at night."

As I managed to stutter out a yes, Clem made a kind of choking noise, while Eggy had looked on with pride. We'd then patiently listened as he'd made Otto promise not to be too much trouble and to go to bed when I asked him. Otto nearly exploded trying to contain his snort of laughter at Eggy's stern fatherly chat. I suddenly developed an urgent need to visit the lavatory.

And now, we were back at my place, and Otto's lips were inches from mine, his breath coming out in hot puffs. "Do I pester you, Christian?"

"Yeah." I grinned at him. "All the fucking time. And I bloody love it."

I dragged his shorts and underwear down to his knees. His swollen cock bobbed between us, and he thrust forwards onto my thigh, seeking friction. Like a pair of well-trained homing pigeons, my hands found their way to his arse. His mouth latched onto mine in a sloppy, hungry, impatient kiss, one we'd been storing up since we'd maddeningly circled each other after I rang Eggy's doorbell.

"Shit, Christian." He rubbed a snail trail across my jeans and pressed his palm against my rapidly growing dick. "I think it's my turn for a trip to the doctor's because any time I get fucking near you, I want to explode."

"Not yet," I whispered back. "Hold on, sweetheart."

Leaving his mouth, I scratched a line with my stubble along his jaw, biting down on his neck. I wanted to kiss and suck all of him, taste all of him. My dick jerked as he let out a needy whine, pressing painfully against tight denim.

"Suck on these." I plugged his mouth with my fingers. God, the obscene moans he made—from the effect they had on me, he could have been sucking my dick. As I sank to my knees, he gripped my wrist, keeping hold of my fingers. My tongue licked a trail from his neat little navel to his groin crease; my cheek brushed his damp shaft. As I buried my nose in his scratchy nest of fair pubes, inhaling the warm, musky scent of sex, the slurping noise around my fingers intensified. I was close to coming myself, without anyone laying a single hand on my dick. Bloody hell, how times had changed.

"Fuck, Christian, touch me, please. I need you to touch me."

Precum dripped from his slit, and I licked it off before dragging a stripe down his length and back up again. He'd finally released my fingers, his hands trying to steer my head in the direction he wanted it to go, and I put the wetness to good use, pressing them up against his entrance.

"Oh, God. Christian, fuck."

With a shaky hand, I yanked down my jeans and boxers, then grabbed myself and gave the base of my dick a squeeze, steadying him with a hand at his hip. My first-ever blowjob was going to be a damn fine one. With that thought, I took a deep breath, opened my mouth wide and swallowed him whole.

Sucking dick and breathing weren't compatible bedfellows, but even if I asphyxiated in the attempt, Otto would receive a blowjob to remember me by. Ignoring my watering eyes and stifling my gag, I ploughed on, even when he grabbed handfuls of my hair and fucked my mouth. My saliva pooled around him, running down my chin. Fortunately, I had a young boyfriend on a hair trigger, so while it felt like I'd been at it for longer than the world free-dive record, it was likely less than a minute. And despite my discomfort, the uninhibited, lustful sounds coming from my man made it all worthwhile. They were fucking hot.

The first jet of spunk hitting the back of my throat took me by surprise. I reflexively swallowed, then swallowed the jets after, every last drop, even licking it off his dick until he pushed me away. Resting on my knees, panting, I gazed up at him collapsed against the fridge, head back, lips parted, eyes fluttering closed. Boneless.

Christ, my boyfriend was fucking pretty.

As he slid down the fridge to join me on the floor, I wiped the spunk and spit off my face, my other hand still wrapped firmly around my knob. I brought myself off, slowly and deliberately, my eyes never leaving his pretty face. I think he knew what I was doing but was too blown to lift his eyelids and watch. Not even when I shoved up his T-shirt and practically signed my name in ropes of spunk across his flat, white belly.

"Do you remember," he whispered at last, "when we were bodyboarding and I said I loved you?"

"Yeah?" My heart quickened, and trust me, it had already been galloping along.

"Well, I want you to know that I didn't mean to say it."

The same heart possibly stopped for a few beats. Blood stopped reaching my brain, I felt as if my entire circulatory system leached out onto the floor. With a rush of nausea threatening, I froze, then suddenly retched, covering my mouth with my hand. Trousers at half-mast, my flaccid knob still hanging out and covered in drying spunk, I felt horribly, foolishly exposed.

"Because," he continued, as if patiently explaining to a customer how he would replace the tailfin on a surfboard, "I didn't want you to know. I didn't want you to think I was a silly teenager with a crush on my older brother's best mate."

Peeling my hand away from my face, he squeezed it in his and smiled gently at me. "It's not a silly teenage crush. I do actually love you. I'd love you if I was twenty-eight. I'd love you if I was forty-eight. I'd love you if I was sixty-eight!"

He wrinkled his brow. "Although if we were meeting now and I was sixty-eight, then you'd be seventy-eight, and you might not love me back. Not in a horny, 'let's give him the best blowjob in the world' sort of way, anyhow. Hopefully, you'd still love me, but perhaps as a friend, like, a much older, wiser friend." He tilted his head to one side, contemplating. "I'd love you if I was eighty-eight, too, but perhaps I'd be too demented to tell you. So you would never know, and you'd die a sad, lonely death, feeling unloved, but all the time being really…"

"Shh." I put a finger to his lips, and he gave it a sharp bite, grinning inanely as he babbled on about being eighty-eight. Oh god, if this boy dropped any more bombshells, reaching even my thirtieth birthday hung in the balance. Once more I found myself wondering if it were possible to faint while sitting down. Not taking any chances, with a groan of absolute relief, I almost fell forwards, my head finding itself in his lap, the rest of my body sprawled across the cold kitchen floor tiles.

"I'll interpret that to mean you don't mind, then." His fingers stroked through my hair. "The 'I love you' bit. Not the demented bit. But by the time I'm eighty-eight, you'll likely be dead anyway, so it won't matter if I'm demented."

"I'm planning on hanging around with you for a lot longer than that," I murmured, closing my eyes. "Thank you, sweetheart. I love you too."

I slept wrapped around him, having finally persuaded Otto's inner Vikingness that being little spoon in no way reflected our comparative masculinity, but simply the most comfortable way for two men with our contrasting physiques to sleep together.

When he woke me with a demanding kiss, it felt like the middle of the night; my bedside clock informed me it was closer to dawn.

"Wake up, Christian! I have supplies," he whispered urgently, shaking my arm. "Are you ready?"

"Eh? Supplies of what?" I cuddled up against him. I could have stayed snuggled under the covers with him all weekend.

He wriggled away. "Lube. I bought some yesterday. Look!"

The overhead light flicked on, temporarily blinding me. His head disappeared over the edge of the bed, and after some rustling, he reappeared, brandishing a plastic bag. Blinking a few times, I hauled myself up to a sitting position, tucking pillows behind me.

"Omg, I thought you were going to sleep, like, forever, and I couldn't wait any longer."

I yawned widely. "It's...um...it's still dark outside?" His concept and my concept of forever were not on the same page.

"Yeah, I know, but I've been watching you since five, and I'm...I'm excited, Christian!" Yep, he was certainly that, bouncing around like a kid on Christmas morning.

Pulling him close, I kissed his nose. "I'm excited too, sweetheart."

"Honestly?" He seemed incredulous.

Why wouldn't I be? I wanted this as much as he did; it had been at the forefront of my mind for days. He worried his bottom lip. "And I thought if I caught you on the hop at, like, now, then you wouldn't have time to overthink it and dwell on, you know, stuff."

He rummaged in the bag and threw a small package across the duvet. I picked it up, trying to work out its relevance to our apparently imminent plans for penetrative sex. "Dude, this is athlete's foot powder. Are you trying to tell me something?"

He rummaged even more. "I know, right? But there was this old biddy watching me in the pharmacy. I looked so shifty; I think she thought I was shoplifting. I had to buy some random stuff, so it didn't seem like I was zoning in on the lube."

He chucked a white bottle, which rattled, in my direction. "I got some multivitamins too. You'll benefit from those at your age."

I squinted at the label. "They're for menopausal women."

"Exactly."

Grabbing him, I wrestled him to the bed, tickling his belly. "Stop, you big bully!"

Another delve into the bag. "Some condoms, too, in case you changed your mind about not using them."

I reached for the condom packet, studying it. "They're luminous green. Glow in the dark. And...um...piña-colada flavoured?"

"I know!" He beamed. "I love coconut, so maybe we'll use them sometime. Honestly, she watched me like a hawk. I grabbed the first packet I saw."

I tossed them onto the bedside table next to me. I would not lose my virginity to a man wearing a luminous green condom. "We're not going to need them, Otto."

Finally, after more rummaging, he triumphantly held up a bottle. "Tah-dah! Found it. And I had a quick wank in the bathroom about half an hour ago so I wouldn't come too quickly."

Bloody hell, how long had he been awake for? Casting the bag aside and onto the floor, he crawled into my lap, looping his arms around my neck. He nuzzled into my chest. "It doesn't matter if I'm not very good the first time, does it? I'll get better. Practice makes perfect."

Gosh, was my confident young Viking lover having a moment of self-doubt? Is that why he'd woken early? Bizarrely, I didn't feel anxious at all. Horny, but not anxious. His skinny arse wriggling around on my dick generally had that effect.

I kissed the top of his hair, breathing in his warm, bedhead smell. "It's going to be great because it's you and me. It's not a performance, remember?"

"I know. I've been doing some reading, Christian." He was chirpy once more.

"Of course you have."

"The best position for a first-timer is either doggy style or you lying on your back so we're facing each other. And Clem says a pillow under your bottom helps get the angle right."

I nearly choked on my own saliva. "*Clem* says? You've asked Clem for advice?"

He shrugged. "Yeah. I mean, only generally—not, like, you know, you and me specifically."

Thank fuck for that.

"I've got a useful website here on my phone if you want to look."

Visions of the phone propped against the headboard next to us, like a recipe book, as we bungled our way through sexual intercourse flitted through my head. I laughed, clutching him closer. "Nah, the second option sounds good. If Clem recommends it, it must be correct. He's had enough practice. We'll work it out as we go along."

Otto sat up straighter, studying my face. "You're very relaxed about all this, Christian."

I was. More relaxed than I had ever felt in my life. I didn't worry about it hurting, although it might, a bit. Neither did I worry we'd be crap at it, or that my dick would stay soft. Or that we'd mess up the sheets, or that Otto would come too quickly. I was happy to bottom this first time, but I wanted to try topping as well one day. Sex with Otto, in all its amateur imperfections, would be perfect.

Of course, it wasn't perfect at all, but it was bloody funny. Otto declared I needed to visit the bathroom first, for a 'clean-up down below' as he euphemistically called it, flushing even as he gave his orders. I'd been doing a bit of quiet reading myself, so yeah, I dealt with all of that business while he made me a cup of tea, then anxiously had another wank, petrified he'd come the second he entered me. At this rate, he'd be so wrung out, he'd not be able to get it up again until mid-afternoon, and I had surf lessons booked in at ten.

From living with Clem, Otto had got it into his head that British men were good for nothing in the mornings until they had a cup of tea inside them. I drank it down obediently before we both brushed our teeth and returned to bed. Otto's face appeared almost as white as the bedsheets. I turned off the harsh overhead light, the flush of early dawn bathing us both in a dim golden glow. Was he having second thoughts?

"What if I have a fit halfway through?"

"Do you feel one coming on?" He'd turned pale before his last fit, although I only realised this in retrospect.

"No, I don't think so."

"Then you probably won't. And so what if you do? At least I'll be very nearby."

I dragged him over to my side of the bed and hugged him close. "Do you remember the first words I said to you in that club, when Alejandro had a crack at you?"

"Yeah," he answered quietly. "You said I was yours. I'll never forget."

I planted a light kiss on his brow. "Well, you are. So stop talking and start making love to me."

Once Otto got going, his determined Eggebraaten genes took over. Stretched out on my belly, he kissed me like he owned me, his tongue marauding through every corner of my mouth. With my arms pinned above my head, he made his way down my body, pausing at a nipple to give it a teasing bite. I yelped with shock.

"I've been meaning to do that for ages," he giggled.

"You've got bloody sharp teeth. Don't do that any lower down."

"But do you like it?"

"More than I expected to, yes."

Cue a tug on my other nipple. I'd definitely need a rash vest under my wetsuit later; that would chafe.

I'm not going to lie. I felt like a king as I lay in the middle of the bed, having my body worshipped. Otto saw my size as a challenge, a mountain to be climbed, not satisfied until every last inch of my flesh had been kissed, nibbled or caressed. And better still, my dick rose to the occasion, tall and proud and straining for attention.

"If only Dr Marchena could see you now." He licked a drop of precum from my slit. Possibly the least erotic pillow talk ever.

Like spilt milk, a little lube went a long way. Not one of the pearls of wisdom Clem had chosen to pass on; by the time Otto had coated his hands, his dick, and my arse with the stuff, I felt as if I was sliding around on a burst waterbed. And it was bloody cold, not that I minded. When the tip of his finger breached me, it felt so fucking delicious my hips snapped up like I'd been electrocuted.

Otto leapt back in alarm. "Shit, did I hurt you? I haven't used enough lube, have I?"

I felt the loss of his finger. "No...no...you've used...ample. It's aah...fuck, Otto, that feels so good."

One finger became two. Prostate homework had paid off— Otto's, not mine. That boy had learnt exactly how to crook his fingers. By now, he lay atop me, fingering me like he'd done it a thousand times before, and our hot, wet shafts slickly rolled against each other with every upwards thrust of my hips.

"I did this to myself earlier," he panted into my neck. "Stuck my fingers inside when I brought myself off. I thought of you as I did it, and how fucking lovely you'd look right now. But I'd got it wrong. You're even lovelier than I imagined, Christian."

This boy was as innocent and inexperienced as me, but

Christ, he'd got a silky tongue as well as a silky touch. The combination of both, added to the insane friction of our rubbing dicks, brought me close.

"Are you ready?" Otto sensed it, his voice in the semi-darkness edged with a needy desire matching my own.

"Born ready, sweetheart."

Pillow in position as per Clem's useful tip, Otto kneeled between my thighs, hand clutching his dick as I spread myself wide. Even though my inhibitions and anxieties had mostly vanished, and I badly wanted this, I was still grateful for the dimness of the room. Otto had a palm on the back of my knee. Pushing my leg backwards, he lined himself up against my dripping hole.

He took it slow, an inch at a time, as much for his benefit as for mine. I'd read warnings about the burn, the stretch, and the weird feeling of fullness. Somewhere, all those sensations hazily registered with me. But mostly, it felt fucking amazing. Otto let out a strangled little gasp, more of a giggle of disbelief as he finally seated. With his arms bracketing my head, I looped my hands around his neck and kissed the perfect wet heat of his mouth.

"How does it feel?" I whispered, neither of us moving.

He sucked in a sharp breath. "Like I've entered the kingdom of Valhalla," he whispered back. "And I never want to leave."

My beautiful lover was nineteen years old, and as much as his head wanted to linger in that tender moment forever, his hormones signalled otherwise. Orgasm denial wasn't his strong suit. But he'd paused long enough for me to accommodate the intrusion. As he found a rhythm, I bucked against him, matching his pace and his downward thrusts with strong upward resistance of my own.

My dick throbbed, trapped between our slick bodies. The delicious press of his belly, wet with sweat, gallons of lube and my own juices, triggered a lightning surge of electricity, leaping from the base of my spine and detouring through my head before landing in the pit of my stomach and my balls. My vision blurred; my hearing faded out; a whooshing pulse of blood pounded through my veins.

Otto slapped against me, a staccato accompaniment to my base grunts of pleasure. His grip at my hips would leave bruises; his breath puffed harshly against my cheek. With a warrior cry of triumph, I came in hot, wet jets between us, pumping on seemingly forever, nudging Otto over the brink and to his own climax. As he filled me with liquid heat, my body melted against him.

"You're going to be an assertive power bottom, Christian," were his opening lines after he'd recovered his breath. His half-hard cock stayed inside me, a comforting sensation. After being filled so completely, I wasn't ready for a sudden emptiness.

I tipped my head back and laughed. "Sweetheart, I don't even know what the fuck that sentence means."

They say surfing was the most blissful experience you can have on this planet. A taste of heaven. It's a great quote, but those dudes had never had sex with Bjørn Otto Sigurdson Egge-braaten.

"You're mine, Christian," he whispered fiercely against my chest. "I'm yours, and you're totally mine."

I hugged the lithe heat of him close, my nose buried in his soft hair, inhaling the scent of sex and fresh sweat. "Tell me something I don't know."

"Will you come to Norway with me this winter?" He twirled my chest hairs between his fingers. "I want you to meet the brothers. They'd like you."

"They might like me, but they'll think I'm too old for you. Eggy will, too."

"Well, they'll be wrong, and you're not. I'm the youngest of six. I've always preferred the company of older people. It's partly why I enjoyed working in the care home."

"I'm not sure how I feel about being likened to the residents of a care home." I smiled, giving him a poke. "We're telling Eggy tomorrow." Whatever happened, I wanted our relationship to be out in the open.

"Good," he agreed. "Given that I want to spend every night here from now on."

The shadowy bedroom had lightened, the wetness around us cooled, and I had a day of surf lessons to get up for. Reluctantly, I started to move, heaving Otto off me. I smiled at his grumbles as I pushed him to his feet, admiring his rounded, peachy backside.

But, as he clambered off the bed, my jaw dropped. "Otto, why the fuck is your dick covered in glitter?"

Oh Christ, not only his dick. His thighs, belly, hands, even his hair was coated in the stuff, tiny silver sparkles glinting in the morning sunshine. As if he'd covered himself in glue, then run naked through a kindergarten Christmas display.

Aghast, I threw back the covers, only to see my own body similarly bejewelled. My bedding, too. "What the fuck?"

I snatched up the bottle of lube from the bedside table at the same time as Otto burst into fits of giggles. "I told you—an old biddy watched me in the pharmacy like she was waiting for me to nick something. I grabbed the nearest bottle and got out of there!"

"*Put some sparkle into your sex life!*" I read out incredulously from the jazzy label. "*Make your thing go with a zing!*"

The plastic bottle was virtually empty, not surprising, seeing as most of its contents drenched my pubic hair. A few globs of pink, glittery residue dripped down the inside of the container.

"Oh, come on, Christian, we did sparkle, didn't we?" Otto

laughed, dancing around the room. "And I don't want to blow my own trumpet or anything, but...er...I, you know, outlasted you?"

He slightly ruined his smug expression by attempting and failing to wipe some of the glitter off his knob. "I'll make myself come twice in the shower trying to get this stuff off!"

Groaning, I buried my head under the covers. An error, as now I had lube all over my face too. I groaned again. They said you couldn't polish a turd, but for the next few days, mine were going to be rolled in glitter.

Chapter Fourteen

When Fifty realises he's quite fond of his toenails

After my day of back-to-back lessons, Clem waited for me on my doorstep. The hours had been a mixture of blissfully reliving my early-morning lovemaking with Otto, interspersed with a heaviness every time I remembered my imminent conversation with Eggy. Clem stopping by was almost a relief in some ways. I'd known the hammer would drop, but not known exactly when or how.

"Cup of tea?" I enquired, filling the kettle with water. To be fair, I wanted to crack open the whisky, but I'd have been drinking alone.

"Yeah, perfect." He reached forwards with his hand. "Stand still—you've got something caught in your hair." I stood patiently while he plucked shiny silver shards out of my hair. One of my clients had done the same earlier. "Been crafting a collage, Fifty?" He examined the pieces in his palm.

I turned away. "Must have picked them up from one of the kids this afternoon."

While I fussed with our tea, delaying the inevitable, he told me Eggy had taken Otto to a college open day over in Puerto del Rosario, both of us pretending I didn't already know. After all,

Otto had sat in my lap earlier this morning, chewing on a piece of toast, and talking me through the online brochure.

With increasing dread, tea in hand, I watched Clem lean against the breakfast bar, casually taking in the rumpled state of my usually pristine sofa cushions, the jar of powdered hot chocolate next to the fridge, Otto's unmistakeable colourful T-shirt carelessly draped across my coffee table.

He almost sniffed the air. "They should be heading back around now," he stated, taking a small sip.

"What? Oh, yeah." Lost in my thoughts, I could too easily see how this would go. Like a cheesy 1970s television detective duo, Clem had elected to play nice cop, buttering up the suspect, getting him to let down his guard, ready for bad cop to pounce.

"Fifty." He indicated around the room with a sigh. "Your apartment is a shrine to Otto's DNA. On the off chance Eggy drops by, he'll put two and two together straight away."

I could have feigned puzzlement, but what was the point? I'd been busted.

"I haven't seen your bedroom, but I'm guessing it's much the same?"

I nodded, a creeping numbness shifting through my brain. At least the bedroom door had been closed when he walked in. The glitterfest still needed tidying up. Sinking into the sofa, I clutched my tea in both hands, sighing deeply.

Clem took his time making himself comfortable on an adjacent armchair, then placed his mug carefully down on the coffee table in front of him. He shot me a quick grin. "From the amount of nights Otto has allegedly spent sleeping over at Alicia's, Eggy has started questioning if he's actually gay." He paused. "Has he stayed at her place at all?"

I shook my head. "No. He's been here. With me."

With me. In my bed, in my arms. In my heart.

"Please, for god's sake, don't tell me you've been shagging old Handsy and Felipe at the same time. As you know, Eggy will pull your toenails out excruciatingly slowly."

"As opposed to really quickly when he finds out it's only been Otto?" Shaking my head, I gave him a wry smile. "No, of course not. I'm a one-man man. And, according to Otto, I'm also demisexual. Which meant nothing to me but makes perfect sense now."

Clem digested what he'd already suspected.

"I'm providing a new chapter for your lonely Californian surfer book, hey, Clem? An unexpected twist? Readers love those."

Running his hand through his thick, dark hair, Clem blew out a long breath. "You're providing me with enough material for two volumes, Fifty. At least Otto's endless questions about sex make sense now. He didn't shy away from the details. That boy doesn't possess a shred of embarrassment."

"Tell me about it." I rolled my eyes at him.

"He's very persuasive. He now knows more about my personal sexual preferences than anyone apart from Eggy ever should." His expression turned from laughing, to serious. "You have to tell Eggy soon. Otherwise, I will. I don't keep secrets from him."

I couldn't disagree. "I'm going to talk to him tomorrow," I promised. "Whatever Eggy thinks, you need to know something. I haven't taken advantage of Otto—he was as willing as I was— but the blame lies totally with me, not him. Because I'm the one old enough to know I should have stayed away. I never set out for this to happen. It just did, and I'm sorry for the upset it's going to cause."

I hated myself for pleading, for believing I had to explain anything. Otto was a consenting adult—we both were. I shouldn't need to seek approval or justify myself to anyone.

Leaning back and stretching out, Clem gave me a slow smile. "If it's any consolation, from the time I've spent with Otto, I believe you. You've got your hands full there. He's an Eggebraaten through and through. If he'd been built to the same dimensions as Eggy, he'd be scary as hell."

He smiled again, a little sadly. "But I doubt Eggy will see things that way. He'll think Otto's infatuated with you, an older, experienced guy, and you've exploited his brother's naivety. Like Svengali."

I frowned. Trust Clem to use an analogy I didn't understand. And experienced? That was a fucking joke.

"Svengali is a character in a story, who hypnotised a much younger girl to fall under his spell," Clem explained. "It's a Victorian novel by George du Maurier. I have it on my bookshelves somewhere."

"Does the book have a happy ending?"

Clem gave me an apologetic look. "Not for Svengali, no."

I drank the rest of my cooling tea, and Clem placidly did the same. I always found it odd knowing one of my best friends was a super-clever, famous writer, with lots of awards to his name. Especially being just a surfer who had smoked too much weed and never managed to form a single, meaningful relationship with anyone until Otto burst into my life. Despite Clem stealing the heart of the man I'd craved for so many years, I'd never been able to dislike him. Far from it, in fact.

"Otto's the first person I've ever slept with," I blurted. "Kissed, even."

Confessing this to Clem felt much easier than confessing to Eggy. Clem dealt with his own feelings of inadequacy for many years before he'd found happiness with my oldest friend. He understood the concepts of loneliness and shyness much more than the big hairy ginger Viking ever would.

"I guessed." He had the grace to appear slightly embarrassed. "I mean, I'd always suspected—not that I'd ever said anything to Eggy. I won't, either. But when Otto asked me some fairly...um...pertinent questions, I, yeah, er...I hope the pillow thing worked out for you."

Bloody hell, this rivalled my first appointment with Dr Marchena on the awkwardness scale. Otto would easily rank it a solid nine out of ten.

"You think I'm an idiot, don't you?" I said eventually.

"Falling for a nineteen-year-old boy? Yeah, obviously."

"I know he's young, Clem, but he's strong. He knows his own mind."

"Oh, I know. Otto will be fine whatever happens. He's got Viking blood pumping 'round his body—as Eggebraaten men are so fond of reminding us. And if you are merely a youthful infatuation, then he'll get over it. No, it's not Otto I'm worried about, but I shan't tell Eggy. It's you, Fifty. I don't want him to break your heart."

That made two of us.

Busying myself with the dregs of my tea, I waited for the lump in my throat to subside. I thought back to that first astonishing kiss in my jeep, when I'd been pissed off with Alejandro and Felipe, with my useless libido, with the world in general. And of Otto's anxious face after I'd fainted in the doctor's waiting room. The way he endured that hideous appointment with Dr Marchena, even though he hardly knew me. And how he basically ignored my erectile dysfunction our first few times together, happily focused on his own pleasure and not giving a rat's arse about mine, which helped me more than he'd ever know.

"For a while now, I imagined I would stay single," I admitted to Clem. "You know, one of those beige, unmarried virgins, who lives alone, or looks after their elderly mothers. We had one down our street when I was a kid. My mum used to say that he was 'a bit peculiar'—by which she meant gay. Every time he left the house he wore a brown mac, and the boys at school said he was a flasher."

Clem regarded me with interest. He loved mundane, personal stories, hoarding them in the way stamp collectors hoarded stamps. No doubt this one would be regurgitated into one of his novels someday.

"I wouldn't end up exactly like him," I qualified, before Clem started feeling too sorry for me. "I want to stay in Fuerte for a start—I love living here. And I haven't got a flasher mac. But being on my own, having everything in my house exactly as I liked it?" I nodded. "Yeah, I could see that. Not the most exciting existence, but doable. I'd have been reasonably happy."

I gazed 'round at my living room: at Otto's T-shirt, his beloved hot chocolate, my usually immaculate sofa cushions, now haphazardly chucked in a random pile. A whirlwind had blown through the place, and I didn't care if I never tidied up again.

"Goodness, Fifty, you deserve more than reasonably happy! What about Felipe, or the other men you go out with? Surely you'll want to settle down with one eventually?"

If only he knew.

"No. I want Otto." I took a deep breath in. "And I'm prepared to take the risk he'll grow out of me one day. And I'll be alone again."

"He's a little on the young side for you," Clem ventured. "I mean, I know you're not that old yourself, but there's a wealth of difference between an age gap of ten years when you are, say, in your forties than when one of you is still a teenager."

"I'm aware of that." God, was I aware. "But with Otto, it's... it's not only about the...er...the sex. He's the first person I've ever felt a proper emotional bond with, too. The first person, apart from you-know-who, with whom I've ever...felt comfortable enough to want to have sex."

Telling him I'd been a virgin was one thing. Exploring my erectile dysfunction and Otto's key-to-the-door theories was another entirely, even knowing how fascinating Clem's lively mind would find them.

"Oh, lordy. But I thought you liked Felipe?"

"I do. He's a nice guy. So is old Handsy, once you get to know him." I filled him in on my matchmaking activities. "It's been a weird sort of love triangle. Felipe wanting Alejandro and me, Alejandro wanting me and Felipe, Alejandro wanting Otto, Otto wanting me..."

"Strictly speaking, Fifty, and maths isn't my forte, but aren't triangles three-sided?"

"Yeah, whatever. But the point is, Otto and I are serious about each other. He's going to move in. We've talked about how we'll make it work through college, how I'll probably look for a bigger place."

Clem's eyes were as big as saucers, his voice barely a whisper. "Oh my goodness. Shit, Eggy is going to..."

"Rip my toenails out. Yes, I know."

Chapter Fifteen

Pistols at dawn

I picked Eggy up early the following day, and we headed out to Caleta for six hours of lessons. We were on a trial run for a long-term contract for classes at a new hotel, so we were on our best behaviour.

He spent the first few minutes of the journey texting. "I'm checking Otto's arrived at the shop. He really struggled to get out of bed this morning. I wondered if he'd had a fit in the night —he looked so washed out. He didn't think so; he said he was knackered from our day at the college. And he'd stayed at his mate's the night before. Came home with glitter in his hair. God knows what he'd been up to."

"Mmm." I concentrated on the road, letting Eggy talk about the nursing college open day. His version sounded pretty much a replica of what I'd heard on the phone from Otto in bed last night. He'd been excited. If he passed the generic Spanish test for foreigners, he'd be starting the course in October.

"He still wants to work at the shop during his college holidays, which is ideal, as he'll need the money, and we're at our busiest. It's a win-win."

Glancing over at me, Eggy grinned, his strikingly handsome

face tanned and healthy. He had exceedingly good looks, what my mum called a proper head-turner. Cocky with it, too, which he'd be the first to admit.

In my eyes, however, he'd become a pale imitation of his youngest brother. Why on earth had I been infatuated with him for so long and wasted so many years? It was difficult to see it, now. Maybe fate had intervened, or the will of those Norse gods he and Otto loved to tell me about, keeping me waiting until the right man came along. But me and Eggy went back a hell of a long way. During the hard times, I'd kept him off the streets and he'd kept me sane. I so desperately didn't want to lose him as a best mate, or a business partner.

"What are you grinning at?" I asked him as he continued to stare at me. Shit, I hoped it wasn't more glitter.

"I don't know. They don't label poo," he chanted in a kid's voice, grinning again.

"God, you're so childish. You're worse than..."

I was about to say Otto and stopped myself in time. Another reason I needed to get our relationship out in the open—I would trip myself up sooner or later.

"I'm smiling at you." He smirked. "You've had a stupid grin plastered all over your face since you picked me up. Anything you want to share?"

Yes, your little brother shagged me two nights ago, and it was fucking awesome. He wants to move in with me, so we can spend every night together.

"Nope, nothing to share."

"Well, whoever he is, he's doing something right. I haven't seen you this chilled for a long time."

Rapidly, I changed the subject. "Have you checked out the surf report? Going to be great conditions back in town later. The wind's dropping to nothing."

"Cool. Shame we're stuck on this side of the bloody island teaching kids all day."

I hesitated. "We could go later? You and me? We haven't for months."

And I'd tell him about Otto. After we'd bonded doing what we did best.

"Sounds great, dude. I'll get Clem and Otto to come down to the beach afterwards, maybe bring some tinnies and grub, make an evening of it." I thought Eggy was pretty chuffed. What with running the business, the roster of lessons, him being wrapped up in Clem and their new house, we'd lost our closeness, despite seeing each other practically daily.

"Sure, bring them along." In for a penny, in for a pound. If Eggy became tricksy, then Clem knew how to manage his mood better than anyone. And Otto, well, I'd be happy to see him anytime.

Our lessons ended close to five in the afternoon, my favourite time of day to go for a surf. In an upbeat mood, Eggy drove us back to our local beach in front of the hotel, and we grabbed our boards from the shop. Otto had closed up early, causing Eggy to frown and me to worry, but I'd see him soon enough and assess him for myself. Aside from a few local families, the beach was predictably deserted. Tourists tended to return to the hotels about now, missing the best part of the day.

Some moments in life, a man needed only three things—his body, a surfboard, and an awesome swell. This early evening was one. Work niggles were cast aside; even thoughts of Otto were temporarily banished. For a couple of hours, Mother Nature, Eggy and I experienced a slice of heaven. Or Valhalla, according to Eggy. I say a couple of hours, but time meant nothing out on a board, sunk deep in that magical pocket where swell and shore collided, conjuring ideal waves. No kids, no tourists, only me and my old mate doing what came naturally.

Although I prayed it wouldn't be, it felt like the end of an era. I determinedly eked out every last minute and caught every last wave, since who knew if Eggy and I would ever do this together again? Commenting on the swells, absorbing the fading heat of the early evening sun, talking shit about tides and our worst wipe-outs, but much of the time saying nothing at all.

"Bro," Eggy shouted after we'd dropped on the same wave and managed to ride in tandem, "We should do this more often. I miss you, dude!"

Choked, all I could do was nod.

"Time to head back in," he observed a while later, breathless and flushed with joy from coming off the last set. The lights of Corralejo twinkled in response to the fading daylight, and I reluctantly agreed. As we waded ashore, he clapped me on the back. "Leave on a high, dude."

Clem and Otto had set up camp on the edge of the dunes a while ago, and I was ready for the promised beer and my young lover's kiss. One of those would have to wait a while longer. As we reached the pair of them, Eggy, like a wet dog, predictably shook out his dripping hair all over a shrieking Clem, before throwing himself down on him for a sloppy kiss. That gag never got old. I'd have liked to have done the same to Otto, but I had to settle for plopping down next to him instead and giving his shoulder a little nudge. He nudged back, side-eyeing me an uncharacteristically shy smile.

"You two were out there for hours," Clem exclaimed, pushing Eggy away.

"Yeah, well," Eggy reasoned, "we haven't done it for ages."

"Aside from, like, lessons all day today? And yesterday? And the day before?"

"That doesn't count, babe." Eggy stripped off his wetsuit

down to his waist, revealing perfectly toned pecs and a grooved rack of abs. "When a man is tired of surfing, he is tired of life."

I covertly admired him in an abstract way, simultaneously reminding myself for the billionth time to stop ordering double helpings of tapas every time I ate out.

Clem hummed. "I seem to remember that quote slightly differently." He shot his boyfriend an amused look. "I don't recall Samuel Johnson mentioning surfing at all in his letters to Boswell."

Eggy shrugged. "His loss, whoever the fuck he is." He turned to his unusually quiet younger brother. Perhaps, like me, he felt apprehensive about our big announcement. "Okay, Otto?"

"Yeah."

A bottle of Tropical stood wedged into the sand next to him, untouched. "Not drinking anything?"

Otto wrinkled his nose. "Nah, tastes a bit funny. I had a can of coke earlier. I'm good."

Wriggling out of my wetsuit in a much less elegant manner than Eggy, I donned a baggy white T-shirt before leaning back on my elbows and digging my feet into the fine, warm sand. I lifted my face up to meet the fading rays of the sun. My board shorts would dry in the evening breeze in no time. Eggy threw me a Tropical and mooched around in the cool box for food. Otto lounged next to me, and Clem sprawled on the other side of Eggy. Out to sea, a small, sleek yacht with yellow sails skimmed across the horizon, outlined vividly by the setting sun behind it. Further along the beach, a pair of giggling toddlers built a wall of sand to stem the incoming tide, ably assisted by their father.

Idyllic, in other words. A preview of heaven, containing the three people I loved most in the entire world. And I was about to blow it.

Eggy munched on a ham sandwich and swigged from his beer bottle. The only one of us blissfully unaware of what was about to follow. Even Clem seemed edgy, and, like Otto, I'd suddenly lost my appetite entirely. It was now or never.

"Eggy?" I glanced up at him nervously. Words and speeches really weren't my thing.

He swallowed and gave me his attention. "Dude."

"I...um...I've, or rather we—Otto and me, have something to tell you."

"Oh yeah, what? Listen, if it's about Otto letting that kid off with cracking the skegs on the Mini Mal yesterday, I know about it. Even though you tried to cover it up for him, Fifty." He took another gulp of beer, then grinned. "You're both too soft."

"No, it's not about that. It's...well, we..."

Christ, could I be any more rubbish at this? Eggy had clocked I had something serious on my mind, though, and gave me his full attention.

"Dude, I'm not...not actually seeing Alejandro. Well, not like, as a...a boyfriend or anything. Although we are friends."

Eggy gave me a quizzical stare, probably wondering why I imparted this information in such a formal, angst-ridden manner.

"I'm...er...I'm not seeing Felipe, either. Not anymore. We're just friends, too."

"Cool, bro." He gave me an open smile, his grey eyes searching my face. "So who's the secret lover taking chunks out of your neck, then? You look like you're about to puke."

The gassy beer tried to make a break for freedom from my belly as my stomach clenched. A wave of prickly sweat broke out across the back of my neck.

"I'm...erm...I've got something to say that I don't think you'll like very much."

I definitely had the full thousand-watt stare now. "Oh, yeah? And what might that be?"

"I...um...I..." Oh, shit, whichever way I phrased it, it would come out wrong. I should have asked Clem to write something down for me. Of the shortlist of opening gambits running through my head, none seemed suitable. As I was about to find out, I wouldn't be needing any of them.

"What Christian is trying to say," blurted Otto, before I could clap a hand over his mouth, possibly permanently, "is that we love each other and we're fucking."

Oh shit. Oh shit. Oh shit. That shocker had not been on the list. Clem's stricken mask of horror no doubt mirrored my own—he looked about to vomit, too. My stomach performed a few backflips. I swallowed down bile.

In the stunned silence that followed, Eggy froze, almost comically. Almost as if someone had pressed a pause button. His hand holding the beer bottle halted halfway to his open mouth. Wide grey eyes, usually soft and crinkled at the edges, narrowed, flashing like a pair of solitaire diamonds. But they weren't focused on his beloved youngest brother and his brash, defiant announcement. They were lasered on me, the interloper, threatening one of his own. A look of pure hatred.

Otto began to speak. "Ragnar, it's..."

Eggy stayed him with a hand and a rapid bark in Norwegian. For once, Otto didn't stand his corner. He answered his brother's questions with few words, his voice quiet, resigned, as if the fight had left him before we really started.

Slowly, Eggy got to his feet and stood legs apart, his brawny arms folded across his impressive chest. An iron breast plate and a sharpened spear couldn't have made him more menacing. "Get up, Fifty. I want to hear it from you."

Otto tugged on my T-shirt as I stood, and I gave his hand a

quick squeeze. "It's okay, sweetheart. We need to have this out. I have nothing to apologise for."

Eggy harrumphed, bristling at the *sweetheart*. "That's a fucking joke, dude. I just haven't yet decided how I'm going to make you fucking start apologising."

We stood a few feet apart in the sand, like cowboys in an old black-and-white Western, ready to draw our pistols and fire. Our earlier surfing bromance seemed like last century.

Most men would have been rightly intimidated taking Eggy on like this. He'd never shied away from throwing his weight around. I wasn't most men and I didn't give a shit. We'd seen each other at our worst. I wasn't good with words, and I hadn't managed to break the news to him in a way I liked, but I could stand up to him like this. I knew I had nothing to be ashamed of, and neither did Otto.

"He says this has been going on a while."

'He' being Otto, who had also risen to his feet and stood apart from us, shoulders hunched over, face buried in his hands. The urge to take him in my arms and crush him against me grew strong, and I would, as soon as his overprotective brother and I had everything cleared up.

"Yep." I nodded defiantly. "It has."

"And you say you haven't been fucking those Spanish blokes at the same time."

"No, I haven't."

He took a step forwards. "Why the fuck should I believe you?"

I shrugged coolly. "It doesn't matter whether you believe me or not. Otto knows the truth, and that's all I care about."

Another step forwards. His tone was low and deadly. "I've worked out what you're doing. I know what this is, you bastard."

Once when we'd been surfing in Biarritz, Eggy had caught some French kid trying to nick our boards out of the vans. He'd spoken to him in the same manner as he spoke to me now, all calm and controlled. But the Viking never lurked far away. Needless to say, the would-be thief had been deterred from stealing for life by the time Eggy finished with him. He held his mad streak under control these days, much more so than when I first met him, but in this mood, he could be capable of anything.

"What is it, dude?" Equally as calmly, I stared back at him, my face inches from his. "Tell me. I'm all ears."

Another step closer. "You've taken your time, Fifty. I'll give you that. But this, this *fucking* with my brother. This is you getting your own back, isn't it? You can't have me, so you thought you'd screw the next best thing? Am I right?"

He brought his face even closer, beer on his warm breath. "Did it feel good, mate, breaking in my baby brother? Did you think of me when you did it, you fucking cunt?"

I hit him. A single hard punch, with a closed fist on the sharp angle of his jaw. Strangely, I felt calm, born of knowing what Otto and I had was worth fighting for. "There's only one person being a fucking cunt on this beach right now, Eggy, and it's you. I'm not explaining myself when you're like this, and neither is Otto. If, and when, you've calmed down, then we'll talk."

To give him his due, Eggy recovered quickly. I smacked him pretty hard—my hand fucking hurt enough, anyway. He stepped back a pace, gingerly fingering where I'd hit him, a trickle of blood seeping out. From somewhere to my left, I heard Clem gasp, and he rose to his feet as if about to intervene.

And then Eggy did what any red-blooded angry young bloke would do. He fucking hit me back.

I'd played this encounter out so many different ways in my head. I'd broached the subject gently, given him a roundabout route towards how Otto and I found each other. I'd even confessed my erectile issues and how Otto had helped me at the doctor's, as a way of explaining how we became close. I'd down-played the sex, as if Otto and I had been chastely holding hands up to this point, seeking Eggy's approval before we ventured further—I wasn't above white lies and massaging his ego.

But never this. Never us wrestling in the sand at dusk, hell-bent on killing each other.

This was no choreographed movie fight, the protagonists managing to both look cool *and* simultaneously kick the shit out of each other. No, this was more of a school playground scrap. I had the advantage of bulk, but a blunt knee to my balls had me contemplating that my sex life might be over before it had scarcely begun. Rather too late in the day, I recalled Eggy was one of six brothers. Impromptu fisticuffs were likely a daily occurrence in his household.

"Pack it in, you two!" Clem shouted, dancing around us. "You're grown men. Stop being so fucking stupid!"

For all we paid him any attention, he might have been screaming at us in Cantonese. We were way too far gone. I managed a jab into Eggy's belly (those honed abs did their job; he hardly flinched). Then he tried to gouge my eye out fending me off. I retaliated by grabbing his hand and bending his fingers back. He returned the favour, then pushed me onto my back, raising his fist for another punishing blow to my solar plexus. My breath came in short, hard gasps, and blood thundered in my head, my brain ignorant of everything except showing the arrogant fucker Otto and I were none of his fucking business.

Suffocating on mouthfuls of red hair might have killed me before any of Eggy's fierce blows. With my eye smarting, I wasn't above playground tactics of my own. I gave a clump a sharp tug, before rolling away and clambering to my feet. Panting heavily, I pushed my own sweat-drenched hair off my face and wiped blood from my split lip. A welcome adrenaline rush dampened the intense pain from a possible broken rib, bruised balls, and a wickedly swelling hand. Clenching my fists, I sized up my opponent from a distance of about four feet.

Around this time, the three of us realised Otto had disappeared. Quickly scanning the immediate area, I rounded on Clem. Eggy wordlessly did the same before rounding on me.

"Otto!" he bellowed. "Otto! Where the hell is he?" he accused, as if I'd fucking had the time to spirit him away while he'd pummelled me to death.

"He was here," Clem insisted, frowning. "When you two started, he was still here. Otto!"

By now, the sun had disappeared over the horizon completely, the yacht had disappeared, and the kids and their dad had gone home for tea. When the northeast trade winds picked up, the tide on this side of the island rolled in at a gallop. The only people remaining on the beach in the growing gloom were Clem and us two fucking idiots.

"Otto!" We all hollered his name, more desperately. Clem headed up a sand dune to get a better view through the fading daylight; Eggy screwed up his eyes at the inky blackness of the waves. Why the hell didn't he answer? Come to that, why hadn't he been pulling me and Eggy off each other, berating us for our stupidity? This was Otto we were looking for, he of countless strong opinions and never-ending back chat.

"Perhaps he went back to the shop," Clem suggested, breathlessly skidding down the side of the sand dune. "He wasn't feeling great when you were surfing—and you two fighting wouldn't have helped much."

He came to a halt in the soft sand, kicking something over— Otto's untouched bottle of beer from earlier, when he'd made a face, saying he didn't fancy it. That it had tasted funny. He'd looked pale then, distracted, but I'd thought nothing of it, putting it down to the showdown we were all going to have. But

Eggy had mentioned he'd complained of feeling knackered and...oh fuck.

"He's gone off because he's going to have a fucking fit!" I yelled angrily. "I knew he wasn't right. You said so this morning, Eggy."

All the colour drained from Eggy's face as his gaze met mine. My blood ran cold. Our precious Otto, alone in the dark, dizzy, disoriented, feeling scared, or however the fuck someone felt when they couldn't convey to the world what they knew inside was about to happen. And the fucking tide hurtled towards us at a rate of knots.

When it became clear we were both paralysed with fear, Clem took control.

"Right, listen to me. He's not up in the dunes unless he's lying in very tall grass. I'd have spotted him. The lights from the carpark illuminated the whole area." He pointed behind him. "I'll go that way, back to the shop and hotel, see if anyone has seen him. You two, run the other way, towards the town. Eggy, go along the shore, and Fifty, you go along the top edge."

Snapping out of it, we set off. Clem resumed calling out his name; his shouts receded as Eggy and I pelted in the other direction. If my body ached and complained from my cuts and bruises, then it didn't register with my brain. I guessed Eggy felt the same. He powered through the shallows, yelling urgently for his brother.

We'd covered a quarter mile and seen no sign of him. The rocky wall separating the main beach and the virtually non-existent edge-of-town beach loomed ahead of us. A set of concrete steps weaved up through the jagged slope. With the current high tide, the steps led nowhere, the small strip of sandy beach now completely immersed underwater.

And of course, as I ran towards the steps, I knew exactly where I'd find him. That first night when I'd collected him from the club, and he'd brought me to his special place. Pleased to be able to show me something I didn't know about the town, he'd led me down the broken stairway leading to the ugly strip of rocky beach, hidden from the road above. The place where the dangerous shoreline reminded him of home. And then weeks later, when we'd raced to my apartment from the club, desperate to rip each other's clothes off, we'd stopped there for a brief snog and a quick grope.

"Eggy! Over here! I know where he is."

With no time to retrace my steps and run up to the road before descending once more via the concrete steps, I scrabbled over the slippery giant boulders, Eggy hot on my heels. Like a pack of rabid dogs, the breaking waves repeatedly snapped at our feet, climbing higher with every bite. God, what if we were too late? Cold, sharp fear pierced my chest. What if he'd had a seizure and been pulled out to sea? What if that beautiful, precious body had been flung against rocks?

As I threw myself against the concrete steps, hauling my bruised body up, I caught a flash of yellow T-shirt tucked away on the rocky outcrop under the other side. Thank fuck. My Otto, my wonderful, sweet, funny Otto lay curled on his side, small hands neatly folded under his head. Almost as if he'd discovered a perfectly comfy corner of the world in which to steal a quiet nap. Peacefully sleeping, except that the frigid waters lapped higher with every roll of the tide, the lower half of his body already swallowed up.

"He's here," I yelled over my shoulder. I half fell, half jumped down onto the ledge of broken steps. My foot twisted awkwardly as I landed. Barely registering the pain, I crawled to him, drenched as a wave crested over me.

"Otto," I shouted, urgently shaking him by a chilled, damp shoulder. "Wake up, sweetheart, wake up. We need to get you out of here."

Post-ictal was the correct medical term—I'd learned that from my reading. Not a sleep at all, not a normal one, anyway. To be precise, an altered state of consciousness after an epileptic seizure, lasting anywhere between five and thirty minutes, but sometimes longer in the case of larger or more severe seizures, like the one Otto had at my house. My shaking roused him enough to groan and perform a couple of the disconcerting lip-smacks, and relief flooded through me. I'd take post-ictal unconsciousness and weird facial expressions any day over stone-cold dead. His thin chest calmly rose and fell with steady deep breaths, his pale face slack in repose.

Crouching down, I cradled his head in my lap, pressing my warm lips against his icy cold ones, eliciting another grunt of displeasure. He can't have lain there too long, but with the heat of the day disappearing and heavily saturated clothing, his temperature would rapidly plummet.

Another wave crashed over me. I lost my balance, slipping into one of the deeper pools between the rocks. The water washed over Otto's face, sleeking his hair down over his head. Fuck, we needed to move fast. I didn't know how high the tide climbed up these rocks, but if it rose any more, in a few minutes we'd both be underwater. Hauling him up, my hands under his armpits, I began dragging his limp body back towards the main steps.

Eggy's horrified face peered over the edge as another wave hit me from behind, pushing me down. Yet again, I lost my footing on the seaweed, as if a tonne of slime had been poured over the rocks. My bare feet struggled for purchase, yet no way would I let go of Otto. I would pass him up to his brother's loving arms or drown trying.

"Lift him to me," Eggy screamed over the noise of the surf. He'd lain flat on the main steps, hanging the top half of his body as much over the edge as he dared. His strong arms stretched towards us. "Come on, Fifty. Push him up to me. I can reach!"

As the next wave receded, I adjusted my hold on the slippery body, then encircled Otto's waist with my arms and hoisted him as high in the air as I could. Otto stirred again, flopping his head back to give me a bleary, almost surprised look, before lolling forwards again.

"Let me sleep, Christian," he slurred in protest. "Leave me alone."

"It's okay, sweetheart. I'm here—me and Ragnar are here."

I talked bollocks to him, all sorts of gibberish that likely fell on deaf ears, but I babbled on anyway. He moaned and tried to push us away as Eggy got a hand on his T-shirt. For a moment, the cheap cotton threatened to rip. But then Eggy had his other hand on it too, and firmly underneath his shoulder. His big strong fingers wrapped tightly around Otto's pale upper arm.

"I've got you, *lille venn*, I've got you." Eggy sobbed with relief as Otto's legs slithered up and out of my grasp at exactly the second another wave hit. His voice cried out a warning a fraction too late. My own legs disappeared from under me, flung forwards like a rag doll. Flailing wildly, I smacked into the high sea wall. Breath rushed out of me in a *whoosh*, the sudden inertia sending my head thudding against unforgiving stone.

Maybe banging my head would knock some sense into me, I thought to myself, almost smiling at the idiocy. My mum always told me I wasn't the sharpest tool in the box. Drowning in the act of rescuing someone else was a pretty stupid thing to do. Safety first—lifeguard rule number one.

I licked my lips, tasting blood and salt. My limbs had lost their heaviness, my arms suddenly floaty and airier. My hands tingled pleasantly; I swore I smelled *patatas bravas* sizzling. The murky waters swirled around my chest in oranges and reds, almost purple, exactly the shade of a board I serviced last week at the shop. I heard a low droning, as if the waves were talking to me, buzzing like a swarm of fat bumblebees, crowding my head. I held out my arms to welcome them in, as the bees turned a dazzling white, the colour of Otto's favourite jeans, the ones with a huge rip across his—

Chapter Sixteen

When Fifty becomes a Viking brother

I wasn't sure what woke me. To be fair, I had no idea how I slept at all with an unholy trinity of nausea, dizziness, and the mother of all headaches battling for supremacy inside my skull. Of course, it could have been none of those. More likely, it was the impatient fidgeting of the warm body laid out on the hard mattress next to me.

I let out a long sigh as dreamlike images floated through my mind—crashing waves, me running along a sandy beach in the dark, Otto wet and cold. Events blurred, separating then merging in my addled thoughts, overlapping and disordered. Flashing lights, a siren, Clem squeezing my hand tightly, reassuring Spanish voices speaking complicated words I didn't understand. Eggy shouting to me, Otto sleeping. Bumblebees.

Sighing again, I shifted on the bed, increasingly aware of my immediate surroundings. I stilled instantly as the movement caused a stab of pain in my head, accompanied by a fresh wave of nausea.

"Ssshhh," I heard Otto whispering. His lips brushed against my cheek. I'd recognise his touch anywhere. "It's okay, Christian, I'm here. You're waking up."

I drifted off again. I don't know for how long, but the next time I stirred, Otto still fidgeted next to me, and the unholy trinity had taken up permanent residency. This time I didn't chance moving and lay quietly, fuzzily trying to work out where I was. In a bed, definitely. On my back, with pillows propped under my head. It didn't feel as comfy as my bed, though, and it didn't smell like it either. It smelt of cheap soap. Cautiously, I opened my eyes. It wasn't my bedroom ceiling; two blinding spotlights roamed above me, dancing towards each other before twirling apart again. Ugh. Bile rose in my throat. I shut my eyes quickly.

The next time I awoke, I only opened one eye, and the ceiling had only one spotlight. Experimentally, I carefully opened the other, and the light split into two. I repeated the experiment, concluding only opening one eye made me less sick. My mouth was drier than a camel's arse, and I felt simultaneously high as a kite and horribly hungover. In my previous experiences, one usually followed the other. Experiencing them both together was unfair.

Otto again, gently stroking my cheek. "Christian, you're just waking up. Lie very still. You're in hospital."

I carefully assimilated that information, possibly for hours or maybe only a few minutes. Whatever, the dry mouth had become difficult to ignore.

"Drink," I croaked. Well, I meant to say 'drink'. It came out more like the slurred honking of a drunken goat. Otto apparently understood goat-speak, as the tip of a plastic straw butted my lower lip.

"Only take a few sips, Christian. Otherwise, you'll be sick again."

Those few sips tasted like the sweetest nectar. Combined with Otto cuddling up against me and caressing my brow, I was sufficiently inspired to try speaking again. Funnily enough, profound thoughts failed to break through the barrier of the pounding headache. Yet somehow, conveying to Otto how wonderful it felt having him next to me became of paramount importance. In my later defence, I'd tried my best.

"You can hump my leg, Otto," I slurred. "I'm…I'm too tired for anything else."

A deafening silence followed. No leg humping, though the head stroking continued. I may have dozed for a few minutes; talking and drinking exhausted me.

"Dude," Otto hissed in my ear, rousing me to consciousness. "We're…um…we're not alone."

Sometimes, sleeping was the best course of action. Or feigning sleep. I did a mixture of the two. By now, I had begun to understand a few things. Firstly, if I moved any muscles what-soever, my body really fucking hurt. Especially my head, but also my chest, my hand, and my left ankle. In addition, a tube hung out of my knob, which stung a bit. I had a similar stinging pain in the backs of both hands. More importantly, hushed voices murmured all around me. I couldn't make out any of the words.

"The nurse says you can have another drink, Christian," said Otto, and I opened my mouth obediently to accept the prof-fered straw. I was getting good at this. "Sit him up a bit."

As if by magic, two pairs of strong arms lifted me up my pillows into more of a sitting position, like I weighed hardly anything at all. The excruciating pain had me grunting in shock, but once I settled again, I felt more comfortable.

So comfortable that, after a few minutes, I chanced opening my eyes. And immediately wished I'd kept them closed. It was definitely my Otto next to me on the bed, even if he did split into two Ottos—double the quantity I could ever handle.

Closing one eye, the two Ottos thankfully merged back into one, and I registered his anxious smile and reassuring hand squeeze. Hopefully delivering a smile in return, although I think it was more of a pained grimace, I opened both eyes again and tried to focus on the room beyond him.

Scanning from left to right, I counted eight versions of Eggy. Granted, my brain wasn't at full power. Shaking my head in confusion (big error—I nearly vomited), I began counting again, this time from right to left. Still eight Eggys, some of them standing, some of them sitting, but all huge and ginger. Squinting one eye closed, I began again from the left. A few of the Eggys miraculously dissolved, but there remained still more than one.

"The brothers are here with us," Otto explained. "They heard how you rescued me and flew all the way from Norway to say thank you and to check I was all right. Isn't it wonderful? They love you already." He leaned closer. "They know that you're my boyfriend. Better not mention the leg humping again, though."

Oh...fuckity fuck.

An internal debate raged as to whether I could pretend to doze off, or at the very least threaten to spew, but my good manners won out. Placing my palm over one eye to lose the double vision, I nodded at the ginger Viking immediately to my left.

"Hello, Christian," he boomed, that singsong accent bright and chirpy. I couldn't lie; it grated on my tender skull. "I'm Dag. Nice to meet you. And thank you for saving our Otto."

"Yes, thank you. I'm Arvid," announced the next one along, if anything even louder. "We are so grateful; Otto means the world to us. If *anything* bad ever happened to him, we'd be devastated beyond belief. The whole family would never recover."

No pressure then. I nodded lamely.

"And I'm Erik. Thank you, thank you, thank you, from the bottom of our hearts."

I nodded again. Erik—I recognised that name. "Your girl-friend Miriam is a really good kisser," I mumbled blearily. "Ten out of ten."

Otto gave a falsely cheerful laugh. "Hah! Ignore him, Erik. Christian is concussed. He doesn't know what he's saying, do you, Christian?"

All things considered, his squeeze of my arm seemed a little firmer than necessary. Could I find a single inch of my flesh not covered in bruises? Deciding saying nothing was the best policy, I gave what I hoped was a bewildered, concussed smile.

"And I'm Egil," boomed someone else. "Me and Arvid are twins in case you hadn't noticed."

Frankly, they resembled a set of quadruplets—quintuplets, if I counted Eggy.

"My brothers really wanted to meet you, Christian," Otto commented. "They've heard everything about you."

Not absolutely everything, I prayed.

"When you are feeling better, you have been invited back to Norway to stay with them—they will show you how to fish, and they will take you surfing."

A couple of the men stood, and the others followed. "We must leave you to rest now," Dag pronounced. Or it could have been Erik. Looming over me, he gave me a pat on the shoulder. I'd endured softer rugby tackles at school. Turning to Otto, they had a conversation in Norwegian, the other brothers chipping in.

Otto's voice was proud. "Dag says you are one of us, now. A Vestvågøy Viking. A true son of Odin himself."

Identical ginger giants nodded solemnly at this pronouncement. From the awestruck tone of Otto's voice, a great honour had evidently been bestowed. I hoped I looked suitably grateful while trying not to vomit up the water I'd gulped down.

"Otto, *lille venn*, Clem will pick you up when you are ready to go home," Arvid reminded him. "Don't wear Christian out."

I endeavoured to respond to their goodbyes in a coherent fashion. After they filed out of the door—first smothering Otto in bear hugs and kisses and every one of them checking that yes, his phone had sufficient charge, and yes, he had money for food if needed—I collapsed back into the pillows, and Otto dived back onto the bed.

"Oh my God, Christian. I've been so worried about you."

I had my eyes closed again. I felt much better that way, particularly as his energetic flump down had created ripples in the mattress underneath me. But there was no mistaking the hitch in his voice. "You saved my life."

And I'd do it again, a hundred times over, I wanted to tell him, but my head hurt, and I was too tired. Instead, I held out an arm. "Come here, sweetheart," I murmured, and he snuggled in, his head resting on my chest.

"I love you so much, Christian." His voice was chockful of tears. "You need to know that."

"I know it, babe. I love you, too." In my concussed fuzzy brain, I remembered a story my mum used to read when I was very small, back in the days when she used to pay me attention, before her marriage turned to shit. The only love I needed now lay in my arms. "To the moon and back."

Chapter Seventeen

Surfing the perfect wave

The next couple of weeks took on a regular pattern. As well as numerous bodily injuries sustained from my punch-up with Eggy, but mostly from buffeting against the rocks, I'd smashed my head against the stone sea wall, causing a small bleed into my brain. Not enough to require surgery, and not enough anyone would notice if a few of my brain cells died a quiet death. Yet sufficient to warrant observation in hospital for a severe concussion. Every time I tried to stand, my nausea, headache, and loss of balance meant obediently taking my medicine, answering the doctors' questions, and then snoozing the days away in a hospital bed was my limit.

Clem sat with me most days, arriving a few minutes after the nurses had made me presentable, then staying until late afternoon. By far one of my favourite visitors, he reliably brought with him a satchel of papers, books, his laptop, and, crucially, delicious homemade food. He didn't speak much, which soothed my tender head, and the tap-tapping of his fingers and rustling of paper lulled me to sleep as well as any medication. Generally, he'd wake me again at lunchtime, we'd share whatever treasures he'd brought to eat, and then I'd settle down to sleep again.

Occasionally, he'd read extracts out loud from his Work in Progress. The hippie, American surfer dude was way more intellectual than me, not surprisingly. Clem had created a real deep thinker. But yeah, I recognised aspects of myself; his insecurities were mine, his fears, his love of food, his general life-fuckery.

"In my mind he's a cross between you and Chairman Mao," Clem explained one afternoon, frowning down at his laptop. "It's tricky."

I bet.

"Mao was that Chinese dude, yeah?"

"If you mean the leader of the communist party and the founder of the People's Republic of China, then yes, that Chinese dude." He smiled at me, wrinkling his nose. Clem, the smartest person I knew, never made me feel stupid.

"What I mean is," he continued, "he made many, many speeches, often comparing his people to nature. Some were trite and some very profound, but the message was always very simple. That's the vibe I'm trying to channel into my hippie surfer. Your aphorisms remind me of him, although yours are surfing-related, but still."

Did I have aphorisms? Were they contagious? I pretended to nod knowledgeably as he began telling me about how Mao considered himself the sun and his people were trillions of sunflower seeds packed into sunflowers bowing down to him. To be honest, he lost me. It wasn't long after my lunchtime meds, and they made me woozy.

"Individually, we are one. Together, we are an ocean," I agreed sleepily as he came to an end. I received a look of astonishment. "You mean me and Mao and the dude in your book spout surfer shit like that?"

Loyal through and through, at that moment, Clem came as close to criticising Eggy as he ever would. "Don't change, Fifty. The fluffball is lucky to have you. And the big hairy Viking will realise that one day. He's hurting, but he needs you. We all do. Promise you'll give him a chance?"

Alejandro popped in to visit, as did Felipe. Together—a very pleasant surprise. Well, sort of together. Felipe presented me with a huge bouquet of flowers—no idea what type—pretty ones, though. Alejandro's eyes lingered on his retreating back when he slipped out to find a vase.

"We're courting," he confided, with a pained sigh. "*Mierda*, it's hard work. We meet for coffee. We talk. We talk. We talk. We don't fuck."

"He's dingling you." I smiled, and he smiled back.

"*Si*, I'm being dingled. But, you know, Mister Fifty, a man has needs. Alejandro has needs. Alejandro does not like dingling."

"He'll come around. He's making you work for it, that's all."

Felipe returned, his face almost hidden behind the impressive bouquet. I'd never received flowers before, or sent them. His gesture touched me. Leaning over the bed, he gave me a quick peck on the cheek. "You look like shit."

I laughed, which hurt my head. In contrast, Felipe's brown eyes sparkled, his skin radiant. He'd never looked so handsome. Being courted suited him.

"I might let him kiss me soon," he whispered with a naughty grin. "He's good for a few more romantic dinners first. I'm quite enjoying being wooed."

* * *

My new Viking brothers also filed in, one at a time, to say their goodbyes before heading back to Norway. Although I'd never admit it to Otto, I was quite relieved they lived so far away. Imagining that lot breathing down my neck on a day-to-day basis scared the shit out of me. I shook four meaty hands, braced myself for each manly pat on the back, and accepted their gratitude all over again. From their subtle warnings, I had the distinct impression they were handing the crown jewels to me for safekeeping. Christ, and I'd thought Eggy was overprotective.

The crown jewels himself, Otto, visited me regularly, of course, but high season ran on regardless. Our surfing business didn't stop just because I'd given myself a clonk over the head. Neither did I want it to—we'd worked too damn hard to build it up. Eggy had arranged for a lad from one of the other surf shops to cover my lessons, but Otto had to man the store. So he generally didn't arrive to sit with me until about four each afternoon, which became Clem's cue to leave. Then he bounced around on my bed giving me a headache until the nurses kicked him out. His visit was the highlight of my day.

"Dr Marchena says hello and get well soon!" he announced after flopping down heavily on the mattress. My brain rattled. "The brothers made me have another appointment with her. They all bloody came along too, which was kind of embarrassing. I felt about five years old, Christian!"

One day Otto would realise how amazing it was to be so loved by so many people, but we were a few years away yet.

"She thinks I've had more fits than usual due to the big upheaval of moving here and everything. So she's not worried. But if I have another one in the next month or so, then we're going to try a different tablet." A sloppy kiss followed this news. "I told her about you and me, and she seemed really pleased. She said we made a cute couple."

I happened to agree with Dr Marchena.

Delving into his pocket, Otto produced a small round tin of Vaseline, from which he applied a liberal quantity to my lips. "You're all chapped," he explained, before kissing most of it off. Eventually, having regurgitated all the news of the day, he settled alongside me, throwing a leg over my thighs and an arm around my waist.

"Next time you go past my apartment, can you pop in and empty the fridge of all the stuff that's going mouldy?" I asked. "I don't fancy returning to sour milk and green ham."

"Mmm," he murmured into my chest. "About that. It's kind of already been done."

"Great, thank you."

"And...um...it's...um...been replaced by fresh stuff."

A little unnecessary, seeing as I had a few more days of lounging around in here, but nice of him anyway.

"And the fresh stuff is being eaten. By me."

I lifted his chin up off my chest. He had the good grace to look sheepish. "Is there something you'd like to tell me, Otto?"

"Well, yes. I...I've, well, I've kind of moved in. You'll need someone to look after you when you get home. You can't manage on your own. And I needed some space from Ragnar after...you know. Ragnar brought most of my belongings over."

I raised my eyebrows in surprise. "And he's happy with this state of affairs, is he?"

Otto rolled his eyes. "Apart from phoning me every half hour to check that I haven't collapsed against a burning gas ring, then yes. I think so. It's difficult to tell. He's behaving quite oddly at the moment. Clem says he's cool with it, but, you know..."

It was the first time anybody had made direct mention of Eggy since the accident. With a sickening pang, I realised I missed the annoying fucker dreadfully. I appreciated no one wanted to upset me while I recuperated, but even Clem had been unusually quiet. Otto even more so. Clearly, they were both uncomfortable, seeing as we had spectacularly fallen out, so I hadn't raised the issue either. But Eggy was pretty much the only person I knew on the island who hadn't visited or sent their good wishes. I had desperately wanted to ask Clem and Otto, but if he chose never to have anything to do with me ever again, then I wasn't sure I wanted to hear the answer.

"You're cool with me moving in, aren't you?" Otto asked me tentatively. "I know we talked about it, and while you are getting better, it will be helpful for you to have me around, you know, helping, and...being helpful and doing...helping things."

"What, like cooking and cleaning and laundry? The washing up?"

He gulped. "Well, you know, I was thinking more, like, helping you undress and get into bed. I could help you undress to shower, wash those hard-to-reach areas and such."

"Moving in is fine, sweetheart," I murmured. It was. Very fine indeed.

As he wittered on, I stroked slow circles up and down his smooth back, my hand sneaking under his loose T-shirt. Stretching like a cat, he rubbed against me, snuggling in. In my fairly limited experience of hospital visiting, most visitors perched on uncomfortable plastic chairs around the bed, occasionally daring to hold the patient's hand. Fortunately, I'd been allocated a single room, as from day one, Otto had treated my narrow hospital cot as if he belonged in it, with me. I didn't know if it was a Norwegian thing or an Otto thing, and god knew what the nurses made of it, but I wouldn't tell him to stop.

"There's a lot of undressing in your plans to help." I kissed the top of his head. He no longer smelt of Clem's expensive shower gel—I smiled as I recognised my own. Slipping my hands under the waistband of his jeans, they drifted onto his arse, cupping it firmly. He responded with a satisfied moan, softly grinding against my thigh.

"I've been reading, Christian," he breathed, and I chuckled.

"Should I be worried?"

"And I discussed my reading with Dr Marchena."

Oh god, this could be anything. "At your appointment? In front of your brothers?"

"Yeah, obviously. They didn't mind."

If a smack on the head didn't kill me, this boy would.

"I read that people who suffered a severe concussion like yours, Christian, sometimes have a problem with sex afterwards."

Marvellous. He'd discussed our sex life in front of the Vikings. I beamed into his hair, relaxing anyway, realising I didn't care. And I guessed what was coming, since he wasn't the only one who'd been reading. Clem hadn't been on his laptop all the time. "Carry on, sweetheart." Continuing with my slow caress of his buttocks, I trailed a finger down his cleft and chuckled again as his grinding picked up tempo.

"The thing is, Christian, you may—aah, fuck that's nice. With your head injury, I read that you may...aaah...have problems initiating sex..."

"What, you mean like now?" I breathed, ghosting over his hole one more time.

"It...yes, although...aah...so nice...you don't seem to be struggling...and, aaah...do that again...she said you might have problems...fuck...sustaining an erection...and..."

He lost the powers of speech while I put the little pot of Vaseline to good use. As my finger found his entrance, he humped my thigh with renewed vigour, struggling to finish his sentence.

"And...I...just...I just want you to know...fuck...that it won't...shit...you're good...be a problem for me, Christian."

He gave up talking, gone past the point of no return as he pleasured himself with abandon, both on my finger and against my leg. He buried his face in my neck, and a hand grasped my hip. Taking that hand in mine, I steered it towards my groin, covered only in thin cotton hospital pyjamas, where my thickened, needy dick desperately awaited his touch.

"I think you'll find it's not going to be a problem for me either, sweetheart."

Chapter Eighteen

When Fifty and the big hairy Viking clear
the air

The day before discharge, I woke from my afternoon snooze expecting Clem tapping away in his familiar corner of my hospital room, only to find Eggy in his place. I had no idea how long he had been there, healthy and handsome, sprawled in his usual hoodie and board shorts. Settled so comfortably, he looked for all the world as if he'd been keeping a daily vigil, not avoiding me completely.

Immediately, I shut my eyes again. "I'm not apologising," I warned, when it became clear he wasn't going to be the first to speak.

"For hitting me, or for fucking my baby brother?"

Ouch. "Neither."

"Maybe not, but you could at least look at me."

"My headache is worse with my eyes open."

"Not anymore, it isn't. Clem told me. Your double vision disappeared eight days ago."

That was interesting. So he'd been following my progress even if he couldn't be arsed to drop by. Christ, I'd missed the arrogant fucker. Although having him here now, all casual and relaxed, irritated the shit out of me. If he hadn't been such an overbearing, overprotective arsehole, Otto would never have wandered off, and I'd never have half-killed myself rescuing him. My mildly aching head began to throb as my irritation grew.

Fuck it. Opening my eyes, I gave him what I hoped was a cool stare. He stared back, effortlessly coolly.

And then, despite myself, I laughed. "Shit, dude, how the hell did you get that?"

I might have had a concussion, but I distinctly remembered that, a few minutes prior to being smacked on the head, I'd punched Eggy across his perfectly fucking square jaw. A faint blueish tinge remained as proof. But I'd been nowhere near his left eye, currently bathed in all the colours of the rainbow.

Unusually for Eggy, he appeared uncomfortable, bringing a self-conscious hand to his eye. "A little gift from Otto. Immediately after he recovered from his seizure and his hypothermia. And before he phoned the brothers to tell tales on me."

I smirked. My boy had quite the left hook on him. I reminded myself to stay in his good books.

Eggy gave me a regretful look. "I suppose I deserved it."

I nodded slowly. "Yep. I suppose you did."

We eyed each other warily, each silently daring the other to go first. I sat it out; I'd always been the more patient.

"Are you going to ask me about the shop? Or what I've been up to?"

"Okay then." I rolled my eyes. "How's the shop?"

"Busy, but we're managing. Christos, the kid I've hired, has been a great help."

We'd have to talk about the business in the near future, especially if a parting of the ways was on the cards, but I needed to be in a much stronger frame of mind before I tackled that particular conversation.

"Your brothers seem nice," I observed neutrally.

He smiled briefly. "Yeah, it was good to see them. Really good. They've grown into nice lads. We won't leave it so long next time."

Another pause. We were done with the polite chitchat. He shuffled restlessly on the hard plastic seat. Sitting still and doing nothing didn't suit Eggy. He was always on the go, be it plaguing Clem, tinkering in the shop, singing (badly), or nagging Otto. Right now, the only thing he managed was raising my blood pressure and worsening my headache.

Lying in this bed, I'd had a lot of hours to do nothing but think. Not only was I angry he hadn't been in touch, but hurt, too. Hurt he'd not even phoned. Hurt that apparently he no longer cared, after all we'd been through together. Hurt he couldn't accept Otto and I had a good thing going and be happy for me.

Tears threatened at my eyelids, and I turned away from him, gazing out of the window at the bland view of the hospital carpark. I'd been warned head injuries caused emotional lability, but this had nothing to do with my head injury.

"Well, thanks for visiting," I managed stiffly. "Don't let me hold you up. I'm sure you must have a lot to do." *Otherwise, you'd have fucking visited me a hell of a lot earlier.*

Aside from telling him to fuck off out of my hospital room, that was about as pointed a dismissal as I could manage without choking up. I'd be damned if I'd give him the satisfaction of seeing he'd upset me.

Two cars, a little blue Mini and a white Renault, both competed for the same parking space. The cheeky Renault driver sneaked in forwards as the other driver, who had found the space first, prepared a careful reversing manoeuvre. A horn blared, windows were opened, harsh words exchanged. The elderly Renault driver refused to budge.

And neither did Eggy. I turned back to him.

"Why are you still here?" I asked coldly.

His face whitened. He rubbed at it briskly with his hands, as if trying to bring colour back into it. Sniffing, he let out a shaky sigh. His mouth opened and closed wordlessly, grey eyes darting all over my face. "Fifty, I...I..." As his voice cracked, he stopped abruptly, shaking his head.

Oh my god. I stared with dismay. Eggy, one of the most self-confident, imposing men I'd ever known, was horribly, desperately upset. I'd only seen him like this once before, when Clem disappeared from Woolacombe and Eggy thought he'd lost him forever.

Sucking in a deep breath, he composed himself and then tried again. "I'm still here because I need to tell you I'm sorry." His voice hardly lifted above a murmur; I could barely make out the words. "I couldn't face you. I was scared you'd tell me to fuck off and never want to see me again."

He sniffed loudly and rubbed his nose. "Shit, I thought you were dead after you hit your head. I thought you were fucking dead, Fifty. And it would have been all my fault." Resting his elbows on his knees, he dropped his head in his hands, that mane of fabulous red hair falling like a curtain over his face, hiding his eyes.

Stunned, I stared at him, lost for words. Of all the reasons he'd not visited, this one had never occurred to me.

"I...I...couldn't come," he carried on. "I fucking couldn't, okay? I couldn't bear knowing you hated me."

Anyone else and I'd swear they were crying. Hate him? Never. If he believed that, then he was more of a bloody idiot than I thought. After Otto, this man was my everything. I loved him like a brother. Was I angry with him? Yes, fucking livid. And not for the first time. Those years in the vans, I'd frequently been angry with him, not that he always knew. Back then, my anger had been a mixture of jealousy, desire and anguish that he'd not chosen me, coupled with frustration at my own uselessness, rolled into a tight ball I labelled anger so I could deal with it better. But never hatred. Eggy had saved me when the rest of my family couldn't be arsed with me, when my life hit a downward spiral of weed, weed, loneliness and more fucking weed.

Pushing back the bedclothes, I swung my legs out of bed. Eggy looked up in alarm. "Don't get up. You're not well. I'll go." He wiped at his red-rimmed eyes and sniffed again.

I stood up anyway. And he stood too, watching anxiously, ready to dive across the space between us if I fell over. I wouldn't, although the room bent out of shape for a few seconds as my bruised brain told itself I'd shifted to vertical from horizontal. I waited for it to tilt back again.

"Dude." I gave him a cautious smile. "According to Dag, I'm now an honorary Viking brother, one of the Vestvågøy Vikings. A son of Odin, didn't you know? I can't ever hate a Viking brother, can I?"

"Christ, that's a load of pretentious bollocks," he scoffed. "Don't tell me that's what I sound like every time I say it."

I snorted. "I couldn't possibly comment, mate."

When I held my arms out wide, he stepped into them, embracing me in a tight squeeze. Relief washed over me. We were good. We could deal with the rest.

"Shit, not too hard, dude," I murmured, wincing as he crushed my broken ribs into his chest. He lessened his hold a fraction, but still clung, which I kind of liked. It was a rare day Ragnar Aleksander Sigurdson Eggebraaten of the Vestvågøy Eggebraatens showed weakness, and hell, I'd make the most of it.

He pushed me back towards the bed. "Sit down again. Clem says you've been told to take it easy for another six weeks at least." He fussed around me, plumping the cushions, and straightening the covers. I let him; it gave us both a moment to compose ourselves.

"So Clem's been keeping you up to date, has he?" I asked, as I settled again.

"Well, yeah, obviously." He grinned, more his normal self. "Why do you think he's been sitting here all day every day? I mean, he likes you, dude, but he fucking hates hospitals. I made him come."

Shit, I nearly started crying myself then. Clem, ensconced in the corner, day after day, pretending he had nothing better to do. And the entire time, Eggy had been with me, every step of the way.

"When I say I'm sorry, I really fucking mean it. I was cruel, saying what I said when you told me about you and Otto. I know that's not why you're with him."

"I should have told you about us earlier," I replied, but he shook his head. "I was fearful for my toenails."

"Nah, it wouldn't have made any difference. I'd have still been a dick, especially as I thought you were shagging my baby brother *and* those two Spanish dudes." He sighed. "Clem says I need to learn to stop biting when a simple growl will do. He's right. And I have to accept Otto is growing up. I'm trying, but it's hard, you know? He's special."

Typical Clem. He read Eggy so well.

Eggy shook his head, exasperated. "I feel so guilty leaving him behind when he was a boy. Not seeing him for all those years. And then when he came to stay here, I felt so proud he'd chosen me, but so anxious about him, too. Especially with his epilepsy. I want to wrap him in cotton wool. And I don't want him to fuck up like I did—I want him to go to college and have a proper career."

"You didn't fuck up, Eggy." I'd reminded him of this

frequently when he was younger, when the raw pain of it still caught him unawares. "Your father did. By kicking you out."

He sighed, blowing out his cheeks. "Yeah, I know. And Clem pointed out that if I was so anxious about Otto, then who better to look after him than you?"

We studied each other.

"I do look after him," I began carefully. "But only in the way that a normal guy would. Like you and Clem are with each other. He doesn't need special treatment from me, and he doesn't want it."

Eggy pursed his lips. "He told me you took him bodyboarding, and I was really pissed off. I thought it was stupid and dangerous. We ended up having a huge fucking row about it—this was a couple of nights ago."

I tensed. "As I said, Eggy, I'm not apologising. For anything. He's an adult. He can make his own decisions about what's safe and what isn't."

"And about who he wants as a boyfriend, am I right?"

"Yeah," I breathed. "He can choose that too. And if he decides it's not going to be me, one day in the future when he's older, then that's a risk I'm prepared to take. What we have—he's worth it."

Eggy sat on the edge of the bed, twisting his hands in his lap. His voice was soft. "He's very young, dude. Ten years younger than you. I've changed a hell of a lot since I was that age. He will, too."

It wasn't a criticism or an accusation, not even a warning. Getting used to the idea of us being together would take him a while. He wouldn't find it easy overnight. And if Otto outgrew me and moved on, then...I wasn't going to think about that.

"Clem says the age gap will seem less as Otto gets older," he continued. "He's probably right."

"He's right about most things," I agreed. "And Eggy, I need

you to know—it just happened. I didn't plan on it, or take advantage of him being so young, or anything like that."

Eggy gave me a funny sort of smile. "I know that now, dude. He's told me everything."

Oh shit. Why didn't that surprise me? Heat rose up my neck, and I held my breath. "Um... everything? Absolutely everything?"

"Well, yeah." He reeled all the ways off on his fingers. "About how he jumped you in the jeep after the hotel gig, about how you always let him beat you at FIFA, how you make better baguette sarnies than me and Clem—we don't spread enough butter on, apparently. About how you let him eat pizza at, like, three in the morning. Basically, you let him treat you like a giant marshmallow. Which I kind of knew you were anyway. You're spoiling him, dude."

Not absolutely everything, then. I could start breathing again.

"Oh, and that you're a bloody animal between the sheets. Fucking gross! I do not want to hear about that! I mean, he's my baby brother, dude."

As if summoned, a knock sounded at the door. Without waiting, the fluffball himself rushed through, arms laden with groceries. While Clem brought me healthy, nutritious lunches, Otto could be relied on to deliver the treats. "Hey, Ragnar, hey Christian."

Beaming happily at the sight of both of us, he dumped the bags on the floor, then squashed in next to Eggy, planting a wet smacker on my cheek. And then another on my other cheek, keeping his face close. His long eyelashes tickled mine. "Butterfly kisses," he chuckled lightly. God knows what Eggy made of that. Most likely that I was overindulgent, way too soppy with my boy, and stupidly, crazily in love. And he'd be right.

"Thank God you two have made up! I thought I was going

to have to give Ragnar another black eye if he didn't come and visit you soon."

Grinning at the both of us, he leaned down to open one of the bags. "I've been doing some reading, Christian, about the best foods after head injury. No more *patatas bravas* for you."

What? I pulled a face as he delved deeply into the plastic bag, flourishing a packet of some pretty unappetising greyish berry things and another which resembled a sack of birdseed. Eggy looked on approvingly.

"You're kidding me," I groaned, falling back against the pillows. For the last two weeks, since the nausea had abated, I'd dreamt of nothing but *chipirones*, *gambas al ajillo* and of course, a mountain of *patatas bravas*.

Two identical sets of wide grey eyes bored into mine. Determined, cocky and beautiful. I didn't stand a fucking chance.

Three days later, after finishing work for the day, Eggy picked me up from the hospital and drove me home. Otto filled the silence in the car with his usual chatter, but Eggy and I weren't totally back to normal with each other. It would take quite some time for the hairy ginger Viking to accept my place in Otto's life, and I'd have to be patient with him. He'd get there eventually, though the pile of board games on my coffee table was an interesting development. I stood in the centre of my living room, bags at my feet, eyeing them curiously.

"Clem's been doing some reading this time," Eggy explained. "You're not coming back to work for at least a month, and I didn't want you to become bored. You have to avoid TV and computer screens for a few weeks, as they can make your headaches worse."

Bloody hell, and a three-hour game of Monopoly wouldn't?

"Don't worry, Ragnar. I can think of plenty of ways to keep

him entertained," Otto interjected mischievously. "We'll be playing our own version of Cluedo: Mr Grey, in the bedroom, with a—"

"Thanks so much for bringing me home, Eggy."

I cut him off, trying not to laugh. The little fucker could wind up his big brother better than anyone else I knew. Experiencing the rare sight of Eggy's cheeks turning scarlet, I decided it wouldn't harm to tease him even more. Raising my arm, Otto immediately snuggled in, wrapping his own tightly around my waist. I kissed the top of his head.

"You're going to have to take it easy with me, Otto, for a few weeks."

That wasn't a lie. Even the walk from the hospital to the car and then from the car to my apartment had left me weak and dizzy.

Eggy nodded approvingly, relaxing once more.

"I'm going to need to spend an awful lot of time lying down. In bed."

Eggy groaned.

"That's fine." Otto threw his brother a naughty look. "And, of course, when we do manage to have sex, I'll make sure that—"

"Okay. I'm out of here." Eggy marched to the door, flustered. "I'm...I'm...yes, anyway. Otto, be good, take your pills and call if you need me." Hand on the door, he hesitated. "Fifty?"

I looked up and smiled. "Yeah?"

"I love you, dude. Stay safe."

After two months spent sneaking around, conducting our love affair in secret, followed by three weeks in hospital, Otto and I were finally alone. In our apartment. My head hurt, my vision occasionally blurred, I felt intermittently nauseous, and my ribs ached.

Life was a funny game. As any gnarly old surfer would tell you, you could never stop the waves from crashing to the shore. You just had to ride the ones you were given and accept them for what they were. Despite my nausea, I still had a craving for *patatas bravas*. I guessed I'd be well padded for the rest of my days. The sculpted six-pack would remain elusive. That was okay. Otto loved me exactly as I was.

And strangers would snigger when they heard my ridiculous name for a few good years to come yet, especially older folk. I couldn't ever change that. Otto would forever be ten years younger than me, and I'd forever worry he'd tire of having an older guy and trade me in for a younger model. Eggy would always be an arrogant arse, but Clem would continue to keep him in check and love him anyhow. As would I, but as the brother I've never had. Epilepsy would plague Otto for the rest of his days. I wished I could shoulder that affliction for him, but I couldn't. We'd roll with the punches together.

I had my own man to love now. Granted, he was still a teenager, and, god knew, sometimes he behaved like one, but a man all the same. And, currently, my man gently led me by the hand to our bedroom.

Soon, he'd carefully undress me and help me into our bed before undressing himself. We'd have very quick sex, because, well, Otto. Afterwards, we'd kiss and cuddle at a more leisurely pace and rediscover the joy of each other's bodies. My brain and my dick would work in tandem, because, at long last, they'd finally made peace with each other. Later, we'd make love slowly, and Otto would fall asleep in my arms. And I'd hold on to him for as many years as I could.

Epilogue

Ten Years Later

It took me months to get used to going to bed alone in the evening, then waking in the morning without Otto beside me. Our house felt too quiet and our bed too empty. Even Freya, our raggedy black cat, missed him; at bedtime, she'd arrange herself on the sitting-room floor in front of the patio doors, swishing her tail and patiently blinking out into the dark night. Gently mourning his absence.

We'd moved out of my little apartment the year Otto finished nursing college and he'd started earning some money. With the extra income, we'd been able to buy an old villa requiring a hell of a lot of updating. Fortunately, I was pretty handy with a paintbrush. It was nowhere near as flash as Eggy and Clem's, but we were within easy walking distance of their place. We spent the next couple of years lovingly turning it into the neat, simple home we both wanted. Rescuing Freya from a cattery had completed us.

Eggy and I worked hard and expanded the business. We now owned three surf shops—two in Corralejo and one in

Puerto del Rosario. Next year, we had plans to open a fourth and maybe a fifth. We still gave a few lessons ourselves, but employed some younger guys, too, to take the summer strain. Occasionally, we'd catch each other's eye, mostly when sitting in front of our bank manager, accountant, or solicitor. We'd smirk at each other, as if to say, "Bro, is this for real?" And then pinch ourselves, grateful for the good fortune bringing two clueless surfer dudes a new start on this faraway holiday island. Fuerteventura—Spanish for strong fortune.

Eggy would declare the Gods were smiling on us, and Clem would roll his eyes. I'd always agree with Eggy because agreeing was easier than not, and after all, I was an honorary Viking brother and us Vikings stuck together.

Next month heralded my fortieth birthday. A few grey hairs had begun to appear in my blond bird's nest, which Eggy took great delight in pointing out. His own thick locks remained annoyingly lush and bronze. His equally hirsute brothers were travelling over from Norway to celebrate my birthday with me, bringing hordes of offspring with them. A veritable Viking invasion. Those Eggebraatens sure knew how to procreate. The four heterosexual brothers had thirteen kids between them and more on the way.

Eggy and Clem were excitedly planning a big, no-expense-spared garden party for me, which I'd enjoy, although fancy shindigs like that weren't generally my scene. Alejandro's hotel would provide the catering, so at least I could guarantee the food would be excellent. He and Felipe were first on the guest list.

I checked the time. Seven in the morning. Freya had woken me by leaping onto the bed and treadling the duvet around my face until I gave her the attention she craved. After a quick tickle behind her ears, I shooed her off. Owning a cat had been Otto's idea, not mine. She stalked out, tail held high, to resume her lonely vigil for her true master by the patio doors. Smiling with contentment, I rolled over and snoozed.

Another hour passed before a rattle of a key in the front door. Otto's voice, deeper since we first met and his Scandi accent fainter, carried through to the bedroom as he petted the cat. Even after all this time, a tingle of anticipation ran through my veins, a flush of pleasure. It would be another ten minutes before he joined me, after he'd showered and made us both a cup of tea. Enough time to perform my own quick ablutions, then dive back under the covers.

His footsteps, light on the stairs, his body as lithe and boyish as the first time I'd watched him dance. Ten whole years ago, when I'd been entranced by the seductive shimmy of his narrow hips and tried desperately hard not to be. I admired him openly now, every chance I got. He still went dancing with his friends, old mates from the early days and new ones from the hospital. Sometimes, I joined in, but increasingly felt more and more self-conscious as the years passed. It didn't matter— we danced together at home every chance we got, and a lot more passionately than was permitted on the dance floor of Gators.

So, more often than not, I propped up the bar, usually with Alejandro and his friends, and we watched the youngsters strutting their stuff, secure in the knowledge we no longer had to play the mating game. Otto liked having me there; performing for me on the dance floor turned him on.

Dropping the towel he'd loosely hung around his waist, he slipped into bed, cool and damp from the shower, and straight into my open arms.

"How was the night shift, sweetheart?" I lightly pressed my lips to the top of his head.

He snuggled down even further. "Same old, same old. Ancient guy with a heart attack, a young lad who crashed his car and gave himself whiplash. A load of tourists drinking too much and falling over. Odin's teeth, they're stupid."

I laughed softly at his disapproving tone. He'd morphed into Captain Sensible in his old age.

"No more night shifts now for another month," he murmured sleepily. "More time to do this."

'This' varied, depending on how busy his night shift had been and how early I was expected at work. Sometimes 'this' was a cuddle and a cup of tea, before I headed out to the shop leaving Otto to settle down to sleep. Today, however, we had plenty of time. Predictably, as the warmth of my body suffused into his, Otto began rocking gently against me. Slowly at first. My impatient teen had become a mature, confident lover, and we were in no rush. After all, we had the rest of our lives. Closing my eyes and breathing him in, I chuckled softly to myself then surrendered to his kiss.

* * *

Want to find out how Eggy and Clem found their happy ever after?
Brushed With Love (Surfing the Waves #1)

Acknowledgments

To the good citizens of the beautiful town of Corralejo: apologies for totally rearranging the geography, the location of the beaches, and occasionally, the direction of the prevailing winds.

Thank you so much to the author Norah Belle for ensuring the accuracy of my Norwegian content – any errors are my own. In addition, many thanks to my editor, M.A., and to Lori, for all your input and support.

About the Author

Fearne Hill resides deep in the British countryside, in the county of Dorset, surrounded by animals. She likes it that way.

Her popular Rossingley series was nominated in nine separate categories of the 2021 Goodreads M/M Romance awards and received an Honourable Mention in the 2021 Rainbow Awards.

She can be found on social media:
Facebook group: Fearne Hill's House
On Instagram: instagram.com/fearnehill_author
On Twitter: twitter.com/FearneHill
On Bookbub: bookbub.com/authors/fearne-hill

Also by Fearne Hill

Rossingley Series

To Hold A Hidden Pearl

To Catch A Fallen Leaf

To Take A Quiet Breath

To Melt A Frozen Heart

Standalone Romance

The Last of the Moussakas